# Red Willow's Quest

## Heidi Skarie

SunShine Press Publications

SunShine Press Publications, Inc.
P. O. Box 333
Hygiene, CO 80533-0333
www.sunshinepress.com

Cover design: Bob Schram of Bookends
Cover illustration: Heidi Skarie

Publisher's Cataloging-in-Publication Data

Skarie, Heidi
    Red willow's quest.
    p. cm.
    ISBN: 1-888604-10-7
    1. Skarie, Heidi  2. Medicine woman  3. Indians
    of North America  4.Religion and mythology  I. Title
1999
E99,C88A54      2000      299'.78          99-68550

Printed in the United States of America
*Printed on recycled acid-free paper using soy-based ink*

# Dedication

I dedicate this book to Harold Klemp, my Spirit Guide and teacher on my spiritual quest.

# *Acknowledgments*

Grateful acknowledgment is extended to all the people who helped me with this project. Nothing in life is accomplished alone but through a circle of friends and experts.

Thanks to Jim Skarie, my husband, who has supported me in my love of writing over the years.

I also want to thank Janet Deemer my writing partner, Ingrid Spindt who encouraged me, Paul Baker and Jan Whiteley who edited the manuscript, and to Bob Raming who believed in my writing.

And finally, I extend special thanks to my editor and publisher, Jack Hofer, for his careful editing and attention to detail, and to Bob Schram the cover designer.

# Author's Notes

I started writing this story as a fantasy. As the story unfolded, I realized that the culture was much like that of the Plains Indians and debated writing the story as Native American. Soon afterwards I was reading a manuscript about a woman who remembered her past life as a Native American woman. I had read only one page when I walked outside to the mailbox. On the way I found a hawk feather in perfect condition standing upright in the lawn. On each of the next two days I found another hawk feather in the yard. For me finding three hawk feathers was a significant spiritual sign that I should write the book as a Native American story. To some Native American tribes the hawk means clear spiritual vision and flying above the mundane world.

As part of my research for the story, I traveled to the Rocky Mountains in Montana. After purchasing a book, I flipped it over and saw on the back cover that it was about a Kootenai Indian girl. I had never before heard of the Kootenai Indians, but had used the name Kootenai for one of the tribes in the story. I took this as another sign that I should write Red Willow's story.

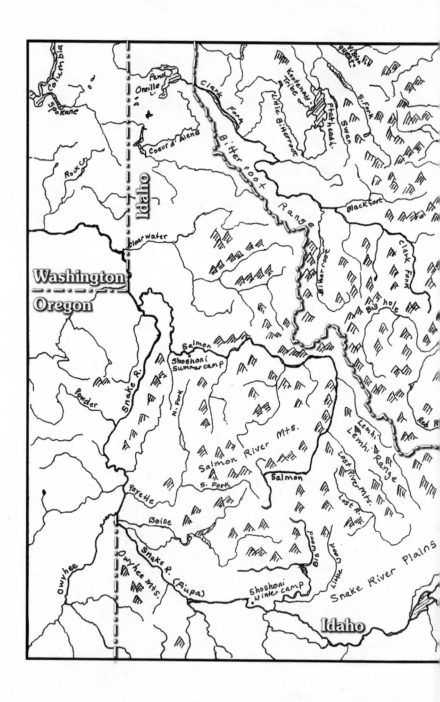

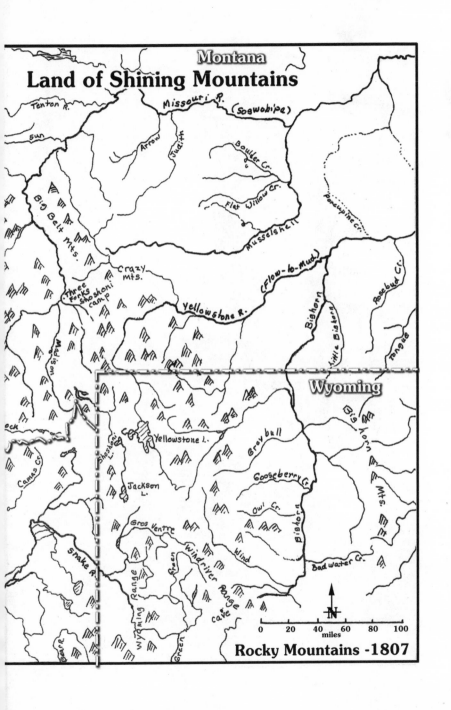

Montana
# Land of Shining Mountains

Tenton R.

Missouri R. (Soswohipa)

Sun

Arrow

Judith

Boulder Cr.

Flat Willow Cr.

Porcupine Cr.

Big Belt Mts.

Musselshell

Crazy Mts.

(Flow-to-Mud)

Three Forks Shoshoni camp

Yellowstone R.

Bighorn

Little Bighorn

Rosebud Cr.

Tongue

Madison

Wyoming

Big Horn Mts.

Shoshoni

Yellowstone L.

Greybull

ech

Camas Cr.

Jackson L.

Gooseberry Cr.

Owl Cr.

Bighorn

Gros Ventre

Snake R.

Wind River Range

Wind

Bad Water Cr.

Wyoming Range

Green

Cache

0    20    40    60    80    100
miles

N

# Rocky Mountains -1807

viii

# Table of Contents

Chapter 1 Hawk Feathers                               1

Chapter 2 Blackfeet War Party                        23

Chapter 3 Masheka                                    39

Chapter 4 The Battle                                 55

Chapter 5 Turning Point                              69

Chapter 6 Sunrise Ceremony                           87

Chapter 7 Journey to Spirit Cave                    107

Chapter 8 Visions                                   127

Chapter 9 Trading Post                              145

Chapter 10 Horse Raid                               159

Chapter 11 The Parting                              173

Chapter 12 Winter Among the Shoshoni                195

Chapter 13 Smallpox                                 217

Chapter 14 Kootenai Village                         233

# *1*

## Hawk Feathers

*1807 in the Rocky Mountains near what is now known as the Missouri River in Montana.*

The Season of Melting Snow had arrived. After hiding in the Shining Mountains during Season of Howling Wind, my people made a temporary camp on the headwaters of the Sogwobipa River to hunt the huge, humpback kotea. It had been a long, cold winter causing food to be short. I walked a long way from camp in search of roots and healing herbs with Wind Chaser, my half-dog, half-wolf companion.

While digging up camas roots with a stick, a strange, uneasy feeling came over me. Scanning the terrain and listening intently, I heard the snort of a horse and the sound of a hoof scraping the ground. I moved to the tall grass and squatted down out of sight, motioning Wind Chaser to follow. He crouched beside me with his ears perked up, sensitive to every sound. I breathed slowly, becoming one with the grass and Mother Earth so my presence wouldn't be detected.

A Blackfeet brave rode into view; his tribe was our worst enemy. White and red lines zigzagged down both sides of his face. He carried a bow and quiver of arrows and a lethal-looking tomahawk. The many feathers in his hair and his war paint showed he was a war chief. When he reined in his horse to look around, I saw that on his stallion was a red handprint, which meant he'd killed someone in hand-to-hand combat.

Five more warriors moved into view and the war chief's attention shifted to his men as they drew up alongside him. I waited in tense silence, hardly daring to breathe. The warriors began talking in their own tongue and my fear grew so intense my stomach ached. If they found me they would know my village was near and they would return with many warriors to destroy it and steal our horses.

Into my mind came images from when I was very young. A Blackfeet war party had attacked our village, catching my tribe unprepared. My mother grabbed me up and ran to the tepee, yelling for my brother, Gray Eagle, to follow us. Instead Gray Eagle had snatched up his small bow and raced after my father who was leading the defense. My mother dropped me and ran after Gray Eagle, grabbing him by the arm and pulling him back over to where I stood crying. She dragged us both into the tepee. Many were killed and the wailing and loud keening cries of the mourners could be heard for many suns afterwards.

Wind Chaser sensed my fear and began to growl. I placed a hand on his thick-furred back to silence him. The leader of the war party looked directly at where I was crouched and I was afraid he could see me through the grass.

Wind Chaser leapt out at the chief's steed and the startled animal reared up. I took advantage of the moment of confusion to quietly back away and slip into the forest. Once I was out of sight, I began to run toward my village, weaving my way through the tall cedar and hemlock trees. I leapt over fallen branches and tore through bushes that barred my way, ignoring the scratches to my face, arms, and legs. My leather

2

pouch slowed me down, but the food and herbs were too valuable to leave behind. Wind Chaser reappeared and ran alongside me with his tail held high; his long, powerful legs allowing him to move in easy loping strides. Wind Chaser looked like a reddish-brown colored wolf except for his larger size and stronger body build.

I ran until I couldn't push myself anymore then slowed my pace. I had gone further than I'd realized in my search for food. Once rested, I began to run again.

I finally reached our encampment in the river valley, and the sight of our peaceful tepees filled me with relief. We had camped at Three Forks, a place where three rivers come together. We had nearly three hundred people in our band, five hundred horses, and many dogs. On a hill near the village there was always a scout and I went directly to that place. As I drew closer I saw that the sentinel was Chased-by-Bear, a war chief and warrior of great courage. He came down the hill to meet me with a concerned expression on his proud face. "What is wrong, Red Willow?" he asked.

"There is a Piegan war party nearby!"

"Chief Gray Eagle's at the river. Go tell him while I round up some scouts to follow the Blackfeet."

I hurried through the village and down to the river where Gray Eagle was spearing fish with Kicking Horse. They stood in the muddy water amongst the tall bulrushes. I dropped my bag and ran to them, calling out Gray Eagle's name. Both men turned upon hearing me and lowered their spears. Kicking Horse came swiftly to shore and I ran into his arms.

"What has happened?" he demanded. His usually cheerful, open face was clouded with concern. He was a young warrior with a beak-shaped nose, high cheekbones, and swarthy complexion. He was wearing only a breechcloth, though the water was cool, and his long black hair was worn loose around his shoulders.

I told him about the Blackfeet war party and felt his body become rigid as his arms tightened around me.

"Did they see you?" Gray Eagle asked, joining us on shore with an air of confidence.

I moved from Kicking Horse's arms and turned to my brother. "No, I hid from them."

"Where did you see them?" Gray Eagle asked. He was broad shouldered, but very lean for there had been a lack of food that winter.

"On the animal trail near the Cedar forest. I'll lead you there."

"No, it's not a squaw's place. I know the trail well. We'll follow them and see where they're headed."

"Let me come along!"

"This is not a game, Red Willow."

"I know that! You've let me come along to steal horses."

Kicking Horse watched me with an annoying smile on his face and his arms crossed over his chest.

"This is different!" exclaimed Gray Eagle. "The safety of our band is at stake."

"I won't slow you down. I can run like the wind and move without making noise."

He replied sharply. "I have the responsibility for our people now. I can't risk bringing along a squaw. Come, Kicking Horse, let's go." He started running up the embankment.

"I should have followed them myself!" I called after him in frustration. Kicking Horse started to follow and I grabbed his arm. "Wait! Convince him to let me come along."

"Kicking Horse is right. You are a woman now and the sister of the chief. You need to be an example for our people of how a squaw should behave."

"I do not want to be a squaw! It's not exciting."

"There might be fighting. I don't think you want that type of excitement." He turned and ran off to catch up with

4

Gray Eagle while I stood there, furious that I was not allowed to go along.

Last summer, before Gray Eagle was chief, he would have let me come. When we were children, he had let me accompany him and Kicking Horse on nearly all their adventures. He had taught me how to throw a knife, shoot a bow, and ride a horse.

My parents had gotten ill during the previous winter and left us for the Land of Shadows. Since then I had taken on all of the duties of gathering and preparing food, and keeping camp. I was sixteen summers and old enough to make a tepee of my own. I was sure that Kicking Horse would have already asked for me if I was not still in mourning for my parents.

Unable to accompany Gray Eagle and Kicking Horse, I washed the roots I had gathered in the river, then walked back to our campsite. I fed pine needles into the smoldering coals and as they caught on fire the smell of burning pine scented the air. Grandfather came over and crouched down near me as I put the roots and some water in a kotea paunch that hung over the fire from a three-legged, wooden frame. He was an old man with wrinkled, leather-like skin and long, white hair. His eyes were clear and filled with wisdom and he seemed to always know everything before I had told him. He took out a pipe, put kinnikinnick and willow bark in it, and began to smoke. I wanted to talk to him, but out of respect for his age and wisdom, I waited for him to speak first.

As I stared into the flames, my thoughts turned to when I was seven summers. Gray Eagle was going on his first Vision Quest to find his song, as all boys of the people must do to become warriors. He was being taught and guided by Grandfather to be the Head Chief some day. Father was currently the Head Chief, and although it was not an inherited position, the people often picked the Head Chief's son if he showed courage and wisdom, and if it was thought that he could guide the tribe.

I adored my brother and wanted to be like him, so I listened in rapt attention whenever he told me of his conversations with Grandfather. I was in awe of Grandfather: His power frightened me as I could feel it around him and around the sacred things he kept for our village. He was quiet and contemplative and he never played with me like father and Gray Eagle. When Gray Eagle proudly told me that it was time for him to go on his first Vision Quest, something stirred deep within me. I wanted to find my song as well, and know why I was so different from other girls who were content to play with dolls and work alongside their mothers. I had this deep yearning inside me to know about the mysteries of life.

I decided to go on a Vision Quest, so I secretly loaded my pony with supplies and left camp. I was drawn to the Sacred Mountains, which were many Suns and Sleeps from my village. There I fasted and prayed, seeking a vision. On the third day a blue light appeared before me. When it drew closer I saw it was a tall, strong-looking warrior, finely dressed in ceremonial clothes. I was frightened but his smile was gentle and reassuring. He told me his name was Oapiche, meaning big man, and that he was my Spirit Guide. When I needed him I was to enter the inner silence where he would be waiting for me. He showed me a grown woman who was full of wisdom and power, explaining that she was whom I would become in this life. He said he would help me become a medicine woman and guide me on my spiritual journey.

Intense joy filled my being for I felt as if Oapiche was an old friend. Oapiche gave me a sacred sound that I was to sing when I was afraid or needed his guidance. The song was Hu-nai-yiee. As I began to sing it, I felt a greater love than I'd ever felt before.

I must have fallen asleep for the next thing I remember is being awakened by someone saying my name, "Red

WIllow." I opened my eyes and saw it was Grandfather. He drew me into his arms and held me close. "A man came to me, Grandfather!" I exclaimed. "He told I am to become a medicine woman."

His concerned look broke into a serene, knowing smile. "Then we will have to start your training." He handed me to Father and I threw my arms around his neck and started to cry.

"You are safe now, little papoose, there is no reason to cry," Father said, standing up with me in his arms.

"I was afraid I would not be able to find my way back to our people."

"You have journeyed far. We have been tracking you for many days. I was afraid a bear or mountain lion would find my little papoose before I did."

"I am not a papoose anymore."

"That is true. I see you have grown to be a big girl." He set me on his large war-horse and gave me pemmican. I had started to eat it when my attention was drawn by the sound of Grandfather's chanting. He was standing in the center of the circle with his hands raised to Father Sky, singing his thanks to Apo, the Great Spirit, for protecting his grandchild on her Vision Quest. He lay down a pipe in the circle as a gift. I was amazed that he would give something of such great value.

"You are thinking of the past," Grandfather said, bringing me back from my inner reverie to the present moment.

I smiled. "I was thinking of my first Vision Quest."

He nodded. "You have always been strong willed. You will need that strength for this next quest. You must leave tomorrow on your Vision Quest despite having seen the Blackfeet war party."

I nodded. "I know. I hear the calling of spirit like the beating of drums. It's growing louder in my dreams."

"Your path is special and soon the people will need

you," he said, lifting up a leather pouch and handing it to me. "I have a gift for you."

I felt the object's power as soon as grandfather placed the leather pouch in my hand. I opened it and discovered an ancient, wooden flute inside. The end was carved in the shape of a bird's head that had been painted red and yellow. It had been my Grandmother's and I remembered the uplifting songs she played on it. I looked at Grandfather and saw the sadness in his eyes and knew he was also thinking of Grandmother. She had gone to the Land of Shadows and we could not speak of her for it would disturb her spirit. She was a wise, warmhearted woman who had told me many stories when I was young.

"This has special powers. When you play it, listen to its sound and it will speak to you and guide you." He looked up at the sky. Following his gaze, I saw an eagle flying high overhead. We watched the eagle for a long time as it soared over the mountains, flying on invisible air currents.

"The eagle is strong medicine and a good omen for your quest. Your thoughts and visions should rise as high as the eagle." Grandfather turned from the eagle and looked at me again with eyes that were clear and focused. "We, the two-leggeds, share life with the wings of the air, the four-leggeds, and all green plants. The sky is our father and the earth our mother and all living things their children." He gave me a warm smile and deep lines appeared in the corners of his eyes. "Try playing the flute."

I put the flute to my lips and played a few notes as the sun sank behind the mountains. "Listen to its sound with your heart, it will lead you home to Apo," said Grandfather.

Grandfather and I ate, then I went into the tepee, which faced east so the morning sun would always greet us when we awoke and went outside. The tepee smelled of leather, dried roots, and sage, and was dark after being outside. I stirred up the center fire to get it going again and added more

8

branches. Reflecting on my conversation with Grandfather, I gazed at inner wall of the tepee, which had painted designs from the men of our family's dreams and hunting exploits.

My brother returned to camp late that night. Grandfather and I were already in our pine-bough sleeping couches, but I sat up when Gray Eagle and Kicking Horse came into the tepee and crouched by the center fire. Wind Chaser was curled up beside me and he raised his head. I could see the men quite well by the light of the fire in the middle of the tepee.

"Did you find their trail?" I asked.

"Yes," said Gray Eagle. "We followed them at a distance until they entered Kootenai territory. We will decide at council tomorrow whether to continue to search for the kotea or move on to our summer camp. It may be too dangerous to go on to the sacred land of boiling water."

"I must leave on a Vision Quest tomorrow. How will I know where to find you?"

"You'll have to follow our trail."

"You should not let her go," said Kicking Horse.

"It is not for me to interfere with her Vision Quest."

"But the Piegan warriors are headed for the Sacred Mountains and that is where she always goes for her Vision Quests."

"Grandfather said that I should go despite the danger from the Blackfeet." I quickly intervened before Kicking Horse convinced my brother that I should not go.

"Your grandfather is a great man but he has grown old and lives in the world of visions and spirits now," said Kicking Horse. "He is no longer aware of this world, otherwise he would not allow his granddaughter to go on a Vision Quest with Blackfeet warriors in our territory."

"Only the world of Spirit is truly real," said Grandfather from his sleeping couch. "My vision is clear; not only do I know what is happening here but I see into the future and that is why I know Red Willow must go on this quest."

I was upset that Grandfather was not asleep, as Kicking Horse must have assumed; I did not want him hurt by Kicking Horse's words. "Red Willow," Grandfather continued in a voice that carried force and power, "must follow her own path. The spirits talk to her for a special purpose. She will never be content to live as other women. An older man of more experience might understand this."

"I did not mean to be disrespectful," said Kicking Horse. "I am just concerned for her safety. If she must go on this quest at least let me go along."

"A squaw does not travel alone with a warrior unless she shares his lodge. You do not think things through clearly."

Kicking Horse's jaw tightened and I knew he wanted to speak out. "I had better go," he said. His eyes met mine with a tense, worried look, and then he left the tepee.

"I cannot remain in our tepee forever," I said to Grandfather. "Most maidens my age already share a lodge with a brave. How long do you intend for me to be in mourning?"

"I do not see Kicking Horse in your future. I will pick a brave for you when your time of mourning is up."

"I love Kicking Horse! I won't marry another man."

"It is not for a maiden to decide whom she is to marry."

I knew better than to argue with Grandfather. He would only become more set against my marrying Kicking Horse if I became rebellious. I lay back down, frustrated and worried. Marriages built alliances between families; a warrior would know he had a brother-through-marriage who would hunt and fight beside him. Fathers betrothed their daughters to warriors, sometimes when they were very young, to ensure a secure future for them. Father had not betrothed me because Grandfather told him that I had a special destiny. Now I worried that Grandfather would not let me marry Kicking Horse, but would marry me to someone else. Grandfather was the wisest man in the band and he could see things in the future and on a deeper level than most. Maybe he saw something I could not see. Sick at heart, I curled up on my sleeping robe.

Early the next morning, my Mother's sister, Talking Goose, came into the tepee as I packed supplies into a buck-skin bag. "So it's true that you go off on another Vision Quest!"

I stiffened, knowing she did not approve. A loud silence filled the tepee and I knew she wanted to speak her mind, but was respectful of Grandfather's presence as an elder and shaman.

"Your thoughts are like rain pelting against the side of the tepee," Grandfather sighed. "You might as well say them out loud."

"Red Willow should not follow the path of a warrior. She should follow woman's medicine, the path of healing and nurturing. Her training should be left to the women of the tribe. Her behavior is causing the women to gossip about her."

"You are wise in wanting her to follow the way of women and yet you do not see everything," said Grandfather. "Red Willow must follow her heart and go on this quest as part of her training to become a medicine woman. It does not matter what the women of the village think. When she fulfills her destiny they'll understand and be sorry for their harsh words."

My aunt looked distressed. "I wouldn't say anything because you are known for your wisdom, but the Blackfeet are on the warpath. It is too dangerous for her to go off on a quest!"

"Trust more in my guidance, Talking Goose. I wouldn't send my granddaughter into the world if I saw only darkness and danger."

I hugged my aunt, then left the tepee and saddled Good Thunder, my brown and white pinto horse. Good Thunder had been one of my father's war-horses and was a small-headed, strong-bodied stallion. Wind Chaser stood beside Good Thunder, eager to be off on a new adventure.

Father had been a great chief and warrior so we had more horses than most other families of our tribe. Not only had father and Gray Eagle broken wild horses and bred them, but they had also stolen many horses from Crow and Blackfeet bands. It was a great test of courage and wit to steal horses, a rite of passage that all young boys were taught.

I was ready to set out on my quest, but I hesitated a moment, looking for Kicking Horse who usually came to see me off. I wanted to speak to him after what Grandfather had said last night. Disappointed I mounted up and rode out of camp.

Kicking Horse was waiting just outside the horse corrals. "I thought we could ride a short distance together."

I smiled. "I was hoping to see you before I left."

"I wish you wouldn't go on this quest. It's far too dangerous."

"Now you sound like Talking Goose! You and Gray Eagle have taught me to survive on my own. Come on, let's race." Before he could reply, I pressed my knees into Good Thunder's side and the horse broke into a gallop. He was trained to be guided by the knees so that my father would have his hands free to use a bow and arrow.

I could hear the sound of Kicking Horse's stallion as he came thundering after us. Kicking Horse loved the freedom and speed horses gave and had gotten his name as a child because he had the spirit of an unbroken stallion. Kicking Horse rode up beside Good Thunder and lifted me off the galloping animal's back and onto his own horse in front of him. He slowed his stallion to a walk. "I'm not Talking Goose who is afraid of the dark. I've never interfered with your quests and I've helped teach you how to ride and hunt, but this time I'm worried. I have a strong feeling that you will run

12

into danger on this quest. You're already weakened from the long hard Season of Howling Wind. If you fast and go without sleep for four Suns and Sleeps you will be even weaker and not able to defend yourself. It frustrates me that your Grandfather will not end your time of mourning and let us marry so I can go with you. He's not blind; he must know how we feel about each other, everyone else in the band does."

"Vision Quests are gone on alone. My spirit guide guides me and I have Good Thunder and Wind Chaser to protect me. "

"You have grown into a beautiful woman. If the Piegan warriors find you, they will want you for a slave and for their sleeping couches.

"They will not find me."

"Grandfather is wrong, Red Willow. I do understand the importance of your training and your desire to be a medicine woman."

"I know you understand. I don't know why Grandfather said he didn't see you in my future."

"Did he say that?" He looked truly alarmed.

I nodded. "Yes, after you left the tepee."

His dark eyes were intense. "Will you be my woman even if your Grandfather does not agree to it?"

I could hardly breathe being held so close and with all the feelings he sent racing through me. "We belong together. Grandfather is very wise; he will see this."

"What if he doesn't?" His expression was fierce and his emotions raw and intense. His horse had stopped and was munching grass.

I slide my arm around Kicking Horse. "He loves me. He wants me to be happy. He will not deny our marriage when he realizes how I feel."

"I cannot wait much longer for you to be my wife."

His breathing was ragged and his voice thick with emo-

13

tion. "When you return, I will ask Gray Eagle and Grandfather to end your time of mourning so we can marry."

"I will think of you often when we are apart." My body was tingling in every place where it touched his strong, vibrant body.

Kicking Horse called to Good Thunder. When the animal drew near, he placed me back on my stallion. He smiled almost apologetically. "You are a chief's sister. We should not be alone like this. I will see you when you return." He turned his horse and galloped off toward camp. I stared after him, remembering every word and touch. He had finally asked me to be his wife and when I returned he would officially ask for me. A smile spread across my face and my joy was so great I could not contain it.

I urged Good Thunder forward and I felt as if I were flying as he raced across the plain. I crouched down low, clinging to his back, and felt him vibrate as his hoofs thundered against the ground. His mane streamed back and mingled with my hair as his body became an extension of my own, giving me power and strength. Our spirits merged as our bodies flowed together.

Wind Chaser ran swiftly alongside us, enjoying our race with the wind. The air was crisp and the sun felt warm and good on my skin. It was the season of year when plants begin to grow again after the long, cold winter and when animals are plentiful.

I was in high spirits and excited about going on this quest. Something special about it made me feel that my life was about to be changed forever. I could feel Oapiche's inner presence, protecting and guiding me.

Toward evening, dark storm clouds rolled in across the sky. I took this as an omen of danger since it came at the beginning of my journey. I reined in Good Thunder and stared into the black clouds as they twisted and curled. A sense of sorrow and deep pain came over me. I realized that the emotions I felt were not mine, but those of the Nimi, the Shoshoni people. In that moment I pierced the veil between the physical world and the spirit world, and I experienced an overwhelming feeling of suffering and loss. I had no under-standing or knowledge of what was causing this great pain, but I knew I had made contact with the future of the Nimi.

The sky lit up with jagged flashes of lightning, then thunder boomed around me. I shivered and nudged Good Thunder forward with my knees, looking for a place to camp for the night. Wind Chaser reappeared and stayed close as if he too sensed impending danger.

I camped in a wooded area and made a lean-to by tying a leather skin between two trees. I sat on my furs with Wind Chaser curled up beside me. Clouds moved across the setting sun, leaving us in darkness.

When the storm broke, it was fierce and wild. I walked out to meet it, enthralled by the force of the wind, which tore at my clothing, and by the driving rain, which pounded against my skin. The thunder rumbled through my whole being and I listened to it with my heart. I watched the light-ning with reverence and although the storm's raw power filled me with a sense of awe, I could not escape a sense of doom and foreboding for the Nimi.

The next few days were uneventful as I traveled closer and closer to the Sacred Mountains; a range of especially high peaks in the Shining Mountains. All my life I had lived in the shadows of the Shining Mountains. Their rugged beauty was as much a part of my life as the sky, the earth, the wind, and the rain.

I traveled through dense forest and rugged mountain passes for ten Suns and Sleeps using land formations and stars to guide me. I felt the power of the mountains and it grew stronger as I rode higher. I stopped near Sunrise Peak, for I had an inner knowingness that this was the place where I was to do my Vision Quest, and I camped by a stream. That evening I fasted to purify myself and sang to Apo, giving thanks and asking for clarity in my quest. The sky was very clear, and as I sat there I studied the stars which I knew by name. I slept that night under two furs as the cold air would produce frost by morning.

Just before sunrise I arose and got out my pipe. I walked over to the edge of the mountain with Wind Chaser following behind me. I held the pipe up to Father Sky, Mother Earth, and then to the four directions of the earth, ending facing east. The sun rose as I stood there holding out the sacred pipe in prayer to Apo, splashing red and purple colors across the land. I felt a sense of deep inner peace and harmony with all life. Inwardly a soft humming sound filled me with joy and I knew that Oapiche was near.

After the colors in the sky faded, I went to the stream and bathed, then combed out my hair with a pinecone. I let my hair flow freely down my shoulders and painted the center part with red, then painted red on my cheeks as a sign of peace. Once this was done I put on a light-colored, fringed leather dress and knee-high moccasins. I had spent many hours during the Season of Howling Wind sewing on porcupine quills and beads made of bones, and animal claws, and shells to make them beautiful. Each design represented something sacred to me. Last I tied on my beaded belt and my medicine bag which contained sacred objects. I dressed in my best clothes to show my devotion to Apo.

I returned to Good Thunder and stoked his mane, explaining that I would be gone for a few days on a Vision Quest. I untied him so he would be free to graze on the mountain grass or run from any mountain lions or wolves that might be roaming the area. I had no concern that Good Thunder would run away for we were brothers in spirit. I hid all my supplies under some bushes by the steam, including my weapons and shield, and walked up the mountain, carrying only my flute, furs and leather water pouch. Wind Chaser followed beside me.

Near the top of the mountain, I was drawn to a place that overlooked the valley. When I reached it I found a hawk feather and a shiver went through me; hawk feathers are powerful medicine. Finding it confirmed that this was the right place for my quest—a sign that I would have clear spiritual vision. I looked up at the sky, wondering if a hawk lived nearby.

I felt a sense of anticipation that something of great significance would be revealed to me on this quest. I wanted to know what path I was to follow in this life and how to serve my people. I picked up the hawk feather and braided it into my hair.

I drew a circle with a stick and sat in the center of it, planning to remain here for the next four suns and sleeps. Once Wind Chaser saw that I was not going on any farther, he disappeared into the woods. I prayed to Apo to give me a vision, then began to sing my song: Hu-nai-yiee. Gradually I felt my consciousness expand until I was one with all life. I was a deer running swiftly through the forest and an eagle flying high in the sky.

My upliftment faded as the hours passed. My legs grew numb and my back hurt. Insects buzzed around, some alighting on me and biting. I moved beyond awareness of the discomfort as best I could. The morning sun warmed me. Though happy for its company at first, toward afternoon I was hot and my exposed skin began to burn. I felt faint and dizzy, then I began seeing sunspots and feeling sick.

The sun finally moved to the other side of the mountain. The wind began to blow as evening came on, giving me some relief, but now it was growing cold and I was tired. The hours passed as I fought off the terrible need to sleep, feeling nauseated, head pounding, and weak from hunger. I began to despair of being strong enough to endure this quest and feelings of unworthiness crept in.

The moon rose and an owl flew by. The owl helped me refocus and to move beyond my physical pain and negative feelings.

Toward dawn I fainted and found myself hovering over my body. Oapiche was nearby surrounded by a shining blue light. He gestured to me to follow him and we walked together to the edge of the mountain. "The people of all Nations are the children of Apo. All are here to learn and will live on as soul when they leave this world. All are your brothers no matter what their Nation. A major cycle is coming to an end and you will see many changes in your life. The only way to survive these changes is to pray daily and to look for Spirit's guidance. Listen to Spirit speak in the laughter of a child, in the wail of the wind, and in the piercing cry of a hawk. Look for its light when you see a fawn, a sunrise, or a fragile mountain flower.

The vision faded and I pondered his words, wondering if I had misunderstood him. The people of my tribe were my brothers but not the Blackfeet or the Crow. They were our enemies. What could this great cycle change that he had referred to be? His words stirred up many new thoughts. My mind finally quieted and I began to listen to the wind blowing through the trees. It called me to awaken and go further then I had ever gone before, to defy the limitations of my physical body and return home to Apo.

The heat grew intense and I became very thirsty. I drank a little of my water, conserving it because I had only brought a small water pouch with me. Flies kept biting me and I longed to get up and move around. In the late afternoon, a tall Kootenai warrior appeared. I had to face the sun to look at him and the light surrounded him so intensely that I wasn't sure if he was really there or another vision. He had black war paint on his forehead and yellow lines on his cheeks and arms. He wore feathered earrings, a bear-claw necklace, leather breechcloth and leggings, and a conch shell breastplate. He stood there so still and his vibrations were so in harmony with his surroundings that I decided he was another vision. I closed my eyes for a moment and when I opened them again he was gone. Where he stood lay another hawk feather. The wind blew the feather into my circle and I picked it up. The feather was in perfect condition as was the first hawk feather. My every sense was alert at this powerful sign of finding another feather. What was spirit trying to tell me? Was this Kootenai warrior somehow connected with my spiritual journey?

I braided the hawk feather onto my hair with the other one, aware that I was in Kootenai territory. We were not friendly with the Kootenai, but they were not our enemies either, for they did not invade our territory or steal our horses. They stayed mainly to themselves.

The next Sleep and Sun blended together in a blur as I slipped in and out of awareness. I did not sleep, yet I was not fully conscious of the physical world. Wind Chaser appeared from time to time to see if I were still there. Occasionally he would enter the sacred circle and sit beside me, his spirit touching mine.

On the third night, Oapiche came again and took me into the spirit world. I found myself in a shimmering white body beside Oapiche outside the entrance to a cave. He led me through the cave to an opening that held many ancient objects. I could feel the power radiating out from them. He told me in thought impressions to find my personal talisman, which would give me strong medicine. I examined a pipe and reverently touched a painted shield with feathers on it, then reached out to clasp a small sculpture. The inner vision faded and I found myself back in my body. I continued to pray in hopes that my Spirit Guide would return and take me back to the cave. He did not reappear. I was left wondering at the meaning of the vision and if the cave existed in the physical world.

The sun rose over the mountain and I watched the red and purple colors lighting up the sky. It is a good sign. I had one day and night left of my Vision Quest before returning to my people. I felt clearheaded and well despite the fact I had not slept or eaten in several days.

I lifted up the flute and began to play, discovering how to put the notes together to make a song. The wind caressed my cheek and I felt blessed as my spirits lifted.

I heard the high-pitched scream of a red-tailed hawk, and looked up. It flew above the mountain, easily riding on invisible air currents. It's sharp cry pierced my being, awakening me to greater awareness. I renewed my trust in Oapiche, knowing he was guiding me and I had the ability to listen to this guidance. I knew my vision would gradually start unraveling its meaning and that I would some day go back to the cave to get my talisman whether it was in the physical world or the spirit world. I watched the hawk a long time as it circled overhead. It swooped down low as if it was flying directly for me, then flew upward and disappeared from view. Another hawk feather fluttered down and landed beside me. I trembled as I picked it up and braided it into my hair. Finding three hawk feathers was powerful medicine. I felt greatly blessed and my heart was so opened that tears of joy rolled down my cheeks. A vibrating hum like the buzzing of bees filled and pulsed through me.

When the morning sun was high in the sky the Kootenai warrior appeared again. I knew he was not a vision this time; his presence and energy were very strong. His face was painted as it had been before and his hair was braided. I felt a sense of danger and controlled power about him. He approached me softly on moccasin-covered feet, moving with a natural grace. He stopped when he was just outside my circle.

I stared up at him, a little unnerved, but with no intention of moving out of the circle until my Vision Quest was completed.

"There is a Piegan war party coming up the trail," he said in Shoshoni, speaking my tongue clearly but with a less guttural sound than my people speak it. I was surprised that he knew my language. I lowered my head, not answering because one does not speak during a Vision Quest. I was not concerned about any possible dangers.

"They are at the pass and will be here before the sun has warmed the land."

I sat completely still, hoping that if I ignored him he would go away. My energy was attuned to the mountain; the Piegan warriors would pass by me as if I were invisible to them.

"No blood should be shed on the Sacred Mountains. The Piegan warriors do not understand this. They will kill you if they find you."

"The Great Spirit, Apo, watches over me," I finally replied, annoyed that he did not understand the protection and had interrupted my quest. "I cannot talk to you until my quest is completed."

"They're following the mountain goat trail. It will lead them directly to you."

I did not reply. He stepped into my circle. I gasped, about to protest, when he grabbed my arm and yanked me to my feet. I was so surprised I did not fight him as he hauled me to the edge of the mountain. Down below I saw six Blackfeet warriors on horseback, coming up the trail in single file. I immediately recognized them as the ones I had seen near my village. The sight of them brought me abruptly out of the world of vision; and fear replaced the inner warmth and love that had been mine only moments before.

## *2*

## Blackfeet War Party

*In what is now known as Glacier National Park*

I followed the Kootenai warrior back down to the stream where his horse was tied. "You shouldn't have interrupted my quest," I said. "The Piegan warriors wouldn't have seen me."

"Why not? I did."

"You're in harmony with the mountain. They're not."

"It is not the place of a foolish squaw to question the decision of a warrior." I didn't reply, for among my people a squaw is obedient to a brave and doesn't talk back. "You will ride with me on Straight Arrow."

"I have my own horse." I whistled for Good Thunder, and then went to get my weapons and supplies. As I squatted down to pull them out from under the bushes, Good Thunder came running out of the woods and over to me. He rubbed his nose affectionately against my back, almost pushing me over. I turned and hugged the pinto around the neck.

The warrior watched us with interest. "This stallion is your horse!" he said with a look of surprise.

"Yes." I grabbed Good Thunder's rope bridle as he started toward the other stallion. There was fire in his eyes and he looked ready for a fight. "No, Good Thunder!" I fought him as he pulled against me in an effort to get at the other animal. Good Thunder reared up, lifting me off the ground. The warrior sprung up onto his own agitated stallion and moved him well away from Good Thunder.

After a short struggle I got Good Thunder under control, then I threw a saddle on him and tied on my supplies.

"Where did you get that saddle?" the warrior asked.

"From my Comanche cousins. They steal horses with saddles on them from the men living far to the south." I picked up my bow, put on my quiver, and mounted.

"You carry weapons, too!" His expression was disapproving. "I thought you were Shoshoni."

"I am Shoshoni." I wove my hands up and down in a weaving motion, the sign of the Shoshoni. "I belong to the band of Tukadukas, the Sheep Eaters."

"Shoshoni maidens do not use weapons." He made a clicking noise and his horse started forward.

"Some of us do," I replied, following him. "Who are your people?"

"They are the San' ka, the water people."

"Who taught you to speak my tongue?"

"My mother is Shoshoni."

"Did your father steal her?"

"You ask too many questions for a squaw. Women of my tribe are more respectful and they do not carry weapons. Are you a chief's daughter that you own a war horse and wear feathers in your hair?"

"I'm a chief's sister," I said proudly.

"Why does your brother allow you to carry weapons? You could hurt yourself."

My temper flared at his arrogance. "I know how to use a bow and arrow! I don't need your protection! There's no reason for us to ride together."

"A squaw with such a sharp tongue will have trouble finding a brave."

I respectfully lowered my head. It would bring shame on my people if I were rude to a warrior helping me.

He led me by a different route than the way I had come. I thought he must know the fastest way down the mountain. It would be easy to wind up at a dead end in this rugged terrain.

The trail looked like it was used only by mountain goats, and Good Thunder had to make his way carefully. Straight Arrow was obviously more used to the mountains for he seemed to be having no difficulty negotiating the trail. We rode down the rocky slope in silence. Good Thunder suddenly lifted his head and twitched his ears. Alert to danger, I patted his neck and looked around just as Wind Chaser slipped out of the woods in front of us. Straight Arrow whinnied and reared up. The warrior swiftly pulled out his bow and arrow.

"No! He is my friend!" I exclaimed. "He won't hurt you or your horse."

The warrior lowered his bow. "Why do you have a wolf for a friend?"

"He is half-dog. His mother mated with a wolf, then returned to camp to have her litter. I have had Wind Chaser since he was a puppy." I ducked down as Good Thunder went under a low branch. There were fewer trees here and the ground was rocky. We rode out onto a narrow path on the side of the mountain. A rocky wall rose up along one side and the other side was the edge of a cliff.

"I'm Masheka," the warrior said. "What are you called?"

His question surprised me. Didn't he know names had power?

"Do you refuse to answer simple questions?" he asked, sounding miffed as he turned to look at me.

"The custom of the Tukadukas is to give their children names that tells something about them. The name may even change when a person does something that distinguishes them. We believe a name has power, so a person shouldn't say their own name."

He nodded. "Shoshoni ways are different. I'll give you a new name. I'll call you Vision Woman since you made a long journey for your vision. Do you like the name?"

"It's a good name." I was pleased with the name for a person who had visions was a person who had spiritual power. The name reminded me of my Vision Quest. "When I first saw you two days ago, I thought you were a vision. How is it that you are still here?"

"I stayed to guard you. Quests are no longer safe in the Sacred Mountains unless one is guarded. I came here because I'm a scout for the Crazy Dog society. We're on the warpath against the Blackfeet who have attacked bands of our people living east of here on the plain. These bands have come here. Together we'll have the strength to drive the Blackfeet from the Sacred Mountains."

I reined in Good Thunder and looked around. "I thought I heard something."

Masheka also stopped. "Ride on ahead of me." As I passed Masheka on the narrow ledge, he said. "They're near. I'll try and hold them off so you can escape."

I urged Good Thunder into a gallop and twisted my hands in his mane. I heard a war cry and turned back to see Masheka, swinging his tomahawk at a Piegan warrior. I brought Good Thunder to a stop and pulled out my bow. My hands shook as I notched an arrow, drew it back, and released it. The arrow missed because I was so frightened. Fitting another arrow, I took a deep calming breath and concentrated on the Piegan warrior. I moved to a place beyond fear—focusing only on what I had to do.

The arrow flew through the air, hitting the warrior in the

chest. He screamed as he fell from his horse and over the side of the mountain. Another member of the war party rode around the now riderless horse on the narrow ledge and Masheka found himself fighting a new opponent. I fitted an arrow to my bow but before I could fire it, Good Thunder reared up as a Blackfeet warrior dropped down from the ledge above onto the trail in front of us. I lost my balance and tumbled from Good Thunder's back, almost going over the cliff's ledge. The warrior sprung at me with his war club; I scrambled to my feet, pulling out my knife.

Wind Chaser rushed past me and leapt at the warrior. The warrior fell over backwards with the wolf dog on top, throwing up his arm to protect his throat. Wind Chaser tore into his arm growling fiercely.

I looked up to see Masheka kill his attacker. The warrior fighting Wind Chaser, drove him off with his war club then regained his feet. I stood facing him with my knife drawn. He swung his war club at me, and I jumped back. Wind Chaser dove at him again.

Masheka rode up from behind and smashed his toma-hawk into the man's head. I screamed, "Masheka, look out!" as a Piegan warrior came riding toward him with his spear drawn. The spear went flying through the air. Masheka threw up his shield and the spear pierced into it, grazing his fore-arm. The spear and shield tumbled to the ground. The Piegan warrior leapt from his horse toward Masheka. The force of his body knocked Masheka from Straight Arrow and both men fell to the ground, the Piegan warrior on top. He thrust his knife toward Masheka's throat. Masheka grabbed the Piegan warrior's arm before the knife could end his life. Wind Chaser attacked the Piegan warrior as I grabbed Masheka's toma-hawk, which had fallen to the ground. My help wasn't need-ed, for Masheka quickly overcame the warrior with Wind Chaser's assistance. Masheka rose to his feet, leaving the war-rior dead upon the rocks.

"Where are the other two?" I looked wildly around, searching for sign of the remaining two warriors. My breath came in uneven gasps in a throat that was raw and dry. I had never been more terrified.

"They are probably waiting for a more open place to attack."

"They will kill us." I expected them to appear at any moment intent on avenging their dead brothers.

"I'm not afraid to die."

"I don't have your courage."

He nodded. "You're a maiden not trained for battle."

"I've never killed before." My knees folded under me and I started to fall. Masheka grabbed my arm, lifting me up and placing me on Good Thunder. "If you're going to use weapons like a warrior, you must accept death like one. Weakness is your enemy and pain to be endured." Masheka mounted his horse and started forward, leading the way.

I kept watching in back of me for the other warriors but they didn't appear. We rode swiftly for a long distance with Wind Chaser running alongside Good Thunder. He seemed nervous and stayed close. I was exhausted, both from the battle and because I hadn't slept or eaten for several days.

Masheka led me down the mountain trail into the woods below. We came to a stream and rode into the water, following the stream's windy course in order not to leave a trail. In a concealed section of the stream, Masheka got off his horse and washed his wounds. I slid off Good Thunder into the shallow water; it was cool and revived me some. Good Thunder began to drink. I cupped my hands and splashed my face, then drank heavily.

"I have to stop this bleeding or I'll leave a trail of blood," Masheka said.

Pulling out my medicine bag, I went over to him. " Sit down. I'll tend to them."

He sat on a large boulder that protruded in the middle

of the stream. He had four angry gashes on his arms and shoulders, but none on his chest, which had been protected by his breastplate. The one on his upper arm, made by the spear, was especially bad and bleeding heavily. I glanced up at his fiercely painted face, a little hesitant to touch so dangerous a warrior. He looked wild and unapproachable. I looked back at the wound and knew it would not heal well unless I sewed it up. I took a small bone needle out of my leather bag and told him to unbraid one of his braids.

"What for?" he asked.

"I'm going to use a strand of hair to sew up your wound. It will heal best if I use your own hair."

He looked doubtful. "Your wound will stop bleeding if I sew it up," I said. He made no move to unbraid his hair so I unbraided one side. I felt uncomfortable under his intense gaze. It was an intimate act usually only done by a family member. I pulled out a hair and threaded my needle. "This will hurt."

He frowned. "Do you know what you're doing?"

"Yes." I pushed the slender needle into the strong skin on the side of the wound. He gasped, then tightened his jaw. I slid the needle out the other side of the wound then tied a knot and cut the end of the hair off with my knife. I made several more stitches this way. Masheka's forehead broke out in sweat but he didn't flinch as I continued to stitch up his wound. I sewed up one of the knife wounds as well. When I was done, I put away the needle. I cleaned and wrapped leather strips around the other two wounds. "The others will heal without stitches."

"I've never seen wounds stitched up before. Are you a medicine woman?"

"I'm too young to be a medicine woman, but I am training to be one." I braided his hair as I spoke, for he could not easily do it with his wounds. When I had finished we mounted again and continued our trek.

We left the stream when it became narrow and swift, staying on rocks to keep from leaving a trail. Dusk came and Masheka still showed no sign of stopping. I was so tired that I slumped over on Good Thunder's broad back and twisted my hands in his mane to keep from falling off.

I must have fallen asleep for I awoke to find Masheka standing next to my horse. "We will camp here until the moon comes out and we can see to travel again."

"What?" I asked in confusion. He caught me as I started to fall and helped me over to a fur. "I'm sorry. I'm so tired." I felt nauseous and the trees spun as I collapsed onto the fur. Wind Chaser came over and curled up beside me.

"Do you want to eat?" Masheka asked, taking a shirt from his pack and putting it on.

I shook my head; darkness was closing over. I thought of rousing myself to check Masheka's wounds and prepare his food but the need to sleep was too strong. I felt a fur placed over me as darkness pulled me under.

Masheka woke me awhile later when the moon was high in the sky. "We must travel on," he said.

"I can't. I'm too tired," I replied, feeling worse after such a short rest.

"You will if you value your life."

I struggled to my feet, yawning and stretching. Wind Chaser was confused by our departure in the middle of the night. I bundled up my furs, tied them on Good Thunder, and then pulled myself onto his back. I was stiff and sore from my fall.

"We will follow the stream again," Masheka said, riding off. I followed him into the water and Good Thunder picked his way carefully through the rocky stream. I was waking up a little in the cool night air. The sound of the lively mountain stream as it babbled through the rocks was pleasant and soothing.

Masheka let Good Thunder catch up with his horse and

handed me a leather water pouch. The water felt cool and refreshing on my parched throat. Good Thunder tried to bite Masheka's stallion; I pulled him back before they could get into a fight.

"He is too much for you to handle, Vision Woman," said Masheka. "He threw you when that Blackfeet attacked you."

"I was not prepared or I wouldn't have fallen. I was getting ready to shoot another arrow. I suppose you still think squaws shouldn't use weapons."

"I found it good that this one could shoot an arrow earlier today. Why did you journey all the way to the Sacred Mountains for a Vision Quest?"

"There is a purity here that gives me my clearest visions. The vibrations in the air are finer and the energy more vibrant. Even before I was old enough to have heard of the Scared Mountains, I was led here by my spirit guide for my first Vision Quest."

"The mountain has its own energy. All my people go there for visions. It is because the mountain is sacred that no blood should be spilled."

"It was spilled today."

"In the lower regions. It couldn't be helped. I don't understand why you came here alone. Surely a chief's sister is valued and many warriors would have been honored to accompany you."

"My visions usually come to me when I am alone."

"But you could have been guarded."

"All our warriors were needed to hunt kotea."

"Not even one could be spared?"

"It was a hard winter leaving us weakened. One did offer, but grandfather would not allow it. He said a woman should only travel with her husband. He would not approve of my traveling with you either."

"So you don't have a husband yet."

"No, I'm in mourning."

"It is not good to speak of the dead, but since I'm not of your people I don't know who you mourn for."

"My parents died of winter fever in the Season of Howling Wind."

We traveled in silence for a long distance. The sun was beginning to rise when Masheka finally said we could rest. We camped near the Flathead River, and I finally broke my fast by eating some pemmican.

Masheka did not look well and I was glad we had stopped so he could rest. "Does your arm hurt?" I asked.

"I've had worse injuries. Get some sleep while I keep guard."

I put my sleeping robe on the ground. "We should both sleep. Wind Chaser will warn us of any danger." Wind Chaser wagged his tail beside me at the mention of his name.

"I don't intend to trust our lives to a wolf."

"He's half-dog," I replied, scratching Wind Chaser behind the ears. "And dogs are valued for their loyalty to man." Masheka made no move to lie down.

"I'll keep guard if you don't trust Wind Chaser. You need rest more than I." I stopped scratching Wind Chaser and he pushed his nose against my hand until I started scratching him again.

"I'll rest once it's safe to do so."

I was about to protest but his expression revealed that he didn't think much of the idea of being guarded by a squaw either. I lay down on my fur, deciding he deserved to go without sleep for trusting me so little. I was badly in need of rest from my quest and fell immediately asleep. When the sun was high in the sky, I awoke to see that Masheka was sitting in the same spot. "You must be tired," I said. "Do you want to sleep while I keep guard?"

"No, we need to keep going." I knew he couldn't be feeling well. The knife wound in his shoulder was deep and traveling this hard would make it slow to heal.

"I'm going to the stream for water," I said, picking up the leather water bag. Wind Chaser and I walked the short distance through the woods to the water. I was limping slightly because I was still sore from being thrown from Good Thunder. Wind Chaser sat on the bank, watching me as I slipped off my moccasins and leggings and waded into the stream. The water was deep and fairly warm in the sun. I washed my face and hands, then began to fill the leather bag.

Wind Chaser began to growl; I whipped out my knife and swung around. A Blackfeet warrior rode out of the woods, looking large and dangerous. His cheeks were painted with black lines. He had a bow in his hands with a notched arrow ready to shoot through the air. My chest tightened, knowing I had no chance of escape.

Wind Chaser was crouched down and still growling. He suddenly leapt at the warrior. The Blackfeet brave fired the arrow at Wind Chaser. I screamed as the arrow hit his body. He yelped and flipped over in the air, landing on the ground. The warrior jumped off his horse and started after me.

I turned and ran through the stream, the warrior splashing in after me. I couldn't run fast enough to get away, so I turned to face him, holding my knife threateningly toward him. What I saw frightened me even more. He wore an expression of such total confidence that I felt as if I were a deer cornered by a mountain lion. He didn't draw a weapon but approached me with wary movements. We both knew he could easily disarm me.

He leapt at me and I stabbed him in the chest. Loosing my footing, I went under water and came up coughing and gasping. He pushed me under again and I fought him desperately. I was beginning to panic. I had lost my knife and had only my hands to fight with. My lungs felt like they were going to burst and I feared he intended to kill me.

Finally, the warrior pulled me out of the water and dragged me to shore. He was bleeding from the chest wound, but it wasn't a serious injury. He came down on top of me, smelling of sweat and dirt. I kicked and pummeled my fists against his chest. He repulsed me; his breath was foul and his hair matted and dirty. I scratched my nails across his face and he struck me ruthlessly. I fell back stunned, unable to stop him as he pulled out a rope and bound my wrists.

In the next instant he sprang away from me and drew his knife as Masheka came running toward him, swinging a tomahawk. I turned away as the tomahawk sunk into the Blackfeet warrior's chest and blood spilled onto the sand.

Masheka knelt beside me, breathing heavily. "Did he hurt you?" I shook my head still frightened. He pulled his knife from its shaft and sliced the rope binding my wrists. I threw my arms around his neck and buried my face in his shoulder, shaking like a leaf in a bad windstorm. Masheka held me tightly, talking softly in Kootenai until I had calmed. I released him, embarrassed that I had been so bold.

My leather dress had hiked up, revealing a large black and blue mark on my thigh. "You're badly bruised. When did this happen?" he asked, pushing my skirt up further to look at it.

"When I fell off Good Thunder."

"He's too hard for you to control."

"He is hard for anyone to control. What about the other warrior?"

"He attacked me at camp while this one attacked you. I killed him."

"Is Wind Chaser...is he dead?" I asked, my stomach twisting.

Masheka turned and looked for Wind Chaser. "He's still alive," he said. He rose, helping me up. I walked toward Wind Chaser who dragged himself to me. I started crying as I knelt beside him. He pushed his head into my lap and his tail thumped against the ground.

Masheka came over and squatted beside Wind Chaser,

taking out his knife. "Hold him still while I take out the arrow." The arrowhead was embedded in Wind Chaser's shoulder, but not too deeply because of his thick fur.

I held Wind Chaser's head as Masheka examined the wound. Wind Chaser growled. I pressed his head against my breast as Masheka cut out the arrow. Wind Chaser whinnied and tried to pull away. My tears continued to fall once the arrow was free. "You're going to be all right. I'll take care of you." I rubbed him lovingly behind the ears. He looked up at me with devoted, trusting eyes. I washed the wound and treated it with a poultice of fresh horsetail.

"We've got to get going," Masheka said. He went back to our camp; returning a short time later with the horses including the Piegan warrior's, which was loaded up with our supplies. "We'll have to leave Wind Chaser behind," he said.

"No! We can pull him on a pony-drag."

"We need to reach your people quickly and warn them that Piegan war parties are gathering on your territory."

"What about your people? You are a scout for them, you need to rejoin the other Crazy Dogs and tell them of the Piegan's activities."

"They know about the Blackfeet. A large Kootenai war party is already on the warpath south of here. I'll rejoin them when I leave your band."

"Wind Chaser is my brother and he has protected me many times. I cannot honorably leave him when he needs me."

"We have a long way to travel and there are still many dangers before we reach your people. We can't afford to be slowed down for even so fine a four-legged as Wind Chaser."

My tears started up again. "He thinks of me as part of his den and we can communicate with each other. You go ahead and warn my people. I'll stay behind with Wind Chaser."

Masheka frowned deeply. "It's too dangerous to leave

you here." He waded into the deep water and dove under.

I followed him into the stream to search for my knife. He came over to me after a short time. "What are you looking for?"

"My knife. The warrior attacked me somewhere near here and I lost it." I was unconsciously staring at Masheka for his war paint had come off in the water and I had just realized that he was younger than I had thought. He looked to be only a few winters older than I was. His features were nicely formed and he wasn't so fierce-looking without his war paint. His strong, muscular body, revealed that his tribe had plenty to eat over the long, cold Season of Howling Wind.

"Why do you stare?"

I felt myself color. "You look much different without your war paint." I turned my attention back to the water.

We both searched for a while then he reached into the water and pulled out my knife. "Here it is. It is well the warrior wanted a slave and not revenge. He probably decided it would be a waste to kill a strong, young squaw with such a pretty face." Our eyes met and held for a moment. His presence and comment disconcerted me. I hurried back to shore.

"I have to change into my other tunic." I was still in the white ceremonial dress that I'd worn for my Vision Quest. Once in the woods, I changed out of my wet dress into my other tunic, tying it with a blue beaded belt. Returning to Wind Chaser, I gave him some meat jerky.

"We have to move on." Masheka came over to me with his breastplate and leather clothing on, leading Straight Arrow and the two Blackfeet horses.

"I'm staying here. Thank you for helping me and my people."

"Do you want to be a slave for some Piegan warrior?"

"You've killed the scouts. I'll be okay."

"It's not safe. You'll travel on with me."

I shook my head. I couldn't leave Wind Chaser even if it meant I might be killed.

"You're a very defiant squaw, in my tribe squaws do as they're told."

"I don't wish to be disrespectful after all you've done for me, but I won't go with you."

He glared at me, his body rigid, all traces of gentleness gone. "San' ka warriors do not tolerate disobedience." He grabbed my arm and roughly pulled me to my feet as I struggled to get away from him. Wind Chaser tried to rise, barking ferociously. Masheka lifted me into his arms and leapt onto Straight Arrow. I found myself sitting sideways on the horse, pressed against Masheka.

"Let me go! You've no right!" I wildly struck my fists against him.

Masheka grabbed my two wrists in one hand. "Do I have to beat you to get you to obey?" His tone of voice was deadly.

I froze, my stomach tightening, and stared up at him in fright. I didn't know him well enough to know if he would carry out his threat. Among the Nimi it is considered a terrible disgrace to be beaten.

Masheka released my wrists to grab Good Thunder by his reins. He tied the stallion to the rope leading the two Blackfeet horses. We started forward. Turning back, I saw Wind Chaser watching us with a forlorn expression. I was filled with grief at having to leave him and started sobbing.

Masheka drew me gently against him. "He'll be all right. Don't grieve yourself so. Where are your people so I can take you to them?"

"Please let me stay with Wind Chaser or take him along."

"Wind Chaser is better off where he is. He can rest and heal, and then come to you."

"I hate you." I pushed my hands against his chest to put

some space between us. I was so angry with him that I stopped crying.

"Why? Because I won't let some Blackfeet kill you or capture you for a slave?"

"Let me ride alone."

"I don't trust you to ride alone."

"I don't know which are worse—Blackfeet or Kootenai warriors!"

His arm stiffened on my waist and I instantly regretted saying it. I knew I had to learn to control my tongue.

"Where are your people?" he asked again, his voice lacking the warmth it had held the first time he had asked the question.

"My people were camped at Three Forks," I replied, "but they will have moved on by now."

"We'll go there, then follow their trail."

# 3

## Masheka

*Journey from Glacier Park in Montana to the Salmon River in central Idaho*

We traveled all day and into the evening. That night when I lay in my furs, I was too tense to sleep. "Are you awake?" I asked softly.

"What is it?"

"What if the Piegans attack us while we sleep?"

"I have not seen any signs of them nearby and I need to sleep."

I was quiet for a moment, then I said. "I was almost taken captive."

"It's not safe for you to travel alone." His words were roughly spoken as if he wanted to impress their importance on me instead of giving me comfort.

"I'm not traveling alone. You're with me."

"For the moment. Go to sleep."

"Do you think Wind Chaser will live?"

"It's hard to say. Life is not easy."

"Wolves are sacred. The wolf created people and the

world and stars."

"My mother taught me Shoshoni stories. The San' ka believe that we each have guardian spirits that we seek on Vision Quests when we're young. All things of nature have spirits. The spirits are found in rivers, woods, and animals. Any time an animal like Wind Chaser helps you it is powerful medicine."

"I'd like to go back and stay with him until he is well."

"And while you take care of him the Blackfeet may attack your village."

I held my tongue, sensing he was becoming impatient with me. He wanted to sleep. I named the stars trying to tire myself, but every crack in the woods caused me to jump and every bird cry or wolf howl left me shaking. I'd never been afraid of the woods and night sounds before. I finally gave up trying to sleep, and sat up with my arms wrapped around my legs.

"Why are you up?" Masheka asked; his voice was heavy with fatigue.

"I think I'll keep guard for a while."

"It's better if you sleep; we have a long way to travel tomorrow." Masheka rose and came over to me. He sat down beside me and put his arm around me. "Wind Chaser's wound was not deep, and he is a strong animal. He's better off resting where he is for a few days."

"But he could be killed by other animals."

"Death is always in reach for all of us. Did the Piegan warrior frighten you so much you cannot sleep?"

I nodded; he drew me against him and lay down. I rested my head on his shoulder. His warm body smelled of pine and fresh air. He pulled my fur up around us both to keep us warm in the cool night air. Though he was nearly a stranger to me he made me feel safe; I knew him to be a man of honor and courage.

"Why are you helping me and my people?"

"We share the same enemy and besides I am half Shoshoni. I care about the people of my blood. As for you, my Guardian Spirit said I must bring you safely back to your people. Your life is important for reasons I don't yet know."

"Where's your village?"

"Our village is west of here on Flathead Lake. We stay there most of the time but after we have driven off the Piegans we'll make a temporary camp on the plains to hunt kotea."

I fell asleep to the sound of his voice.

Upon awakening I was upset to realize I'd broken custom by sleeping beside a man, even though it was only to ease my fears and I was still a maiden. We were between the furs and Masheka was still asleep with his arm around me. I didn't want to awaken him, so I didn't rise. He needed to sleep since he was still recovering from his wounds; moreover, we'd traveled hard and slept little. His color looked much better than it had the day before. I enjoyed studying him while he was unaware; his face was pleasant to look upon.

As the sun rose, his eyes opened. He smiled upon seeing me. It was the first time I had seen him smile. His smile was beautiful and transformed him from a dangerous Kootenai warrior to someone not so different from the men in my village. His expression was warm and unguarded and his eyes were an intense brown.

I reached out and touched his pleasingly shaped mouth. "I was beginning to wonder if you ever smiled."

"You've only seen the warrior side of me so far." My pulse quickened at the feelings between us. "My spirit guide expects a lot in asking me to return you to your people. I'd prefer to take you to live with mine." My eyes widened as the meaning of his words sunk in. He arose and I watched him go off into the woods, aware of him as a man.

I'd spent most of my life around a small group of families.

I knew all the young men. Kicking Horse I had known since I was born; I knew him as well as I knew my brother. Learning about Masheka was a new and fascinating experience. Although he was quiet and said little about himself or his people, I was getting to know him by his actions. He'd gone to great lengths to help me, putting himself in constant danger. I felt guilty about the growing warmth between Masheka and myself because of my relationship with Kicking Horse.

Masheka killed a ptarmigan for breakfast, and we roasted it over a fire. After we had eaten and packed our supplies onto our horses, I said, "There's no reason for you to continue to travel with me. Our paths lie in separate directions." I mounted Good Thunder, then looked expectantly at Masheka.

He was on his own stallion, watching me. "The danger from the Piegans still exists."

I looked uncomfortably down at Good Thunder's mane. "Masheka, there's a brave who waits for my return. He and my brother will be angry that I have traveled with you."

"Then they shouldn't have let you journey so far alone."

"They were reluctant to."

"You've no choice but to accept me as your guardian." He started off, heading south.

I frowned, then started after him, knowing he was right.

We covered a great distance swiftly, going southeast to the Angry River, then following it to the Sogwobipa River. We rested only when it grew dark and took turns guarding the camp at night. Masheka killed game as we traveled. I gathered winter cress, dandelions, wild leeks and onions, and dug up jerusalem artichokes tubers, wild carrot roots, and eastern camas bulbs. Masheka was easy to be around, and I enjoyed watching him move and do things. He was a fine horseman who rode as if he was born on a horse. His bond with Straight Arrow was strong.

I was careful to keep some space between us after that first night when we had shared my furs. I was more reserved with him and didn't talk much, as was proper for a maiden when with a warrior. Despite my taciturnity, there were warm, strong feelings rising up between us.

One afternoon we stopped earlier than usual. After we had set up camp, I told Masheka it was time to take out his stitches. The wounds had healed well leaving only small scars. I cut the stitches with my knife and pulled them out.

"This sewing up of wounds is a good thing," said Masheka when I was done. He moved his arm round and flexed his muscles. "It will move fine, soon. It's just a little stiff."

"Let me knead the stiffness out." I began to knead the muscles of his arm and shoulders. "My Grandmother taught me how to rub sore limbs when a person is injured or numb with cold." After I finished his shoulders I worked on his broad back. I liked the feel of his strong, sun-warmed skin beneath my hands. I could feel the tension ease from him.

"Ai, it feels good. You will make some brave a good squaw." My hand stopped moving on his back and I felt suddenly shy, realizing I had been bold.

He turned to look at me. The warmth in his eyes made my heart race as I backed away from him. Rubbing his shoulders and back was an intimate act, something a squaw would do for her man. I felt myself redden at the thought of Masheka being my man.

He grinned as if reading my thoughts. "How many horses do you think a squaw with so many talents is worth?"

I didn't know what to reply.

"I see for once this outspoken squaw is without words."

"I'd better go gather some roots." I went into the woods disconcerted by his remark.

When we finally reached the place where my village had been, we found they had moved on to their summer camp. We followed their trail west along the foothills of the Shining Mountains. The sun was up longer each day and it grew warmer. The Season of Ripe Berries was drawing near. We saw signs of the Blackfeet and continued a constant lookout for them. As we drew nearer to where I thought to find my village, I was sad that I would soon be separated from Masheka. We reached the Salmon River and followed it west.

After two more Suns and Sleeps of traveling, we spotted my village off in the distance. My people had set up camp along the river at a place where a strong breeze blew to keep insects down. Since the sentries recognized me, no one made an attempt to stop us. We rode directly into the center of camp. People gathered around, looking at Masheka with guarded curiosity. A Kootenai warrior had never ridden into camp before with a Shoshoni maiden. Upon asking for Gray Eagle, I was directed to his tepee.

When I spotted Gray Eagle, I leaped off of Good Thunder and ran to him. Upon seeing me, he swung me around laughing. "I feared I might never see you again, Red Willow," he said, setting me down. I was delighted to see him and my people again. Grandfather came out of the tepee, and I ran to him. He embraced me, unembarrassed to show his affection.

One of the men made reference to Masheka and my brother looked up, noticing him for the first time. Masheka sat on his horse, heavily armed and looking like a formidable warrior. He had put on face paint and his expression was dark, almost hostile. Gray Eagle's smile disappeared and there was immediate tension between the two men. "Why do you bring a Kootenai warrior into our camp?"

"Masheka journeyed here with me."

Masheka sprung from Straight Arrow and walked forward. The men stared at each other with growing antagonism. Masheka had a taller build, lighter complexion, and finer features than my dark, stocky built brother.

"Why were you with him?" My brother's voice held anger.

Masheka answered before I could. "There is a large Blackfeet war party on Shoshoni land. I have come to warn you and to bring Red Willow safely back to her people."

Gray Eagle looked surprised. "You speak Shoshoni?"

"Yes, I know your language well. It would be best to break camp and leave this place. I saw signs of a war party of over a hundred warriors on your land."

"Why would you come to warn us? The Kootenai are our enemies."

"Masheka is not our enemy. Please, Gray Eagle, we're tired and hungry. We've ridden hard for many days with little sleep, and the Blackfeet wounded Masheka. Will you keep us standing here all night or show us Shoshoni hospitality?"

Gray Eagle's eyes did not leave Masheka's. "Red Willow doesn't need protection. She is trained to survive alone."

"Gray Eagle doesn't mean to be disrespectful," said Grandfather. "He has been worried about Red Willow and is grateful for her safe return. I know that you were sent to protect her by Apo." He put his left arm over Masheka's shoulder and clasped his back, then pressed his cheek to the younger man's and said "Ah-hi-e, ah-hi-e" as is the greeting of my people.

My brother scowled at Masheka, looking even angrier, before finally greeting him in the same way Grandfather had. "We'll talk, follow me." Gray Eagle and Grandfather went over to my aunt and uncle's lodge and sat down at the fire outside their tepee. One of the men took Good Thunder and Straight Arrow and tied them to our tepee. They were too valuable to be kept in the corral with the workhorses where they could be stolen more easily.

"Go with them," I said to Masheka. "I'll join you shortly." I started to go into our tepee, but Masheka grasped my arm.

"Who's this man to you?"

"He's the head chief."

"Your brother?"

"Yes."

Masheka immediately relaxed and his expression softened. He left my side to join my grandfather and brother.

After changing into a light tan buckskin dress with fringe and blue and yellow beadwork, I combed out my hair until it was shiny and free from tangles. It had already grown dark when I stepped out of the tepee.

I went over to the fire and Masheka's eyes lit with pleasure upon seeing me. Gray Eagle was telling him that our scouts were out searching for the Blackfeet war party. I took a bowl of stew from the leather pouch hanging over the fire, then sat on a log near Masheka. Using a spoon carved from a bone, I began to eat.

"I'm a scout for the San' ka," said Masheka. "Our warriors are on the war path. The Piegans have driven my people from the plains, but they won't drive us from the mountains. We're too strong here. Your people should go back into the safety of the mountains until the warring is over."

"We'll meet with the elders in the morning and decide what we must do," said Grandfather. "Masheka, you are welcome to sleep in our tepee tonight."

Masheka rose. "I can't stay. I need to report to our war chief."

"You're leaving?" I exclaimed, springing up.

"I have been gone too long; the Crazy Dogs will be searching for me."

I was sad, knowing I'd never see him again. "Thank you for helping me."

"If the Crazy Dogs were not on the war path, I'd take you with me."

"Red Willow, go to the tepee," said Gray Eagle.

I immediately left, knowing my brother was angry that

Masheka had spoken intimately to me.

My brother entered the tepee a short time later. "You shouldn't have traveled with a Kootenai warrior!" said Gray Eagle. "They're our enemies."

I looked up at him from where I was sitting on my furs. "Masheka rescued me from a Piegan warrior who shot Wind Chaser and captured me. You should be grateful to him instead of angry."

"I'm surprised he brought you here. He obviously wanted you for himself. The people of our tribe are talking about you."

"There's nothing to talk about."

"There's plenty to talk about. You're the chief's sister and you're in mourning. You shouldn't have been alone with a man, especially not a Kootenai warrior. Perhaps Kicking Horse won't want you now."

"Where is Kicking Horse?"

"He's with the scouting party."

I was immediately worried. "I'll pray for his safe return."

I was exhausted from my journey and slept well into the next morning. I woke up with a feeling of emptiness and loss, knowing that Masheka had gone. I hurried from my sleeping couch and slipped on my tunic, surprised that no one had awakened me.

Grandfather came into the tepee, carrying herbs that he had been gathering. I helped him tie and hang them up, ashamed that I had slept in instead of going out with him to gather them. He knew I was waiting to speak to him but there was never any rushing Grandfather. When we had finished hanging up the herbs, we sat down. He studied me for such a long time that I felt there was nothing he didn't know about me.

Grandfather had taught me many things, like how to understand the hidden meaning and language of my dreams. I sewed symbols from my dreams into my clothing with beads. He also helped me to understand the meaning of my visions and to see the ways that Apo spoke to me.

Grandfather added a few sticks of wood to the fire and watched the smoke thoughtfully. "A dwelling is incomplete without grandfather fire. It is sacred as is grandmother water." He turned to me. "You've seen more of your quest, and now it is time for you to go to Spirit Cave. You'll go there in search of truth and knowledge that only the spirit world can offer."

A rush of excitement went through me and I spoke without allowing him to continue. "Does Spirit Cave exist in this world? Do you know where it is?"

He looked at me sternly for being so impatient and I lowered my head. "Some of the tribe think I can no longer serve the people. They think that I am so much in the spirit world now that I can no longer advise our chief."

"Only those who have lost sight of the importance of the spirit world would say that!"

"Our lives are part of the universal circle of the nation. Our tepees are round representing the circles. Everything is a circle, the seasons, suns and sleeps, and life—it all has order. We're born at the beginning of the cycle of life and die at the end. My cycle is nearly complete. My spirit will be released soon and fly to the spirit world."

I drew in a sharp breath. "No, we still need you!"

He looked at me so long I began to feel uncomfortable. It came to me that my time of training with him was over. "No," I said, shaking my head. "There's so much I still need to learn."

"Only those who are to serve are called on to journey to Spirit Cave. You'll be a great holy woman someday. Stop fighting your path and flow with the river. It'll take you where you're meant to go. You'll face many difficulties before you reach Spirit Cave. It's in a part of the country you've never been to before. It would be best if you left soon; I feel a sense of urgency about this quest."

"Gray Eagle will resist this journey. Blackfeet war parties are close-by."

"Leave Gray Eagle to me. Journey in the direction of the rising sun. Your guardian spirit will guide you to the cave if you're worthy. If your path becomes unclear, pray until you see the light again. Only those who are pure of heart will ever find the cave and be able to go inside it."

"I'm afraid."

He stared into the flames for a long time before he spoke. "You must face your fears. The difference between life and death is merely an illusion. All that we go through is to teach us. What does it matter whether we learn here or go on and learn in the spirit world?" His eyes became distant; I knew he was seeing a vision. "The cycle of our people is changing, for our children I see pain and suffering." The mystic look cleared from his eyes and he looked sad and weary. I realized he had grown old and frail. I'd always thought of him as strong and invulnerable, it was a shock to realize he was not. "You must leave as soon as you have supplies packed. There is little time."

I trembled, afraid that when I returned from my journey he would have crossed into the Land of Shadows.

"Have courage, child. You'll find the strength to do as you must." His expression softened. "I wish I could keep you beside me to enjoy your company, but your path calls out loudly for you to follow it. Learn all you can before our ways disappear."

I started preparing food for my trip as Grandfather left to join the council meeting. My brother was also there, so I could pack without him questioning me. In the afternoon there was shouting. As I ran in that direction, I saw scouts riding into camp.

The scouts dismounted and started talking to the people gathered. I quickly spotted Kicking Horse and a tremendous sense of relief went through me. Although I longed to speak to him, I stayed at the edge of the circle; it would be bold for a maiden to go directly to a warrior.

It was not long before he noticed me. He moved away from the people, who had surrounded him to find out about the Blackfeet, and came over to me.

"I am glad to see you made it safely here," he said, his voice gruff with emotion. I could see that he was worried.

"What's wrong?"

"The Blackfeet war party will reach us when the sun rises again."

The base of my stomach tightened into a knot. "How many are there?"

"Over a hundred and fifty warriors. They want to drive us from this land and keep all the kotea for themselves."

My mouth went dry; I felt like I needed to sit down. In our tribe there were less than a hundred warriors, moreover, our men were not at their strongest after the scarcity of food during the long, cold winter. There were over two hundred women and children for them to defend.

"I have to join the council," he said gently. He touched me cheek. "Do not be frightened, we will win the battle." He walked a few paces away.

"Kicking Horse."

He turned and looked at me. I looked down, twisting my hands, then raised my face to his again. "What is it?" he asked.

"There is something you should know. You will hear soon enough, but I would rather you heard from me."

He frowned. "Go on."

"Not here." We walked away from the center of camp, moving back toward my tepee. "I did not travel alone back to camp." I stopped walking and glanced around to be sure we were alone, then looked at Kicking Horse. The sight of him looking at me with such grave, worried eyes filled me with a rush of deep love for him. "A Kootenai warrior brought me

50

here because a Blackfeet war party was in the Sacred Mountains. Some feel that I should not have traveled with him. If you feel that way and no longer wish to marry me I will understand."

He clasped my upper arms in his strong hands. "I was afraid I would never see you again, Red Willow. Gray Eagle and I were going to set off in search for you as soon as we drove off this Blackfeet war party. I'm glad to see you safely here. If it was a Kootenai warrior who brought you here then I am indebted to him. It is no longer safe to journey across our land alone. I have no concerns about your virtue or honor. A more pure woman cannot be found. You have never done anything to make me jealous."

His grip became less fierce as he continued, "Since you were little you have gone on Vision Quests and followed your guardian spirit. If I wanted a woman others would not talk about I would have looked elsewhere for a wife long ago." He drew me intimately close and I put my arms around him, relieved that he was not angry.

Kicking Horse's nearness made me forget my worries. He whispered, "Grandfather must soon give his permission for you to share my lodge, I cannot wait much longer for this beautiful, wild-spirited woman to be mine."

"Kicking Horse!" my brother said as he made his way over to us. "My sister has caused enough of a stir in the tribe without you adding to it."

I sprung apart from Kicking Horse, but when I looked at Gray Eagle I saw that he was smiling.

"There's no one in the tribe who does not already know how I feel. I have made it no secret," replied Kicking Horse, grinning back.

"I would be glad enough to have another man take responsibility for her, she has grown far too independent for a woman. But enough talk of women, what of the Blackfeet?"

Kicking Horse and Gray Eagle walked off to join the

council meeting and I went back to the tepee to continue my packing.

I planned to leave camp and ride back to where I had left Wind Chaser. I had an inner feeling that he was still alive.

The fear of my people grew stronger. It was decided that the women and children would hide by the river and the warriors would ride out to meet the Blackfeet. I delayed leaving on my quest, not wanting to desert my people when danger was near.

In the evening Wind Chaser appeared. His eyes gleamed in the firelight. He limped over to me and I knelt down and put my arms around him. Never had I felt such great joy. "Wind Chaser, you are alive! But look at you, you're so thin." I ran my hand over his sides and examined his wound, then dipped a stick into the stew pot, spearing a piece of meat, and gave it to him.

My brother arrived back at camp and squatted down by Wind Chaser. "So you are feeding my meat to Wind Chaser."

"Look at how thin and weak he is."

My brother affectionately examined Wind Chaser. "If he has lived this long, he will survive, Red Willow."

I fed Wind Chaser more meat along with water in a bowl made of pine needles covered in pitch. Afterwards, I scratched him behind the ear, thanking Apo for his life.

My brother and I ate, and then I helped him get the weapons ready. I checked our bows to be sure that they were in good repair, put rattlesnake venom on the points of the arrows, and sewed my three hawk feathers to my shield for protection. Wind Chaser put his head in my lap as I worked. I could hear singing and dancing not far away as the warriors prepared themselves for battle. Gray Eagle left me to join them. We expected the war party to attack in the morning.

Later, my brother came into the tepee as I tied the last of my food supplies in a bundle. "What's this?" he asked, his eyes meeting mine in the dim firelight.

I didn't answer. I wished that Grandfather were there to explain everything to my brother.

"Where are you planning to go?"

"On a quest to Spirit Cave. It's east of the sacred land of boiling water."

"You aren't going anywhere! I have decided your time of mourning is up. After we drive off the Blackfeet, you will go live in Kicking Horse's lodge. I gave him my consent this afternoon. The other squaws think that you have too much freedom. They do not like it that you ride a fine war-horse and spend so little time doing squaws' work. Talking Goose says that once you share a lodge with Kicking Horse the talk will stop."

"Has Grandfather given Kicking Horse permission to marry me?"

"It is no longer his decision." Gray Eagle's face was full of pain. "He grows old and tired. This summer will be his last with our band. He has decided to stay behind when our people move on to our winter camp."

"No, he must stay with us!" I said horrified. It was a common custom among the people for an older person to stay behind if the journey would be too difficult for them to make, or if they felt they were a burden to the tribe. The food that they would eat in the cold winter months could go to keep others alive. "Grandfather is too valuable to be left behind. The tribe needs his wisdom and guidance."

"It's for him to decide."

"No, you're the head chief! You must convince him to stay with us! Who will take care of the sick, interpret dreams and visions, teach the children of the spirit world, and foretell of the future?"

"I love Grandfather as you do, but if he doesn't have the strength to make the long, hard journey to winter camp, we can't slow down the whole band for him. He's so much a part of the spirit worlds now that the people are growing afraid of him and his power. He no longer has the energy to tend to the sick or teach the young."

"His connection to the spirit world, knowledge of healing herbs, ability to see into the future, and stories of our tribal ancestors make him one of the most important people in the band. Promise me you will talk to him." Tears streamed down my face. "He is the last of our family. I cannot bear it if he dies."

Gray Eagle drew me against him and covered us both with a robe as is the custom when two are of the same family. "I'll talk to him. Perhaps I can make him see how much the band needs his wisdom; I'm too young to be head chief without his guidance. Now you must forget this quest and do as I ask."

I moved away. "I will stay to help our people tomorrow, but once the battle is over I must leave. I will marry Kicking Horse when I return from my quest."

"After the battle you will marry Kicking Horse. Convince him of the necessity of this quest. If he thinks it is worthy, I'll give you both permission to go. I won't have you going off on your own again."

"What if Kicking Horse doesn't want me to go on a quest?"

"Since when has he not strove to please you? Now enough about your quest, tomorrow we fight the largest war party we've ever fought. Let me get a few hours of sleep so I will have a clear head when I lead our men into battle." The strain showed on his face and in the rigidness of his body. The happier days of our youth were gone forever.

I did not say anything further, ashamed now that I had troubled my brother when he had so much on his mind. I was happy knowing Kicking Horse and I could finally marry, but worried as I thought of the danger my band faced.

# 4

## The Battle

I rose before dawn on the morning of the battle, fastened on my quiver of arrows, and went outside with Wind Chaser, carrying my shield and bow. I had slept poorly after a night filled with nightmares of the coming battle and death.

My brother and Grandfather were in council with the war chiefs. I ate a piece of meat jerky, feeling strangely calm. Kicking Horse came over to me. He was wearing a breastplate, had war paint on his face and chest, and feathers in his hair. He wore only a breechcloth, so if he were wounded in battle the leather of his clothing would not be driven into his body. "Why are you still in camp?" he asked. "You should be hiding with the other women."

"I'll join them shortly."

He scowled. "Don't join the battle."

"Kicking Horse, I'll battle to the death if the Blackfeet break through our warriors and attack our women and children."

"If that happens our warriors will be defeated and there will be no other way." He drew me close. "I don't want to waste time arguing. Your brother has given us permission to share a lodge."

"I know, he told me last night."

"You don't look happy about it."

"I'm just worried. What if we lose this battle?" I asked,

my fear for him was strong and I clung to him, not wanting him to leave me.

"We'll win. The Blackfeet warriors fight like squaws."

I smiled at the absurdity of his answer in spite of my fears. "Come back to me and give me many papooses." My eyes moistened with tears. "I love you."

"And I have loved you, Red Willow, since before I understood what it was to love a woman. You are my soul."

"I see only darkness. Don't take risks and ride out in front with my brother." Tears rolled down my cheeks.

"I'm a warrior. I must show courage and not be afraid of death."

"You must not die! You are a great warrior!"

My brother came riding up to us on a white stallion. He was wearing a fine war bonnet made of eagle feathers and he carried a spear and a shield. "It's time to leave for battle. Red Willow, go down to the river."

Kicking Horse tossed me up onto Good Thunder's back before I could protest. "A battlefield is not the place for a squaw," he said. "I know what you are thinking."

He mounted his own horse and galloped off with my brother to the edge of camp. All the men in our tribe, except the grandfathers, were fierce warriors. They gathered around Chief Gray Eagle and the war chiefs. Every one of them was prepared to fight to the death, even the young braves fresh from their manhood ceremonies.

The grandfathers rode down to the river to guard the women and children. I reluctantly followed them. Kicking Horse was right in suspecting that I wanted to join the battle, I couldn't stand the thought of waiting with the women and not knowing if we were winning or losing. At the river I dismounted and hid Good Thunder in the woods before crawling into the rushes under the edge of the riverbank where the other women were hiding. Wind Chaser wiggled into the rushes beside me.

56

We waited in tense silence, fearful of the upcoming battle. Before long we heard war cries, the screams of horses, and loud cracking noises that sounded almost like thunder.

"What's that loud noise we keep hearing?" I asked Antelope who was beside me.

"I don't know. It frightens me." Antelope and I were close in age. Several warriors had wanted her to share their lodge for she was a pretty woman of strong family, but her father had turned them all down because he was waiting for Gray Eagle to ask for her.

The women were trying to keep the papooses and children quiet, but they grew restless as the sun moved across the sky. Little Cloud, Sweet Clover and Chased-by-Bear's papoose, began to cry. He was over a year old and wanted to run around.

"Keep him quiet!" hissed Yellow Flower, Chased-by-Bear's first wife who was six or seven summers older than Sweet Clover. Her own two little girls were sitting quietly next to her. She was strict with them because we were in hiding, though at home she was lenient with her daughters because among the Nimi being too strict was thought to crush a child's spirit.

Little Cloud cried louder at the sound of her voice. Yellow Flower clamped a hand over his mouth and nose so he could not breathe. When she removed it he had stopped wailing, though he still cried. He crawled onto his mother's lap and clung to her as she rocked him. He had been taught since he was first born that he must not cry for we have strong enemies. When we're hiding or fleeing from them a crying papoose could endanger us all.

I took a blue-green stone and a feather from my medicine bag and gave them to Little Cloud to play with. Yellow Flower moved over by one of her friends to gossip.

"Yellow Flower is always mean to Little Cloud, except when Chased-by-Bear is around," whispered Sweet Clover.

"Chased-by-Bear is proud of his only son and would be angry. I've been tanning hides so by next winter I will have my own tepee. I don't want to spend another winter being a servant for her."

"She's just bitter because Chased-by-Bear took a second wife," said Antelope. "She used to be good tempered."

"I thought it would be nice to be a second squaw," said Sweet Clover. "I thought Yellow Flower would be like one of my sisters and that we would be friends. I thought we'd share the work and enjoy having each other to talk to, especially during the Season of Howling Wind when you have to be inside the tepee so much. Mother always complained that there was too much work for one squaw, and it is good to have women around because we are not allowed to talk freely to men. I'd like it if you became Chased-by-Bear's third wife, Red Willow. He likes you; I have seen the way he looks at you, and heard the praise in his voice when he speaks of you. He says you'll be a powerful medicine woman someday."

"I'm going to marry Kicking Horse. Father and Grandfather have finally given him permission." Little Cloud was bored with the feather and stone, so I put them away and lifted him onto my lap. He fingered the beadwork on my dress. "I don't want Kicking Horse to take a second wife after we marry."

"If Gray Eagle and I marry, I wouldn't want to share him either," said Antelope.

"Chased-by-Bear is a good hunter and a brave warrior," said Sweet Clover. "I'm glad he asked for me. I'm honored to have a man of his experience who is respected by the tribe. Besides, too many of the warriors die in battle, or when out hunting for us to all have our own brave."

"The battle goes on so long. I wonder how it is going," I said, wanting to leave the shelter of the rushes to see what was happening. Battles often took all day because warriors hid behind shields and trees and shot at each other from a long distance. They fought hand-to-hand combat only when one group had overpowered the other and was sure of success.

Battles were a chance for young warriors to prove their bravery. A man who was daring enough to ride up to an enemy weaponless and hit him with a coup stick could become a war chief. But this battle was not to count coup. The Piegans came for our land and to revenge their warriors killed in past battles. Our warriors would fight hard to keep them from attacking our village.

I was worried, for whether we won or lost, many of our warriors would be killed fighting against so many enemies. My people might never fully recover from the loss of so many warriors. The tension grew and the squaws stopped talking. They were holding knives, ready to defend themselves and their children if the Blackfeet found us.

Antelope whispered softly, "Our warriors have no chance against so many Blackfeet warriors. We should gather up the women and children and run away from here."

"Gray Eagle said we were to stay here until he sent a warrior with instructions."

Her eyes lit up brightly at the mention of Gray Eagle's name. "Then we will wait, but I wish I knew how the battle was going."

"I will go find out," I whispered, unable to contain myself any longer.

"No! You mustn't. It's too dangerous."

Wind Chaser and I were already crawling out of our hiding place. I climbed up the embankment and went into the woods to find Good Thunder. I rode back to camp and from the hill above it I could see the battle. The warriors from both tribes were fighting fiercely from horseback. Many men and horses were lying on the ground dead and wounded, while other horses were running off riderless. I anxiously searched for my brother and Kicking Horse among the warriors. I finally spotted Gray Eagle at the center of the battle, Kicking Horse and Chased-by-Bear close beside him. Moments later Blackfeet warriors swarmed around them and they were lost from my sight. I panicked, afraid they'd be killed.

My stomach was in knots by the time I spotted Kicking Horse again—relief swept over me. Near him a Piegan warrior pointed his firestick at one of our warriors. It made the big thunder noise I'd heard when in hiding. The Piegan warrior jerked back as smoke burst out of the firestick. Our warrior fell from his horse. The Blackfeet warrior leapt from his painted war pony and scalped the fallen brave. Raising the scalp over his head, he yelled a triumphant war cry. Kicking Horse went galloping toward him swinging his war club. The Blackfeet warrior began to put something into the end of the firestick. I was afraid the firestick would spit out another cloud of smoke, killing Kicking Horse, but it remained lifeless and Kicking Horse bashed his war club into the Piegan warrior's head. I watched as other Blackfeet warriors shot their fire sticks. They were terrible weapons of death that could kill from a great distance but they couldn't be immediately refired. Most of the Blackfeet warriors did not have them.

Our men began to give way and I knew we would lose the battle. There were simply too many Blackfeet; moreover, with this new weapon they had the advantage. One of our young warriors, of no more than thirteen winters, came riding up the hill toward me with a Blackfeet warrior chasing after him. I notched an arrow to my bow, then sighted the Piegan warrior and let the arrow fly. It hit the warrior, and he fell from his horse as the youth reached me. "Gray Eagle says I'm to warn the women and children!" he shouted. "We can't hold the Blackfeet off any longer."

"Go and warn them!" I shouted. He rode off and, looking down the hill, I saw that many Blackfeet had ridden into our camp. They were searching for the women and children and setting tepees on fire. I rode down the bluff and into the fighting with Wind Chaser close beside me. Some of our men were losing heart and beginning to retreat. The new weapon had struck fear into them and it is always a warrior's right to refuse to fight. "Die with honor!" I yelled over and over as I rode among them into the middle of the battle. Seeing my courage made many turn back and continue the fight.

I held onto Good Thunder with my knees while I readied an arrow and shot it at a Blackfeet warrior. I missed. It was too difficult a shot with Good Thunder running beneath me. An enemy warrior was riding toward me, swinging a tomahawk, and rapidly closing the distance between us. I brought Good Thunder to a stop and shot again. The warrior crumpled over on his horse.

Blackfeet warriors were riding off into the woods, going after the women. I started to follow them when I saw grandfather fighting a warrior in hand-to-hand combat. I rode toward them and shot another arrow. I killed the warrior, but as I drew closer I saw that Grandfather, though still standing, was bleeding in many places.

When he saw me he shouted, "Go, Red Willow, ride from here and go to Spirit Cave!"

I was desperate to get to him and nudged Good Thunder forward, but now there was fighting all around me, separating us. I sent Wind Chaser from me to go help Grandfather. The stench of death and blood and fear was all around me. I heard the scream of a dying horse. All is lost, I thought. I threw up my leather shield as a knife came slicing toward me. The knife tore through my shield but left me uninjured. Good Thunder reared up and attacked the warrior's horse. The warrior was unprepared and was thrown from his steed.

Suddenly I became aware of a new cry as Kootenai warriors came riding into camp. They began fighting the Piegans and some of our warriors set off into the woods after the Blackfeet who were searching for our women and children. I caught a glimpse of Masheka and in the same moment he also saw me. His eyes widened with concern upon seeing me in the middle of the fighting. He tried to ride toward me, but was immediately blocked by a Piegan warrior. I fitted an arrow and fired it at the brave Masheka was fighting.

I do not know if it hit him or not because at that moment another warrior swung his war club at Good Thunder, hitting him in the head. Good Thunder screamed and I was almost thrown from him. As I scrambled to stay on him, the warrior brought his club down again, this time hitting my shoulder. I lost my grip and tumbled from the saddle. The breath was knocked out of me when I hit the ground and I struggled to stay conscious as waves of pain went over me. The Blackfeet warrior pulled out a spear and threw it at me. I rolled away but not quite fast enough and I felt it pierce my side.

The warrior leaped from his horse and picked up his spear. He lifted it into the air to thrust it at me again. I felt an odd sense of detachment, knowing I was going to die.

Wind Chaser growled as he came racing toward us. The warrior turned to him as Wind Chaser took a flying leap. The warrior was knocked to the ground with the snarling wolf-dog on top of him.

I tried to get up, but my body no longer seemed to function. I slid off into darkness, seeing a light in the distance. I was flying through a beautiful sky with billowing clouds around me. Grandfather appeared before me in a body that was strong and youthful and surrounded by light. "It is not time yet, Red Willow," he said. "You must go back."

I felt a wet tongue on my face and came back into my pain-ridden body. Wind Chaser stood protectively over me. Masheka appeared a moment later. He gently lifted me up and I cried out in pain, almost losing consciousness. He mounted Straight Arrow with me in his arms. The fight surrounded us, but I saw my brother and Chased-by-Bear keeping the Blackfeet away from us so that Masheka could escape with me. Masheka rode through the battling warriors and into the dense smoke from the burning tepees with Wind Chaser at his heels. I began to cough and my eyes watered, but soon we were clear of the fighting.

Masheka kept riding until the battle noises were behind us. "Where are the women and children?" he asked.

"They were hiding by the river bank, but by now they will have fled from the Blackfeet into the woods." We reached the spot where I had hidden with Antelope and Sweet Clover. Wind Chaser started smelling the ground and soon discovered which way they'd gone; he ran off after them with us following. It was not long before we saw the bodies of some women and children. I was sickened with grief by the sight. Masheka rode on and soon we heard the sound of fighting again. Our warriors had caught up to the Blackfeet and were trying to stop their pursuit of our women and children. Masheka rode past them into the woods. I was bleeding profusely and barely conscious.

Masheka stopped when he reached several of our women who were running from the battle with their children and papooses. "Stop!" he called out in Shoshoni. "Red Willow needs help." He swung from his horse still holding me. Pain sliced through me at the jarring his dismounting caused. He placed me on the ground and Antelope and Sweet Clover, who was carrying Little Cloud, came over to me. "I will hold off any Blackfeet that find us," said Masheka. "The worst of the battle is over; many Kootenai warriors rode with me to help your people."

My aunt, Talking Goose, appeared beside me. She cut away the side of my dress and examined my wound while Wind Chaser guarded me.

"How badly is she hurt?" Masheka looked greatly distressed.

"She'll live to have many papooses if I can stop this bleeding. The spear has only grazed her side, slicing it open as a knife would."

"Go back and help save my people," I whispered to Masheka.

"No, I'll stay here to guard you and the others." He went off to check the nearby woods for other Blackfeet warriors.

Talking Goose started to sew up my side and I passed out from the pain.

When I awoke, I found both Masheka and Wind Chaser sitting near me. The sun was low in the sky. "How are you feeling?" Masheka asked.

"Not good. Do you know what happened back at camp?"

"Yes, I rode back. Your warriors were able to drive off the Blackfeet once the Crazy Dogs arrived to help them. The women and children are returning to camp. I'll take you back, if you're strong enough to be moved."

"I'm strong enough." Masheka lifted me into his arms and I gasped in pain, breaking into a sweat. I couldn't move my arm or shoulder where the war club had hit me and my side throbbed unmercifully. He mounted Straight Arrow and we started back with Wind Chaser running alongside us.

"Do you know what happened to Grandfather?" I asked.

He looked sadly down at me. "His name can no longer be spoken. Your people mourn his loss."

I clung to Masheka, glad to be in his arms. Tears came to my eyes as I thought of Grandfather and how much I would miss him. I had feared that Grandfather had gone to the Land of Shadow when he had come to me in the inner worlds in a young man's body. I barely had the courage to ask about my brother. "And Gray Eagle?"

"I was told he was injured."

"Seriously?"

"I don't know."

We rode into camp with Wind Chaser close behind. Masheka dismounted and carried me over to my tepee. It was one of the few that had not been burned by the Piegans. My brother and several other warriors lay on furs with Antelope and Talking Goose attending to them. Talking Goose came over to Masheka as he stooped down and came through the tepee opening. "Put her on this sleeping couch." She led him to it. "Be careful of her" Masheka placed me on the fur, then she covered me with another fur, looking worried.

Gray Eagle went over to Masheka. "Thank you for my sister's life, and for helping my people."

"Your sister is seriously injured and it will be your fault if she dies," Talking Goose said, starting to cry. "You taught her to use weapons and ride a horse like a brave. She shouldn't have been fighting. Your mother wouldn't approve of how you have let her run free. The women of the tribe are all talking."

"Enough, Talking Goose," commanded her husband, White Bull, from where he lay on his sleeping robe. "Do you want our chief to cut off the end of your nose for being so outspoken?"

She covered her nose with her hand. "I meant no offense."

"It's all right. I know you are upset," said Gray Eagle.

Masheka still crouched beside me. "You will be strong again," he said. I grasped his hand, reluctant to let him go. "Rest now. I will come to see you later." He squeezed my hand then rose up and turned to my brother.

"Thank you for saving my people," said Gray Eagle. "I thought all was lost until you and your warriors arrived."

"When I reached our war party, I found out the greatness of the Piegan's numbers and that they were headed in the direction of your village. We were only sixty men strong, yet I convinced them that it was better if we fought alongside your warriors. We could defeat them together, but if we let them destroy you, they would come and attack our village next."

"They would have slaughtered and enslaved our women and children if you had not come."

"I know; I feared for Red Willow's life. We rode here as swiftly as the horses could carry us." He looked meaningfully at me. "I want to speak to you about your sister."

Gray Eagle glanced at me, his expression distressed. "Let's talk in private," he said, leaving the tepee.

Antelope was tending the wounds of one of the warriors. I noticed her tense as she watched the men leave. What's wrong?" I asked.

"Your brother will tell you."

My chest constricted and I felt as if a band had been tied around it. "Tell me what?"

Distressed, she lowered her head not answering. Shortly Gray Eagle entered the tepee and sat beside me. "Many died in battle." A terrible dread went through me, seeing his stricken face. "We can no longer speak of your betrothed."

"No! Say it's not so."

"You must be strong."

"You're wrong! He's strong and fearless—no weapon could hurt him!" There was no denying the sorrow I saw in my brother's face. I began to weep wildly, as the horror of his words became reality for me. Wind Chaser started howling, sharing in my misery. I would never see Kicking Horse again. My brother put his hand on my shoulder. "Leave me! I want to be alone!" I cried. He left me and went to the fire. I struggled into a sitting position, causing sweat to pour from my brow for I was as weak as a papoose. I began chanting as I pulled my knife from its shaft at my side. I planned to honor Grandfather and Kicking Horse by grieving them in the ancient way of my people. I gritted my teeth and sliced the knife across my forearm. Blood poured from the deep cut. So great was the pain in my heart that I barely felt the wound.

"No!" screamed my aunt. "Stop her! She'll kill herself!"

I slashed my arm again as my brother came swiftly back

over to me. He grabbed my wrist and with his other hand he pried my hand open until the knife fell from it.

"I have the right to mourn them!" I fought to break free of his hold.

"You have lost enough blood." He drew me against him and held me close until the fight and wish for death went from me. I wept in his arms, inconsolable in my grief. Wind Chaser whimpered and pushed his nose against me. "Let me cut off my hair at least," I sobbed.

"This is not the time for mourning rituals. You need to rest and grow strong again." He held me, sharing in my misery while my aunt tended to the bloody knife wounds on my arm. I felt lightheaded as my brother gently lowered me onto the sleeping couch. I slid into darkness.

In the morning I awakened to the sound of the whole camp wailing as they mourned our warriors and loved ones. Wind Chaser was curled up beside me, warming me with his body. I put my arms around him and buried my face in his thick fur as I started crying. My grief was overwhelming. I was still in mourning for my parents, and now Grandfather and Kicking Horse had been cruelly taken from me. I wanted to follow them into Land of Shadows.

I could not imagine life without Kicking Horse. We had been close since we were young; I had expected to share my life with him. It didn't seem possible that he wouldn't walk through the tepee flap at any moment, as he had always done, with a ready smile on his lips.

I keenly felt the loss of Grandfather as well. He was my teacher and the only person who could guide me in my spiritual training. I didn't know how I would complete my quest to Spirit Cave, and become a medicine woman without him. Yet my tribe needed a healer more than ever with Grandfather gone.

## 5

# Turning Point

*Village on Salmon River in what is now known as Idaho*

I developed a high fever and drifted in and out of consciousness over the next few days. I thought I was dying; in many ways I would have welcomed death so great was my grief. Several wounded men were in the tepee; my aunt and uncle had also moved in since their own tepee had been destroyed. Talking Goose and Antelope attended me, trying to bring my fever down, putting healing herbs on my wound, and bringing me food.

Once my fever finally broke, I was again aware of my tribe and concerned about its survival. My brother sat next to me that evening. "Looks like you're going to live," he said.

"Yes, I'm much better now. Are the burial ceremonies completed?"

He nodded. "As is fitting for his place in the tribe, the elder of our family was mourned for three days, and all touched his body and wished him well in his next life. His war-horse was killed so he would have it in the next life. His horse and weapons were then put into a ravine and buried under rocks. We covered him well, so no animals could disturb his resting-place. The other warriors were buried in a like manner."

I lowered my head, knowing he spoke of Kicking Horse. "How many were killed?"

"Thirty-six Shoshoni warriors were killed in the battle, but more have died since then from wounds caused by the new weapon the Piegan warriors carried."

"How many women and children were killed?'

"Nine women and five children were killed, and four women and two children were stolen."

"Will anyone go after them to try and get them back?"

Gray Eagle sadly shook his head. "We have been weakened too much from the battle to spare any men to go after them. They're mourned as if they are dead."

"How many San' ka warriors died?"

"Twelve. The other San' ka warriors wrapped their bodies in leather robes and put them over captured Blackfeet horses. They'll be taken back to their own tribe where they'll be placed on a platform and mourned before being buried under rocks."

"Where did this new weapon come from?"

"Masheka said that the Blackfeet must have traded for them. There is a wooden lodge, called a trading post, where men go to trade in Kootenai territory. The men at this lodge have these weapons and call them flintlocks. These men are very different from us and do not understand our ways. A Lakota brave at the trading post told Masheka that his tribe calls these men Wasichus. Their holy man says the Wasichus are bad medicine. They are driving tribes from their land to the east of us, forcing the tribes onto Lakota land. The Wasichus are from a far away land that is many moons from here. You must travel east across the land then cross a huge body of water to get there."

I felt uneasy hearing about these Wasichus. "How could

so few men drive tribes onto Lakota hunting land?"

"You ask a lot of questions. A squaw is to leave the thinking to the men. Others in the tribe complain that you do not know your place. The women are jealous of you and the men do not like it that you hunt and fight like a brave."

I frowned, knowing my brother was criticizing me only because he did not know how to protect his people from the flintlock. "Our warriors were inspired by my courage to keep fighting when they would have retreated."

"You speak the truth and make me ashamed of my words. The Lakota brave said there are so many Wasichus in the land to the east of here that they number more then the trees in a forest."

"These flintlocks do not seem that powerful to me. I saw a Blackfeet brave fire one and before he could get it ready to fire again he was killed." I said, remembering Kicking Horse killing him in battle.

"The flintlocks are a tube that shoots out an iron ball. They can be fired from a long distance; the men that are hit are killed or badly wounded. They are powerful weapons. We must find new ways to fight against warriors and the Wasichus that carry the flintlocks."

I pondered his words, for I was worried about these new people on our land who supplied our enemies with such dreadful weapons.

My brother sat silently in thought; he reminded me of how grandfather always took his time speaking. Grandfather never spoke hastily on important matters and when he did speak his thoughts were deep. At last Gray Eagle said, "We're so greatly weakened by this attack that there was talk in council of joining up with the Agaiduka, the Salmon Eaters, for protection. I think it is a good idea."

"We have many relatives in Few Tail's band. We'll be welcomed if we joined them."

"We'd be welcome when game is plentiful but in the

Season of Howling Wind, we must separate from them so we are not hunting the same game." My brother went to his own furs. There had been little time for him to rest and get over his own wounds. He had been busy with the mourning ceremonies, seeing that the injured were taken care of, and meeting with the council to decide the future of the tribe.

Sweet Clover came with Little Cloud, to visit me. She was sad because their tepee had been destroyed. She and Yellow Flower would work during the Season of Ripe Berries to make a new one and would have to share it when the Season of Howling Wind came. I enjoyed her company for I was bored from being forced to rest.

Masheka hadn't come to see me since first bringing me here. As many Suns and Sleeps passed and he still did not appear, I wondered if he had returned to his own people. I finally asked Antelope who told me he had not been seen in camp since the burials. Most of the Kootenai warriors had left our camp, taking their dead with them. I was sad that I would not be able to thank him for helping my people and me.

One warm evening I heard many voices outside our tepee. Antelope was sitting beside me, sewing a pair of moccasins. She looked toward the flap. "I wonder what all the excitement is about." She went outside and returned a moment later grinning with Masheka beside her. "Look who's back."

Wind Chaser began barking, but after sniffing Masheka he started wagging his tail. Masheka petted Wind Chaser then sat down near where I lay on my sleeping couch. He had a serious expression. "You're looking better."

"I'm healing. I have been quite ill...you might have come to see me sooner." My voice had an accusing tone in it.

Antelope gasped at my disrespectfulness, her smile fading. She had a quiet, gentle nature and was always a proper squaw.

"I stayed away out of respect for your time of mourning,"

said Masheka. "Your brother told me you were to share a lodge with a brave of your tribe who was killed in battle."

Tears filled my eyes and my throat constricted at the mention of Kicking Horse. I looked away until I was more in control of my feelings, then said, "Masheka, I am glad you are here. I was afraid I might never have a chance to thank you for all you've done for me and my people."

"I won't leave here until you are ready to leave with me."

"Leave with you! Why would I leave with you?"

Antelope put her hand in front of her mouth and began to giggle. I wished she'd leave rather than staying to hear what should have been a private conversation. At the same time I knew she wouldn't leave for a maiden and warrior are always chaperoned.

The corners of Masheka's eyes wrinkled and a smile slowly appeared. "Your brother has given me permission to marry you."

"But I'm in mourning!"

"Your brother has decided to end your time of mourning so that you can return with me to my people."

I ran my hand across my buffalo robe in confusion. "It is an honor to have you ask for me, but I can't leave with you. I must leave on a Vision Quest as soon as I'm strong enough."

Masheka's smile disappeared. "Your brother has already accepted my gift of horses and given you to me."

His words angered me. "What horses!"

"I just gave him nine Piegan ponies for you. They are tied outside your tepee."

My color rose. Everyone in the tribe would have heard of this by now. Nine horses were a lot to give for a maiden, and it was unheard of for a Kootenai warrior to ask for a Shoshoni woman. "Gray Eagle will return the horses when I tell him I won't share your lodge!"

"I have no intention of returning the horses," said Gray

Eagle, stepping into the tepee. "My sister can be stubborn but
she will make you a good squaw." Gray Eagle gave Masheka
a knife that had been Grandfather's and several buffalo hides.
"I'd give you more gifts since Red Willow is a chief's sister but
I have little to spare after this recent attack."

I watched uneasily, knowing I was expected to accept
whatever brave my brother chose for me.

Masheka thanked him for the gifts, then looked at
Antelope. "How much longer before Vision Woman is well
enough to travel?"

"After she has rested another seven Suns and Sleeps
perhaps she will be strong enough for the trip if you travel
slowly."

"I'll be back then. In the meantime I'll hunt for our journey." He left the tepee.

My brother was scowling. "You're too outspoken. This
man will soon be your brave; you must show him more
respect. He has saved our band from being completely
destroyed. We owe him our lives. You shame me by refusing
so great a warrior when I have already accepted his gift of
horses."

Tears sprang to my eyes. "Gray Eagle, don't be sharp
with me! Please try to understand the importance of my spiritual training. I wish Grandfather were here to explain it to
you. I miss him and Kicking Horse so much that sometimes I
wish I had died of this wound." He sat down where Masheka
had been a moment before and drew me into his arms. I wept
harder. My sorrow upset Gray Eagle; I knew he was as heart-
broken as I was over losing our grandfather and Kicking
Horse, who had been his best friend. The loss was difficult to
bear after having lost our parents so recently.

"Hush, Red Willow, we must not speak of them anymore."

"I was to share a lodge with Kicking Horse and he
would have given me strong papooses."

He stroked my head and rocked me as if I were a small child. "He was a good man, but he is not part of your path. I see the Kootenai warrior in your future. The energy that flows between you is powerful."

"Masheka wants me to live with his people!"

"They're good people."

"But you will need me to cook for you and our tribe needs a medicine woman."

"If you become a medicine woman, you will serve Masheka's tribe. I will soon have my own squaw to tend my fire. You need to start your own life. I don't need another mouth to feed when it grows cold and food is scarce."

I glanced at Antelope and she smiled back at me. "Have you asked for her?"

"No, but I will soon and I know her parents will accept."

"They'll be honored," whispered Antelope. Her eyes were shiny with happiness and she was especially lovely despite the fact she was wearing only her work clothes and was tired from many days of helping with the injured.

My brother helped me lay back down. I drifted off to sleep, slipping into the dream world. I was in my tepee working beside Grandfather. We were hanging up strong medicine herbs that would help those that were injured in the battle. It felt quite natural to be working beside him, but suddenly I realized he was dead. "Grandfather, what are you doing here?"

"Helping our people for their need is great. Time is short; you must go to Spirit Cave. Do not be afraid to travel there alone. In the next instant I was in a cave surrounded by a blue light that seemed to come from the cave itself. I felt its healing light flowing through me, giving me the strength I needed to continue my quest. Grandfather was standing beside me.

I slept late into the next morning not awaking until my aunt brought me food. After I had eaten, she helped me put on a leather dress. I then went outside for the first time since I'd been injured. The bright sunlight hurt my eyes, and I was so stiff and sore that it hurt to move. Over the next few days I began to heal rapidly. I spent time outside each day, sitting up with the help of a backrest and doing small tasks like sewing and helping to prepare food. Antelope and Sweet Clover with Little Cloud often came and worked beside me, making the work much more pleasant.

My friends and relatives brought me gifts of baskets, clothing, and furs since I was soon to leave for Masheka's village. I knew it would be discourteous to refuse the gifts and would cause suspicion, but I was uncomfortable accepting them. I was not planning to go with Masheka; moreover, I knew my people had so little they could scarcely afford to give anything away.

The night before Masheka was to return, Wind Chaser and I crept out of the tepee after everyone was sleeping. Good Thunder was tied to a tree right outside our tepee. After saddling him, I tied my leather pouches on his back. I had packed them with food and supplies during the last few days for my journey to the Spirit Cave.

Because of the wound in my side, mounting him was difficult. It was dark outside the tepee with only a sliver of a moon that was partly covered by clouds. I managed to slip by the guards without being seen.

Riding caused me discomfort, but I was determined not to let anything stop me. I rode southeast in the direction of Spirit Cave. I was very tired, having no reserve strength to draw on after being sick. I grew gradually weaker; it was too soon for me to be riding.

I was finally forced to stop and rest. I laid out a fur and went to sleep. The sun was high in the sky when Wind Chaser awakened me with his barking. Three riders were galloping toward us. I pulled out my bow and an arrow and jumped up. When the riders drew nearer I saw that they were

Kootenai warriors and I lowered my bow, awaiting their approach.

Masheka was in the lead and when he drew up close, I backed away from him for I could see that he was extremely angry. Wind Chaser stopped barking and started wagging his tail when he saw it was Masheka.

"How did you find me?" I asked. I held one hand over my eyes to keep the sunlight from blinding me as I looked up at him on his horse. "I thought you were out hunting."

"I returned early this morning and went right to your tepee to see if you were ready to leave for our journey. It was then that we discovered you were gone. Gray Eagle knew you would be headed for the land of boiling water, so I immediately set out after you. Since you did not travel far, you were easy to find. Mount up, we are going to my village. I have been gone too long already."

"I'm not going with you! I have a quest to fulfill."

"You aren't in any shape to go on a quest. It must wait." He sprung off his horse and saddled up Good Thunder. I rolled up my kotea-sleeping robe, wondering how to gracefully get out of going with him. I was reluctant to argue with him in front of the other two warriors—not wanting to be disrespectful to him.

I glanced at the two still mounted Kootenai warriors. "Masheka, can we speak privately?"

"We have lost enough time."

I went over to him and began to tie the fur onto Good Thunder's back. "I have to go on this quest"

"Your determination is evident, but your life is like a stream that has changed direction and you must accept this new course it has taken." He helped me tie the rest of my supplies onto my horse.

"I am in training to serve my people. I do not want to live with yours."

"I know you are still in mourning and that it's hard for

you to leave your people, but now you are my woman and will do as I wish." His voice held the undercurrent of a threat and brooked no defiance.

I turned to Good Thunder, feeling defeated, for I knew Masheka would force me to come if I refused. I tried to mount, but I was too weak to pull myself up. Masheka lifted me on and again I felt his anger. "You wouldn't have gotten far if you can't even mount a horse," he said.

"I'd have found the strength to complete my quest." I replied, looking down at him from the top of Good Thunder's back.

"Where exactly is it you were going?"

"Some things can't be shared except with the elders."

"You're a stubborn squaw. I don't know why I bother with you." He leaped onto his horse with an agility I envied now that I was so stiff.

We rode north into the late afternoon without taking a break. Wind Chaser stayed close to Good Thunder most of the time. I was exhausted and my wound started hurting again, even worse than the night before, but I didn't say anything.

It started to rain and soon I was drenched and shivering. I knew a warrior would never complain about the weather or stop traveling because of it, so I didn't ask Masheka to stop. My discomfort grew unbearable and I rode slumped over Good Thunder, not caring that I looked as miserable as I felt. Thunder boomed and the rain became harder. I was worried that all our supplies would be soaked.

Masheka finally stopped and dismounted. "We'll spend the night here."

It was a relief to stop moving, but I was too weak to dismount. My hair stuck in wet clumps to my face and the cold rainwater was running down my neck. The other two warriors had also dismounted and were starting to set up camp.

Masheka lifted off his pouches and furs, then looked at

me. The rain was pouring down in a heavy torrent now. "Dismount. We can't continue traveling in this storm," he said, coming over to me.

"I need help," I reluctantly admitted.

"You look terrible." He reached up for me and I slid off Good Thunder. He caught me and lifted me into his arms when he realized I was completely without strength. "You are bleeding, Red Willow," he gasped. The side of my dress was covered with blood; I had thought the moisture was merely from the rain. "You should have told me!"

He carried me over to where one of the other warriors had laid out some furs under a large pine tree and placed me on them. We were sheltered here from the worst of the rain, though I was hardly conscious of anything besides my pain. Masheka unfastened the ties on my soaked leather dress and started removing it. I didn't protest as darkness pulled me under.

When I awoke, I felt dry and warm. The throbbing pain in my side had dulled to a much more bearable level. Wind Chaser was beside me, sleeping soundly. I could feel the heat of a nearby fire and could smell smoke and wood burning. I opened my eyes and realized I was between two dry furs, under a lean-to Masheka had put up. Masheka was sitting nearby, putting a stick into the fire. The other two warriors were also there and they were all talking softly together in their own tongue. Their language was melodic sounding. The firelight lit up Masheka's finely boned face. He looked tired and drained. As if he sensed that I'd awakened he turned to me.

"How are you feeling now?" he asked upon seeing that I was awake.

"Tired." I felt myself flush as I realized I was naked beneath the furs and that Masheka must have removed my wet clothing and bound my wound.

He nodded and looked back at the fire. I watched him,

feeling comforted by his nearness. I could hear the storm still raging outside. Masheka got out some pemmican and gave it to me with water. I ate it in silence. After awhile the two Kootenai warriors left the shelter.

"Where are they going?" I asked.

"They have set up another shelter nearby here. They were sharing the fire with us to dry off, but now Targhee will keep guard while Pocatello sleeps."

"What about you? Aren't you going to sleep?"

"There isn't room except beside you. Almost all our supplies are wet."

"Then sleep with me. You have to sleep or you'll be too tired to travel tomorrow."

"You are the one who won't be fit to travel tomorrow. Did you even think about what you were doing before you set out on this quest?"

I sat up, clutching my furs to me and wincing at the pain my movement had caused. "I don't blame you for being angry with me. You have done so much for my people and me and I have repaid you by running off. I did so only because this quest is so important." I could see that his clothes were soaking wet as mine had been.

"You shouldn't have run off and you should have told me your wound had broken open so we could have stopped sooner. You won't be fit to travel for many Suns and Sleeps and we are in dangerous territory."

"I'll be ready to travel tomorrow. I just need to rest. Traveling was harder than I'd expected." I put my hand on his shirtsleeve. "You should take off your wet clothes before you get sick."

He flinched. "The fire will dry me."

"It will take them a long time to dry." I touched his hand. "Your skin feels like ice."

His eyes bore into mine. "Have you changed your mind about sharing a lodge with me?"

80

"It's not a matter of not wanting share your lodge. It's just that my path lies in a different direction."

"You can't make it on your quest alone."

I saw no point in arguing and changed the subject. "If you won't sleep with me, do you want me to sit up so you can rest?"

"No, lie back down and get warm. I'll share your sleeping robes."

He stripped off his wet clothes and climbed under the furs beside me. His body was cold. He slid an arm under me and drew me against him so that my head was resting on his shoulder.

"You're warm," he said in a hushed whisper, "and soft."

"And you're cold—and hard," I added. I slid my hand across his chest, fascinated by the feel of his muscles. "I like the way you feel."

He rolled onto his side so he was facing me. "I like the way you feel as well. If you weren't so recently wounded I'd make you my squaw tonight." He slid his hand down my back and over my buttock, then clasped my bandaged side and pushed me onto my back. I gasped as pain shot through me.

"Did I hurt you?" he asked, removing his hand. His voice was unusually husky.

"Just a little."

"I am sorry." His breathing was heavier than normal and he seemed tense. "I hope you heal quickly," he groaned, rolling onto his back.

I snuggled against him and put my arm around him. The great pain I had carried in my heart since my village was attacked was beginning to ease. Masheka lightly played with my hair, running his fingers through it. I was worn out and fell asleep, comforted by the knowledge that Masheka guarded me.

I awoke as the sun began rising. I was lying in much the same position as when I had gone to sleep. I shifted my posi-

81

tion so I could see Masheka's face. He was awake and his dark eyes looked back at me with a serious expression.

I sat up and said softly so as to not anger him. "It's important to the future of my people that I continue my quest today instead of traveling on to your village. My Spirit Guide has come to me in my dreams to tell me this."

His brow furrowed. "I'm not your brother who lets you go off on your own as if you were a warrior. You can't bend me to your will. We're going to my village." He got up and went over to Straight Arrow.

"I don't have to obey you! I'm not your squaw!" I slipped on my dress and followed him into the rain.

We stared at each other in anger. He was wearing nothing but a breechcloth and he looked at me threateningly. "Share a fur with me again and I'll make you my squaw!"

I stiffened. "I refuse to go to your village!"

"Get back under the tree!" he said, in a deadly voice. "You're shaking with cold. I'm going to go scouting to see if the Piegans are close-by." He grabbed up his bow and quiver of arrows and called to Targhee. The two men left camp while I stood there fuming. The rain was running down my face and neck. I went back under the tree. I wanted to gather up my things and leave without him, but he had left Pocatello to guard me. I took off my already wet dress and crawled back in between the furs. They weren't nearly as warm without Masheka beside me. Pocatello came over and got the fire going, for it had died down to coals.

"How far is your village?" I asked him.

He gestured in sign language that he didn't know what I was asking. I realized he could not speak the Shoshoni language. I asked again in sign language. He replied with his hands using rather abrupt gestures that it was a long journey. I went back to sleep frustrated that I couldn't easily converse with him. I wanted to learn about the Kootenai people since they were soon to become mine.

82

When I awakened I smelled meat cooking over a fire. Masheka was sitting near it and the rain had died down to a drizzle.

"Are the Piegan nearby?" I asked, sitting up.

"They are headed north back to their own territory. I don't think we're in any immediate danger from them. I have decided that we will remain here a few Suns and Sleeps to give you time to grow stronger."

"I'm sorry we exchanged angry words this morning."

"So am I. I did not sleep well and have little patience."

"How long will it take to reach your village?"

"My village is several Suns and Sleeps journey west from where you did your Vision Quest in the Sacred Mountains. Our village is on the shores of Flathead Lake."

That evening I sat near the campfire with Masheka and his two traveling companions. Now that I was feeling better I paid a little more attention to Targhee and Pocatello. They were both close in age to Masheka. Targhee resembled Masheka, and I suspected he was an older brother. The men talked freely with one another as if they were all close friends. I wished I could partake of their conversation.

Finally, I lay down and tried to sleep. Wind Chaser appeared and curled up beside me.

Masheka stayed up to guard our camp. The other two warriors went back to their own lean-to. When the moon was in Father Sky I felt Masheka crawl into the furs next to me.

"I don't think we should share a fur," I whispered, groggy with sleep.

"You're always a little late in thinking about the consequences of your behavior. Last sleep you invited me to share your fur and now this sleep you object."

"It was raining. I only offered you a place to sleep."

"You still think I am as easy to manipulate as your brother. Did you always get your way growing up?" His hand lightly stroked my arm.

"Not always."

"Do you play games with a Kootenai warrior, testing how far you can push him?" He lifted the hair off my neck and began rubbing it.

"I don't play games." My breathing had quickened; I had the feeling I was not in control of this situation.

"Good, because I wouldn't want a squaw who does. Go back to sleep. I'm only sleeping beside you to protect you."

Relieved, I snuggled up to him and slipped into the world of dreams. The sun was high when I awakened. Masheka and Pocatello were not around, but Targhee was sitting by a fire cooking fresh meat over it. The meat had been cut into chunks that were on sticks over the fire. When I sat up Targhee smiled and handed me a stick with a piece of meat on it. "Have something to eat. Masheka killed an antelope just for you this very morning. He'll give you the hide as well. I have never seen him so taken with a squaw."

"You speak Shoshoni!"

"Yes, Masheka and I are brothers. Our mother is of your people and taught us your language from the time we were small. Masheka and I enjoyed having our own private language that no one else could understand." As we talked he built a drying rack.

"Tell me about your people." I began cutting the meat into thin strips to hang on the rack and dry in the sun.

"We live in the Season of Howling Wind in permanent dwellings made of earth, wood, and stone. In the Season of Ripe Berries we use tepees like the Shoshonis when we hunt the kotea. We also catch fish and are traders. We trade with the tribes to the west of us, traveling down the rivers on canoes. The rivers go all the way to the Big Water."

"What is the Big Water?"

"The Big Water is a lake so big you can't see across it or travel around it. There are fish in it that are bigger than several canoes tied together. From the tribes that live on this

Big Water we are able to get special shells and other unusual things."

"Are your men all great warriors?"

"You ask a lot of questions for a squaw."

"I want to know about Masheka's people."

"Every man is a warrior. The warriors that helped your people are the Crazy Dogs. We defend our people and see that the rules of our village are followed. Masheka was searching for the Blackfeet when he found you. A Crazy Dog war party had been sent out to search for the Blackfeet who have been attacking other Kootenai bands to the east of us, forcing them off their land. Masheka asked us to help your tribe."

"Our people are indebted to yours. Is Masheka a War Chief?"

"He is too young to be a War Chief. He is a Fish Chief. Our tribe is led by a Band Chief, and under him is the War Chief, Fish Chief, Deer Chief, and Duck Chief."

"What are your women like?"

"Women of the Kootenai nation are not as bold as you, not even Mother who is Shoshoni. None of our women are allowed to use weapons except for knives," he smiled. "I am happy to have you for a sister. You will give Masheka strong and beautiful papooses. I will train your sons to hunt and fight and to break wild horses. Mother will help you raise your daughters. You will never be burdened with too much work. If Masheka is killed while hunting or in battle, I will provide for you and your children, so you will never be without food and shelter. "

Masheka and Pocatello came out of the woods and over to us. "I see you're finally up," Masheka said.

"Yes. The morning's half gone, I'm sorry I slept in."

"You needed the rest and there is no great hurry now." He seemed in a good mood and his eyes twinkled. He and Pocatello looked clean and he smelled good as he sat next to me.

"Were you bathing?" I asked, looking around for a source of water.

"The Bitter Root River is on the other side of the hill." He pointed toward it. "We decided to go for a swim since this lazy squaw was still sleeping."

"I want to bathe, too."

"It's too soon. I'll bring you water to clean off with."

# 6

## Sunrise Ceremony

Masheka and Targhee rose early the next morning. After praying for a good hunt, they left camp. I rested by the river with Pocatello. When the sun began to set, I was pleased to see Masheka when he and his brother returned with two antelopes. Masheka gave me his antelope hide. His brother teased him, but gave me his as well. I put the hides in the river to soak overnight. In the morning, Masheka helped me peg them out on the ground with wooden stakes. Over the next few suns, I laboriously scraped off the flesh with an antelope leg bone. Masheka helped me once he realized that it was too much work for one injured squaw. Once the hides were fleshed, I poured water over them to clean them and left them to dry in the sun.

On the following morning, I turned them over and began to scrape the hair off the other sides with an antelope antler. When I was done, Masheka began pounding it smooth with a rock while I began to scrape the hair off the next hide. I was pleased with the skins because I could use them to make a shirt for Masheka. I planned to do bead work on the shirt that would tell of Masheka's part in saving my village.

Targhee came over to where we were working. "Brother, this woman is turning you into a squaw. She sits in her warm furs and lets you gather wood and carry water, and now she has you tanning a hide. Mother won't be pleased when you bring home a worthless squaw." Although Targhee grinned as he spoke the words, I lowered my head feeling ashamed.

"It is too much work for one squaw to tan three hides," said Masheka. "A squaw's work will not make me less of a warrior. You should help instead of complaining. Go get some water." He threw the water bag to his brother. "If she was not here you would not think twice about cooking your own food and getting your own water."

"You would have done better to have picked a strong woman. She is too thin." Targhee smiled directly at me with a mischievous sparkle in his eye. I knew he liked me; his insults were only meant to annoy Masheka.

"Her people were near starvation over the winter. She will grow fatter among our people. You are just jealous that I have found such a beautiful squaw to share my lodge."

Targhee looked me over with piercing eyes. "She is beautiful, I'll give you that," he replied with laughter in his voice. "But will she bear you strong papooses? My wife has already given me two sons."

"So you remind me often enough."

I rose. "I will get the water." I knew Targhee's words were making Masheka mad—though done in jest. I took the water bag from Targhee and picked up the second one from where it lay near the fire.

"Do not try and carry two full ones back at the same time," said Masheka.

"She will make you as weak as she is," said Targhee.

Masheka's expression darkened as he stood and took the second water pouch from me. "Her side is not healed and could break open again. You would not think she is weak if you had seen how she battled the Blackfeet, and if you think

I am weak I will gladly fight you to remind you of my strength."

"I saw her fighting as did many of our warriors. None of us thought it was good that she did. She only injured herself as is to be expected of a squaw."

"She didn't injure herself—she was wounded in battle after shooting an arrow into the Blackfoot warrior I was fighting. Do you dare criticize her to my face?" Masheka asked, his voice low and dangerous.

Pocatello said something in Kootenai and Masheka relaxed. Pocatello and Targhee left us and headed toward the woods with their weapons.

I went to the river with my water bag and Masheka walked beside me in silence. At the lake, he filled the water bag he was holding, then filled mine and handed it to me. "I'm not a lazy squaw," I said. "I would not bring shame to your family."

"I know. When Kootenai girls are young they go into the mountains to seek their animal spirit guardians. A few grow to be very wise and have special powers from the Master Spirit and even become shamans. You are compelled to follow your quest the way a shaman is. Perhaps it is not right to take you to my village when you are so strongly led in a different direction. I don't want an unwilling squaw, nor do I want to offend the Master Spirit."

We walked back to the lean-to in silence. I was quickly getting my strength back. If I were to convince Masheka to let me go on my quest I had little time left, yet I hesitated to press him. My feelings for Masheka had grown steadily stronger; I was no longer so anxious to leave him to go on my quest. Masheka would be a good brave to share a lodge with. For the first time, the idea of having a papoose was pleasing and not something to put off for a long time. Living in a place where the people did not go hungry in the winter, also sounded good; moreover, the idea of trading with people that lived on the shore of the Great Lake had stirred my imagination.

When we reached camp, I took out a small piece of tanned leather from a deer Pocatello had shot and sewed it into a ball, stuffing the insides with rabbit fur. It was done by the time Pocatello and Targhee had returned to camp with several squirrels. I tossed the ball to Masheka. "Get some exercise while I tan this hide."

He got up and the three men started kicking it around. They set up one goal by a distant cluster of aspens and another off on the other side of a hill. Targhee and Pocatello fought against Masheka, trying to kick the ball to their goal. The game was rough and I could see that there was a lot of competition between the two brothers. It was not a fair contest and after a while Masheka yelled for me to join him.

"Squaws don't play men's ball games—and for good reason," I yelled back.

"We won't play so rough. It will do you good to get some exercise."

I was tending a tanned hide that was on a cone-shaped frame over a small, smoky fire of green pinewood. The fire gave off little heat and I was sure the hide wouldn't burn if I left it unattended. I went to join the men with Wind Chaser at my side. He was excited by the game.

Masheka and I stood facing Pocatello and Targhee with the ball in the middle. All three of the men were out of breath and breathing heavily. "Begin," said Targhee. We all went for the ball. Targhee kicked it out from under me and passed it to Pocatello who ran off with it. Masheka and I ran after him. It felt good to run again, but I was still weak and couldn't run far without stopping to catch my breath. Masheka was well ahead of me and I watched him. He ran with good form and speed. Masheka tackled Pocatello and they wrestled for the ball. Targhee joined the fight moments later.

Masheka broke away from them with the ball and

hurled it to me. It slammed into my chest with such force that it took my breath away then it fell to the ground. I grabbed it up and took off running with Wind Chaser at my heels. I had a good head start and the fear of being tackled by Targhee or Pocatello kept me running even after I was winded.

I panicked once I got over the hill and realized I did not know which tree was the goal. "Where is the goal?" I screamed to Masheka, turning around. The men were just a few yards from me.

"That big tree!" Masheka yelled back.

At that moment Targhee jumped Masheka and they both went down wrestling. Pocatello put on a burst of speed to catch me. I fled, but he was on me in moments. We went down hard with me on the bottom. I curled my body around the ball, trying to keep it from him. Wind Chaser sprung on top of Pocatello growling and barking. I released the ball and grabbed Wind Chaser around the neck, afraid that he might injure Pocatello. Pocatello grabbed the ball and ran back toward their goal. Targhee stopped his attack on Masheka and ran after his teammate.

Masheka ran to me. "Are you all right?"

I still had my arms around Wind Chaser's neck for he was eager to run after Pocatello. "Yes, but I'm not up for any more of this game. Go after the ball." I watched him run off smiling to myself. Wind Chaser finally settled down. My smile disappeared when I moved, for I was bruised all over and my side had started throbbing again.

I limped painfully to the river, thinking that a refreshing dip would make me feel better. The sun was warm and I was hot and sweaty after running. I undressed and slipped into the water. It felt wonderful. Wind Chaser splashed into the water next to me, spraying water all over me. I put my arm around him and let him swim with me out to the deep water.

Masheka appeared shortly with the other men. "They

won," he shouted to me from the shore. He stripped off his breechcloth and moccasins and dove off the bank into the water. The other men followed his example and soon they were tossing the ball back and forth in the water. Finally, Masheka swam over to me. "I think you've recovered enough for us to move on. Tomorrow we'll leave for my village."

The lightness of the afternoon disappeared for me. "I'm not going."

Masheka drew me against him. "You have been living with me as my squaw ever since we set up camp here. It is a little late to protest."

"I am still a maiden."

"Only because I didn't wish to risk hurting you. Tonight you should be well enough."

"I thought you said you didn't want an unwilling squaw." I struggled to make him release me.

"I think you just like to pretend you are unwilling. Earlier today you said you were not a lazy squaw and wouldn't bring shame to my family."

"And you said it would offend the Master Spirit if you were to take me to your village."

"That's not exactly what I said."

I pushed my hands against his shoulders. I would not be a maiden much longer if I didn't get away from him quickly. His need for me was all too apparent. Wind Chaser began to growl and Masheka had to reluctantly let me go rather than risk being attacked.

I swam away from Masheka and kicked water in his face, then swam back to shore. I scrambled out of the water, grabbed my buckskin dress and ran into the woods. I slipped on my dress, then went back to the bank to get my moccasins. The men were still swimming. As I headed back to camp, I remembered the hide. I began to run, afraid it would be burnt and that I would have disgraced myself and made Masheka the brunt of Targhee's teasing again.

The fire had died down to coals, so the hide wasn't ruined. I built up the fire again and tried not to think about Masheka.

That evening when Masheka lay beside me under the furs I said, "Tomorrow I will rise before dawn to greet the sun and give prayers to Apo, the Great Spirit. I want you to come with me."

"It will be a good thing," he replied and drew me close to him. "Are you well enough to be my squaw, Vision Woman?"

"No!" I moved away from him.

"Are you afraid of becoming a woman?"

I shook my head and he started to untie my dress. "Don't!" I felt him tense, then he rolled over and presented his back to me. I was upset by his withdrawal from me. I felt lonely for my people and for those who had gone to the spirit worlds. I wanted Masheka to hold me and to give me the warmth of his friendship. I put my hand on his back and I could feel his strength. "Please be patient with me, Masheka. I would gladly go to your village if my Spirit Guide had not shown me that I must take a more difficult path. I do not know if my future includes you or not. I'm waiting for a clear sign that will tell me if our paths go in the same direction. Tomorrow when we greet the sun I will share my vision with you and then you can help me decide my future direction."

Masheka rolled over and put an arm around me. "I will pray to the spirits to give you a sign that will convince you that we should travel in the same canoe down the river of life."

I slept peacefully snuggled against him. Wind Chaser awoke me just before dawn. In the gray light I started putting on my moccasins.

Masheka also stirred. "Why is he howling?"

"To wake us up." I went over to my bags and pulled out my sacred pipe.

Masheka stretched. It was a warm morning and he did not bother putting on his leggings.

We walked away from camp to a small hill overlooking the river. I held my pipe to Father Sky, Mother Earth, and to the north, then slowly turned to the west and held it out again. There was a soft humming sound in my head and I could feel my Spirit Guide's presence.

I held my pipe to the south and last faced the east. I felt a great love for Mother Earth and for all life, as I held out the pipe and watched the sun rise up in the sky, making the world come alive with color. Masheka stood beside me and there was a feeling of great harmony between us.

I shut my eyes and began to chant Hu-nai-yiee. I heard the pounding of distant drums and then was transported to the spirit worlds. My body was made of shimmering light with an aura of blue, and I was filled with a sense of peace and love.

Masheka appeared in a body of vibrating light. The blue light around him was intense and it radiated out until his light overlapped mine.

In the next instant we were in front of the Spirit Cave. It beckoned for me to enter it. The sound of drums grew louder. The light of this world became so intense it nearly blinded me. I knew that I was hearing the drums of an ancient people and seeing the light of the Great Spirit.

I opened my eyes and stared at Masheka, aware now that he was part of my spiritual journey. His eyes were still closed and he looked to be lost in prayer. I felt a deep warmth for him as a kindred spirit. There was a spiritual connection between us that I never had with Kicking Horse.

Masheka opened his eyes and smiled at me. "It's strange," he said. "I feel as if Wind Chaser spoke to me, telling me he is my brother."

I smiled. "Wolves are den orientated. Wind Chaser has accepted you into his den. You will start to learn his language now. He feels the connection between us. Last night I promised I would tell you of my vision." I hesitated, Masheka was not a family member, an elder or a shaman, the only ones a vision is usually shared with, but his path was intertwined with mine, so it felt right to share my vision with him. "As you know I am in training to be a holy woman. I went to the Sacred Mountains to clarify my spiritual path. While on my Vision Quest I had a powerful vision. My Spirit Guide took me to Spirit Cave, which is a place of visions and ancient truths. He told me I must journey there to get a talisman, which will give me strong medicine. I am compelled to follow this vision. That is why I left my band and started this quest even after my brother had given me to you.

"The cave lies to the southeast of here, beyond the Shining Mountains and the sacred land with boiling water. It lies someplace in the Big Horn Mountains."

Masheka listened attentively. His face revealed that he listened with an open heart and mind.

"Apo sent you to me to guide and protect me," I continued, "but I don't think I am to share a lodge with you. One of my animal guides is the hawk. I have chosen to fly high like a hawk rather than be earth bound. It has not been an easy path to follow. I have to go to Spirit Cave, then return to help my people now that we no longer have a shaman. Will you let me follow my vision?"

I lowered my head, waiting in silence for his answer. He was a man who listened to the Great Spirit. He would understand that to ignore my guidance would cause great inner agony.

At last, I looked back up at him. His eyes were dark with anger and I began to tremble. "You know that I can't refuse you when you have told me of such a vision. Visions should only be shared with shamans who know how to interpret them. I do not want a squaw who is discontent sharing my lodge and raising my papooses. Go on your quest and I will not stop you. I will delay here no longer and return to my people."

He left before I could reply. I didn't want him to leave, but to come with me as I had seen in my vision. I knelt down in prayer. "Masheka is leaving me, Grandfather. He doesn't understand that he is part of this quest. Give me the strength to go without him. I have lost so many already and I do not know how I can bear to lose him too." I felt the familiar tingling of tears behind my eyes and fought to gain control of my emotions. I didn't want to show my weakness before Masheka and the other men. I finally gained a semblance of control and walked back to camp.

When I reached it, the men had already packed up their horses. Only my things remained.

Targhee came over to me. "Masheka says you are continuing your quest." I nodded. "It is dangerous for a woman to travel alone into Crow land. If I were Masheka, I wouldn't let you go."

"Masheka understands the importance of my journey."

"My little brother thinks with his heart and not his head. I wish you the Master Spirit's protection, and hope that our paths cross again. You're a brave woman."

Pocatello also said goodbye, gesturing with his hands. Then Masheka came up to me. "We have left you plenty of meat from the antelopes. Be careful when you enter Crow territory."

"Thank you for helping me, Masheka." Tears blurred my vision, and my heart was on the ground. I struggled to not cry, keeping my gaze fixed straight ahead on his bear-claw necklace.

"If your path ever brings you to the Sacred Mountains again come to visit me."

"I will." My voice was unsteady. I couldn't bear the thought that he was leaving me. Tears escaped and started rolling down my cheeks.

He drew me against him and I clung to him, breaking down completely. "Don't go! Come with me." I choked out between sobs. "We are meant to go on this quest together. I don't want to be separated from you."

"Hush, Vision Woman, do you want Targhee and Pocatello to see you so upset?"

Pressing my face against his conch-shell breastplate, I fought for control. It took a few moments before I was able to step back from him. I couldn't look at him or the other warriors, so great was my shame. Going to my furs, I started rolling them up. I heard Masheka say something to the other men in his own language then heard the sound of horses riding off.

I took a deep breath to stop the tears that threatened again. I accepted that it was the will of the Great Spirit that Masheka had left me, for Vision Quests were always gone on alone. I heard a soft step behind me and turned around. Masheka stood just in back of me. I flung myself against him.

"What does this mean?" I asked.

"It is not yet time for us to part. I will journey with you to Spirit Cave and see that you get safely back to your people."

"But you need to return to yours!"

"My brother and Pocatello will convey to the elders all that they need to know of the Piegans."

"I'm glad you decided to stay with me."

"It is too dangerous for you to go into Crow country alone," he said curtly, moving away from me.

Hurt by his gruff words, I wondered why he stayed if he was angry with me. I tied my things on Good Thunder, and then we left, heading south.

It felt good to be traveling again. I was excited to at last be on my way to the Spirit Cave. It had called out to me and haunted my dreams. I wanted to share with Masheka how I felt, but he was quiet and moody.

We saw several mangy-coated kotea bulls and a herd of graceful, antlered antelope as we rode. Game was plentiful this time of year. We rested several times, because Masheka wanted to make sure the traveling didn't exhaust me. In the late afternoon we set up camp in a grassy area where the wind kept down the insects.

We watched the sun go down together and I gave prayers of thanks to spirit for providing me with a traveling companion. The land around the Shining Mountains was familiar to me but we would be journeying east of them to country I'd never been to before. I was glad that I wouldn't be alone. After dark, Masheka unrolled his furs and lay down on top of them. It was a warm night, so there was no need to have a fur over him.

I began to unroll my fur next to his when he said, "I don't want you to sleep beside me anymore."

"Why not?"

"I prefer to sleep alone."

I gathered up my fur. "Fine! I'll sleep with Wind Chaser. He's a better sleeping mate than you." I went to the creek where I could listen to the sound of the water. Wind Chaser walked over to me, howled, then walked over to Masheka as if he didn't know where to sleep. He came back to me and after walking around discontentedly; he threw his head back and howled. Off in the distance another wolf answered his cry and his ears perked up. He glanced at me a moment before running off. I knew I would not see him again until morning. "Fine, I will sleep alone," I said, annoyed with both Wind Chaser and Masheka.

The next morning was uneventful as we continued our journey south to the Salmon River. I felt the power of the land. My Spirit Guide's presence was strong. I knew that I would find Spirit Cave, but felt a wave of fear for what I would learn there. Masheka's moodiness had passed and he was pleasant company once again.

We left the Salmon River where it turned south and entered the foothills of the Beaverhead Mountains. Traveling became slower as we had to search for routes though the rugged mountainous country. I enjoyed the journey immensely; it was beautiful with many spectacular views through the dark green pine trees. We passed by crystal clear aqua-colored lakes and babbling streams. Scampering on the ground were small gray and tan hoary marmots. Their sentinels gave out shrill whistles of warning at our approach. On one alpine slope we came across a large Bighorn sheep. Masheka drew out his bow and notched an arrow, killing the noble creature. He gave thanks to the Master Spirit, then helped me skin the sheep and cut off the meat. The massive coiled horns are highly valued in my tribe. I was pleased when Masheka gave me one of them.

We camped that night near a small lake and I went for a swim. Several whooping cranes were wading along its shoreline. Wind Chaser ran toward them barking; they gracefully flew away. After Wind Chaser and I had swum in the cold water, we went back to camp where we found that Masheka had left on Straight Arrow. It did not surprise me for he often went off to hunt or scout the area.

I went to the woods, searching for wild onions. I soon found some and began pulling them out of the earth. Suddenly Wind Chaser started barking and I looked up to see a black bear within a stone's throw of where I was squatted. Fear swept over me; I had vivid memories of tribal members who had been killed or mauled by bears. I willed myself to not move so I wouldn't startle it. A black bear was not as dangerous and unpredictable as a grizzly. It would not charge if neither Wind Chaser nor I provoked it.

I called Wind Chaser to me, but he kept barking, staying just out of reach of the bear. Wind Chaser's hair bristled up along his back. The bear stood on its hind feet and growled. It was a large animal, and I was afraid it would kill

Wind Chaser. The bear swatted at Wind Chaser who jumped back and circled to the side, staying between the bear and me. I heard an animal cry in back of me and, turning toward the sound, saw that a cub was behind me. I had inadvertently gotten between the mother bear and her cub.

The mother bear barked at the cub and it ran up the tree I was standing beside. The mother bear was growling and becoming even more agitated by Wind Chaser who was commanding most of her attention. I took a slow step away from the tree and the bear immediately lunged toward me. Wind Chaser rushed forward and closed his teeth around the bear's leg. The bear swatted Wind Chaser and sent him flying. I dropped onto the ground and curled up playing dead as the bear came charging toward me. Wind Chaser regained his feet and sprung between us again. He lunged for the bear's neck.

I ran to a nearby pine tree and began climbing it. The lower branches were short and the bark covered with sap. The bear swatted Wind Chaser and lunged toward the tree just missing my feet with her claws. The tree was too small for her to climb so she stood at the bottom and shook it. I clung to the tree terrified of being thrown from it. She finally backed off, looked toward the tree her cub was in, and growled.

I spared a look for Wind Chaser and saw him on the ground. His side was bleeding from the bear's claws. He crawled into the bushes out of the bear's view. I was worried about Wind Chaser. If the bear attacked him, I planned to climb down the tree and try to drive her off with a branch. She stayed under her cub's tree for a long time. I became quite uncomfortable in my tree perch, and climbed higher until I found a more secure place. I wondered when Masheka would return to camp. I wasn't sure how he would respond to finding me trapped in a tree. He might decide to try and shoot the bear and, although the hide would make a fine robe, I didn't want the mother bear to be injured. She had a cub to care for. My concern for Wind Chaser had grown since he had not risen. I heard Good Thunder whinny, frightened by the bear's presence so close to camp.

I looked within and began chanting my personal song. "Hu-nai-yiee." My fears and strong emotions left me and I called out to Grandfather. "Please help me!" His inner voice said, "Talk to the mother bear so she will not fear for her cub." Opening my eyes, I said, "It is safe for your cub to come down. I will not harm it. I am only passing through your land on the way to Spirit Cave." The bear became calmer, and I began to slowly climb down the tree. The bear sat and watched me. I dropped onto the ground on the side of the tree opposite from the bear and backed slowly away. I stopped when I thought I had gone far enough. The mother bear barked to her cub, and it came scrambling down the tree. The mother bear led it away from our camp.

I began shaking violently now that it was all over. I walked to the bushes I had seen Wind Chaser crawl into and found him stunned and lying on the ground. He lifted his head and thumped his tail happily on the ground when he saw me. I knelt beside him and examined his wounds. The claw marks were not deep and I led him down to the lake and washed them. He followed me back to camp and sat down. I took herbs from my medicine bag and treated the wounds, then went to Good Thunder and stroked him until he calmed.

I lit a fire and began to cook some chunks of the Bighorn sheep over it. Masheka finally returned to camp and with him were three Bannock braves. Wind Chaser began to bark as the men dismounted. The men came over to the fire. One was old and the other two were close in age to Masheka. The horses they rode were fine animals and they led two other horses that were loaded down with packs.

"They are friends, Wind Chaser," said Masheka, squatting down next to Wind Chaser and examining the wounds on his sides. "How was he injured?"

"Defending me. I got between a mother bear and her cub."

"Mother bears are very dangerous," said one of the younger Bannock warriors, sitting down at the fire. The Bannocks are part of the Nimi Nation and their language is close to ours, so I could easily understand him. "It is good so beautiful a squaw was not injured. You should not have left her alone for so long, Masheka." He smiled at me. "I am Hard-to-Hit, my companions are Beaver Tail, an elder in our tribe, and Little Robe. We've come from the Wasichus's trading post."

I was frightened at the thought that we might be close to the Wasichus. "Is this trading post near here?"

"No, it is a long difficult journey east from here. It lies in the direction of the rising sun past the Absaroka Mountain Range. It is on the mouth of the Bighorn River. They have many beautiful things to trade for."

Hard-to Hit pulled out some blue beads and handed them to me. "The Wasichus have beads of all colors and many other useful things. They will trade them for furs."

I started to hand them back. "No, keep them. They are a gift." I smiled and reverently touched the pretty beads. The warrior pulled out some tube-shaped beads that shone like the water on a clear day.

"These are made of silver. For your kindness in sharing your fire you can keep them as well." He placed many of them into my hands. "You can sew them on a dress. You should have fine things to complement your beauty." I looked up from the silver beads and saw that he was smiling at me.

Masheka scowled and sat with the other two men. "You are wasting time chattering like a squirrel, Red Willow, when there are guests to be fed."

Embarrassed, I quickly put the beads away in a leather

pouch, then sliced more meat. I put the chunks on sticks over the fire and passed out the meat that was already cooked.

"The meat is delicious," said Hard-to-Hit. "You are fortunate to have a squaw to travel with."

"Squaws are more trouble than help," replied Masheka. He fed several fat pieces of meat to Wind Chaser even though he hadn't eaten anything himself, then scratched Wind Chaser behind the ears.

I felt Beaver Tail's eyes on me and turned to him. He was a man of many years with a prominet nose and ears, deeply etched wrinkles and white braids. He was old to have set out on a journey to a trading post. He was studying me intently. There was great power in his eyes. "Where are you journeying to?"

"I'm headed for a place I've seen only in my visions."

He was silent for a long time and out of respect everyone quietly waited for him to speak again. "The bear is one of your guardian spirits," he finally said. "The mother bear did not kill you even when you came between her and her cub. Bear medicine is the ability to look within. In the Season of Howling Wind the bear sleeps in the cave to gain understanding as he dreams. In the Season of Melting Snow he awakens with greater awareness. You will enter the cave of Bear, and find your pathway into the spirit world. To accomplish your goals and dreams, you must go within, quiet the mind, and enter the silence; then you will know the answers to what you are seeking and be reborn as the bear is."

The truth shone in his words; it was as if we were alone. "Are you a holy man?" I asked.

He nodded, continuing to gaze at me with his powerful eyes. "I came with Hard-to Hit and Little Robe on this journey to the trading post because I knew that we would meet. When darkness comes you will give your people strength."

"Do you know where this place is that I am seeking?"

"I have been there, but I could not tell you how to get

103

there. A person is led there when the spirits call them."

"I hear drums."

"Yes, this is sacred land and others have walked this way before. Listen to the drums and hear what they have to say. The spirits have given you guardians for your journey both in the inner and outer worlds. It is important for you to survive." He closed his eyes and appeared to go to sleep though still sitting.

The other men started talking about the trading post. Masheka became interested and posed many questions about it.

I stared at the flames, letting their words fade and thinking of what the holy man had said. Strange that Beaver Tail should know of me and my quest. My attention was diverted back to the men when I heard Hard-to-Hit ask Masheka if I were his squaw. Masheka tensed beside me. "She's on a Vision Quest and I am traveling with her to give her protection."

"If you wish to return to your people, I would gladly serve in your place." The way he boldly looked at me made me uncomfortable.

"No, I have been told by my Spirit Guide to protect her." Masheka sounded affronted by the offer, and his voice lacked the respectful warmth usually given to a guest. "It is time to sleep, Red Willow. We have a long journey ahead of us." He took my hand and led me to his sleeping robe. "You will sleep with me tonight."

"I thought you preferred to sleep alone."

"Tonight you are safest with me." His manner was sharp and I didn't know what I had done to offend him. I removed my moccasins and lay down between the kotea robes. Masheka joined me; I could feel the tension in his body. Wind Chaser limped over and curled up on the other side of me.

Masheka put his arm around me. "Were you injured?"

"No, Wind Chaser distracted the bear long enough for

me to escape to safety."

"Wind Chaser is truly our brother. I was wrong to make you leave him when the Blackfeet warrior shot him."

"Did you give Wind Chaser your meat because he is our brother?"

"I gave him meat for protecting you. I will have to watch you more carefully. Hard-to-Hit was right to reproach me. A maiden should be guarded constantly when away from her people."

"I hardly need constant guarding. I can fight—"

He cut me off. "I know, but even the Bannock warriors are not so foolish as to travel alone."

"What did you think of Black Feather's words?"

"He spoke with wisdom. The animals' spirits do protect you and give you power. I should have seen it myself. The wolf is your most powerful animal spirit and that is why Wind Chaser protects you. The wolf is a teacher and pathfinder."

I lay in Masheka's arms listening to the sound of a distant wolf pack howling. Wind Chaser rose to his feet and paced restlessly. When they were finally quiet Wind Chaser began to howl as if answering them. I fell asleep to the sound of his moanful howls.

In the morning, I awoke to find Masheka still beside me. He was looking at me with warm eyes. I started to sit up but he pulled me back down on top of him; his hand burned a trail as it moved up my bare leg onto my buttock. His actions drove away all reason and my breathing quickened.

I heard the sound of footsteps coming toward us. Masheka groaned and set me from him. "It is not easy sleeping with a woman who wishes to remain a maiden," Masheka said, then he left. I went to haul water and start a fire. I didn't want the Bannock warriors to think I was lazy.

After eating, Beaver Tail asked me to walk with him. We went down to the lake and on the way he said, "Spirit Cave is filled with spirits and power. It will not be easy to go inside, but you have courage and a strong heart. That is all you need." After our walk, the Bannock men headed west, back to their village, and we continued our journey east across the Beaverhead Mountains.

# 7

## Journey to Spirit Cave

*Near what is now Yellowstone National Park*

During the next few days the weather was warm. We passed streams that were swift and full from melted snow rushing down the mountains. Horseflies buzzed around our heads and black flies bit our arms. We traveled through a dense forest of tall hemlock trees with a rich undergrowth of ferns and moss. Then we rode into rugged, mountainous country where it was difficult to find routes that weren't too steep for the horses.

At dusk one evening, I killed a deer. We ate some of the meat along with seeds from the lupine plant, a bluish-purple plant that grows in the mountains. After we had eaten, I washed the deer hide and began scraping off the remaining flesh.

I went into the woods before I slept and I discovered my bleeding had started. I gathered moss, wondering what to do. At an encampment, when a woman has her bleeding she goes to the lying-in-lodge, located outside the village.

Masheka looked up from where he was sitting by the

fire, making an arrowhead from the deer antler, when I returned to camp. "You were gone a long time," he said, putting out the campfire so there would be less chance of an enemy finding us.

"I was gathering moss." I lifted up my sleeping robe and started into the wood.

"Where are you going?" he asked.

"You must stay back where you were."

"Why?" His voice was sharp as if he had taken offense at my words.

"My bleeding has started and I must not be near you. The elders teach that a man will die if he is near a woman when she is bleeding."

An uneasy expression crossed his face. He looked torn with indecision and was silent for a long time. "I must think on this," he said finally.

I went deep into the woods with Wind Chaser beside me and found a moss-covered spot to sleep on. When I awoke in the morning, I discovered that Masheka had placed his sleeping robe near mine. I sat up, wondering at the significance of his actions.

He opened his eyes; he slept half-awake, always coming fully alert at the slightest noise, as a brave must when on the trail.

"You should not be beside me," I said.

"I prayed to my Spirit Guide and asked him what to do. He said to stay beside you to protect you."

"Are you sure you want to take such a risk?"

"I don't think there is a risk. I think the custom of women's lodges is based on superstition. Anyway, we travel alone and so are not endangering the tribe in any way or offending anyone. In case the people are right, we should be cautious and talk only when necessary and avoid touching one another. I'll prepare my own food as well and pray regularly to keep my connection with my Spirit Guide strong."

We stayed at this campsite for a quarter moon to dry the meat, wanting to have a supply for our journey. On our last morning there, I walked up to Masheka as he packed supplies on Straight Arrow. I had missed not talking to him. "You can touch me now," I said.

He slowly grinned, a mischievous light coming to his dark eyes, then drew me against his hard body and stroked my neck. My body tingled from his unexpected assault. I pulled away from him and stepped back, my heart racing. "That is not what I meant."

"Are you sure?" he asked still smiling.

I turned away in confusion and went over to Good Thunder.

The next day we reached a wide river that I recognized as Flow-to-Mud River. My band often camped north of here when hunting the kotea in the Season of Melting Snow. We swam our horses across the river. My excitement grew, knowing we would soon be in land considered sacred by the Nimi—a land of boiling hot springs and geysers. I wanted to show them to Masheka who had never been there. On the following day we reached a large hot spring. The pools of bubbling hot water and steam that arose from the terraced land fascinated Masheka.

We went south along the Obsidian Creek until we reached Obsidian cliff. There we stopped to gather the black, glass-like obsidian rock that was used to make knives and arrowheads.

"My people have traded for knives made of this material. The rock makes for a fine sharp blade," said Masheka, "I never knew where the rock came from. I will bring some back for my tribe."

"Members of my band come here annually to gather the rock. It is the only place that we have found it."

We spent the afternoon collecting obsidian. In the morning, we set out early. I wanted to show him the huge geyser my father had taken me to see when I was a child. The geyser was quiet when we arrived. Masheka did not believe me when I told him that it would erupt, sending steaming water high into the air. We sat down to wait.

Masheka grew impatient with me after awhile but I begged him to stay. Finally, steam and boiling water started shooting into the air. It sprayed high into the sky, as high as an eagle flies. Masheka stared in amazement as it continued to rise and rise.

"It is powerful medicine," he said when the geyser was quiet again.

I nodded, in awe of this land. "The land is sacred." We rode from the geyser into a forest of lodgepole pines and quaking aspens where we came upon a large herd of antelope. We startled them, and they bounded gracefully off with the young kids running alongside their mothers. A break in the forest opened onto a meadow where wildflowers of every color grew in abundance. Finally, we reached Shoshone Lake and set up camp.

On the following day we circled the lake and continued south to another larger lake. We camped along its shores at the base of the Teton Mountains, a place of spectacular beauty. There were no foothills, just mountains that rose straight up into the sky with jagged, snow-covered peaks. Masheka went off hunting, and I began working on the shirt I was making for him. I had finished the slow process of cutting out and sewing the leather pieces into a shirt and now was working on a beaded design using died porcupine quills and the blue and silver beads from the Bannock warrior. Wind Chaser curled up on the ground beside me.

Masheka returned to camp some time later, carrying a deer over his horse. He slid the deer to the ground and began to skin it. I came over to help him. After we had finished cutting up the deer meat, I showed him the shirt. "See how beautiful these beads look on your shirt."

110

"You're sewing the beads, that Hard-to-Hit gave you, on my shirt!"

"Yes, I want to give you a gift that will be special. You have helped me so much. You will be the most richly dressed warrior among your people. The blue beads look like the sky and the silver beads reflect the firelight."

He didn't look appeased. "You don't need the beads Hard-to-Hit gave you. We'll go to the trading post and I'll trade furs for as many beads as you want."

"I don't want to go there. The Wasichus frighten me."

"The Wasichus are nothing to be afraid of, and they have flintlocks to trade for."

"Bows and arrows are better than flintlocks."

"No, flintlocks are more powerful and can shoot further. A few warriors with flintlocks can kill many enemy warriors. You saw what they did to your warriors."

"Yes, I saw what they did." Images of Kicking Horse in battle came to me. I wondered if a flintlock had killed him. A great sorrow came over me and a stabbing pain pierced my heart. I remembered how Kicking Horse had held me close before the battle, excited that we would soon share a lodge.

"I have made you sad." Masheka reached out and covered my hand with his.

I felt suddenly guilty that I had allowed my growing friendship with Masheka to lessen my pain. I slipped my hand out from under his. "I need to be alone." I ran into the woods and sank down onto my knees. I had never mourned Kicking Horse properly, never given him the honor he deserved. I had been too weak and sick from my own injuries. Crossing my legs under me, I began to pray and sing songs of his courage and virtues to Apo. I reached for my knife but it was not in its shaft for I had left it in camp. I don't know if I would have gashed my arms and legs or merely cut off my hair to mourn him properly. As it was, my anguish was expressed in my prayers and songs. My mourning lasted most of the night until I finally collapsed on the ground in total exhaustion and slept.

When I awoke in the late morning, I found I was covered with a fur and that Masheka was sitting nearby. "I didn't mean to be disrespectful of your need for solitude, but I was concerned about you," he said.

"I loved him," I whispered. Looking up, my eyes met his and I saw he was troubled. "I knew him all of my life. We always thought we'd share a lodge someday. I expected to hurt for a long time and to never feel for another man as I did for him, but now I think more often of you than of him and it confuses me." I looked away uneasily then back at him. "When you are close to me my heart is lighter. I didn't want you to return to your village with your brother and Pocatello." I lowered my head. "I speak too boldly."

He drew me close. "It's good to mourn for those who were close to us, but when the pain begins to ease there is no reason to feel badly. I'm glad you like being with me for I enjoy your companionship above all others." I wrapped my arms around him happy that he was near. We were both tired from the long night, so we lay down on the fur and slept, entwined in each other's arms.

Much later in the day we continued our journey, traveling in the direction of the rising sun. We reached the Togwolee Pass, a passageway we had heard of from the Bannock warrior. It was the best place to cross in this mountainous countryside.

That night we camped at the head of Wind River. I climbed up on a large boulder to do my evening prayers and play my flute. I gazed out across the water and feeling a gentle breeze against my face. Then I prayed for guidance in finding Spirit Cave. The sound of drums beating caused me to open my eyes and search for the source, which seemed to be some nearby cliffs. Yet I knew the sound of the drums was coming from the inner worlds. Its rhythm haunted me.

In the middle of the night the ground began to shake and there was the sound of thunder. Masheka pulled me from my sleeping robe. "Dress quickly."

I slid on my tunic as Masheka began to tie our furs and supplies on the horses. "What is it?" I asked in sleepy confusion. Masheka lifted me onto Good Thunder's back. The stallion started prancing around, and I could hardly control him. His nostrils were flared and his ears flat.

"A herd of kotea!"

"Where's Wind Chaser?"

"He's off hunting. When they reach us stay on Good Thunder at all costs and make for the edge of the herd so you can escape."

The thunder now distinguished itself as pounding hoofs. A huge sea of dark forms was coming toward us. "Masheka, mount!" I yelled in terror. Masheka sprung on Straight Arrow and both horses started running as the kotea crushed in around us, catching us up in its wave. We were suddenly in the middle of a herd of racing kotea. The huge beasts surrounded us on all sides, packing us in tightly. Their size and power were frightening and yet magnificent. I could hear the sound of their bellows and their snorting breath. Dust billowed up all around us. Their huge dark-furred bodies would have instantly crushed me if I hadn't been on Good Thunder. Father had used Good Thunder for hunting Kotea and the horse was experienced in keeping clear of the sharp horns on their shaggy heads.

At first I was close to Masheka, but it was beyond the power of either of us to be more than led along by the thunderous herd. We soon became separated. I was frightened, for I had never been allowed to accompany the men on a kotea hunt. I did not know how to escape from the panicked, stampeding herd. Then I saw a white kotea racing among them— the most sacred of all animals. My fear began to subside. I was in awe at being a part of this powerful herd.

113

My arms and legs began to ache from the effort of trying to stay on Good Thunder's back. I became aware that the rumbling was lessening and the huge furred bodies were fewer around me. The herd was slowing down and swerving as it came to a forest. Good Thunder was soon able to make his way clear of the herd. I slipped off of him as the sound of thundering hoofs faded.

Good Thunder was covered with sweat and his breathing was hard from racing. He pushed his nose against me and I put my arms around his neck. My own heart was pounding in my breast. I wondered if Masheka, Straight Arrow, and Wind Chaser were safe. "They were magnificent, Good Thunder. I felt almost as if I were one of them."

Good Thunder snorted.

"Yes, you were also magnificent," I told him as I stroked his neck.

I heard Masheka calling me and yelled back. He rode into view moments later and sprung from his horse. I ran to him, and he crushed me to him. "I feared you wouldn't be able to control Good Thunder among the kotea. If he had thrown you..."

"He is better trained than that. Father used him for hunting kotea. I found it both terrifying and wonderful to be in the middle of the thundering herd. It's something I'll never forget. And I saw a white kotea!"

"It is powerful medicine. You are trembling. Are you injured?"

"No. I'm fine. We must find Wind Chaser." I yelled his name and started walking back in the direction where our camp had been, leading Good Thunder. Masheka also called for Wind Chaser. Beneath our feet, the ground was torn up from the herd. We went a long distance. Finally I was too tired to go any farther. The rush of energy that had kept me going until now was suddenly gone. I sank to the ground. "He might have been killed," I said close to tears.

"No, he went off hunting. He was high in the mountains when they came through our camp." Masheka placed our furs on the ground. Then we lay down and held each other. Life seemed a little more tenuous and precious than it had before the kotea herd had awakened us.

I awoke to the feel of Wind Chaser's thick tongue licking me. "Wind Chaser!" I exclaimed, hugging him.

We broke camp early the next morning and traveled along the shore of the Wind River. As we journeyed I asked, "Do you think there is any significance to the herd running through our camp?"

"I have wondered that myself. It is not so unusual for a panicked herd to come through a campsite. I have even heard of them running through a village and crushing everything, but it seems more than just chance. The kotea gives our people all that is needed to survive. If we are grateful for the gift of the kotea then our tribes will prosper. When we see a kotea we are reminded that we can only accomplish our goals with the assistance of the Master Spirit. We must ask for Its guidance in humbleness."

We left the Wind River and went south. Large mountains loomed ahead. The following day we reached them and traveled high up into the peaks. From there I got my first look at the Wind River Mountain Range. The cave lay to the southeast of us. Seeing the mountain range made the cave real and reaching it seem possible.

"Look, Masheka, the cave is down there somewhere. How long do you think it will take to reach it?"

"It depends. Did your grandfather tell you how to find it once you reach the Wind River Mountain Range?"

"No, he said I would be guided."

"Then let's hope he's right."

I looked around. "I have the feeling we are being watched."

"I sense it too."

A chill went through me at his words. "Do you think a Crow war party is following us?"

"No, not them, something else. Come on. The horses are nervous." I glanced down at Wind Chaser. He had his ears turned to the side, listening.

Masheka scanned the woods. Neither of us could see anything as we headed down the mountain. The feeling continued and I kept looking behind me. My spine tingled. I finally stopped Good Thunder to look behind me. There was nothing there, but the eerie feeling stayed.

We went a little farther, then stopped again, sure that we were being hunted. The silence sent a stab of fear through me. The birds and other forest creatures were all unusually quiet. "They know something is here," I said to Good Thunder as I continued to look. At first I didn't see anything. Then suddenly there came into view two large yellow eyes staring out from the branch of a large tree. I made out the form of a huge mountain lion in amongst the leaves. The hair stood up on the back of my neck.

"Masheka!" I called. He was a little ahead of me and he stopped his horse to look back. "There, in that tree." I pointed to where I had seen the lion, but he was no longer visible.

"What did you see?"

"A large mountain lion. It's very close to us."

"Wait here." Masheka pulled out his bow and an arrow and tried to get Straight Arrow to ride toward the trees, but the horse wouldn't budge.

"Let's just get out of here," I urged.

"You take the lead."

I started down the mountain, following an animal-made trail. We startled two Bighorn sheep. They caught the scent of the mountain lion and ran off in confusion. I heard Masheka behind me then the scream of the cat.

I turned back and was petrified by the sight of a huge

mountain lion that had now come openly onto the rocky trail to follow us. He made easy leaps covering huge distances at each bound. He didn't seem to want to catch us but only to follow us. He could easily have caught up to Straight Arrow. Masheka turned toward the creature with his bow drawn. "No!" I yelled. "If you only injure him, he will kill the horses and maybe us as well." Mountain lions feed mainly on deer, but occasionally they killed and ate squaws, papooses, and horses. Wind Chaser started barking wildly. I urged Good Thunder into a gallop and we raced down the steep mountain at a perilous speed. I could hear Straight Arrow behind me. Rocks sprayed out beneath Good Thunder's hoofs and rolled down the slope.

I kept glancing back and occasionally caught a glimpse of the elusive cat. He was keeping the same distance between us. We finally reached the base of the mountains and raced toward the woods. I led the way weaving through the trees. Good Thunder was tiring beneath me and he stumbled, nearly throwing me. I brought him to a stop and Masheka drew his horse up alongside us. "The horses can't go any further," I said. I scanned the trees and saw no sign of the mountain lion, but still felt its presence. Wind Chaser sat down, panting heavily.

"Then I must shoot it." Masheka drew out his bow and arrow.

"No, I think he is part of my vision."

"Vision or not, better to kill him now than to wait until night when he will be hard to get a good shot at."

"If he wanted to kill us, he would have already. It will anger the guardian spirit if we kill him. The bear, the kotea and now the mountain lion have come to give me their medicine for my quest. What does it mean among your people when a person has a mountain lion as one of their guardian spirits?"

Masheka notched an arrow to his bow and drew back

the string. "I admit the mountain lion is a powerful sign. If he's a person's totem they have courage and can become a powerful leader. But you are a maiden and it isn't likely that you'd have a mountain lion for a totem. This mountain lion is stalking us. When he shows himself I will kill him."

"Mountain lions are secretive creatures. It is quite unusual to see one let alone to have one follow you in broad daylight. I don't think he is an ordinary mountain lion. You only want to kill him because you are afraid." The cat suddenly appeared in the trail ahead of us. Wind Chaser started barking. Good Thunder reared up on his hind legs. Caught off guard, I flew off him and landed dangerously close to the mountain lion. I stared into his yellow eyes, realizing he could be on me in one bound. I heard the twang of an arrow as the cat disappeared from sight. The arrow struck the ground where he had been.

"Mount quickly," said Masheka. "He is still watching us."

I managed to slowly get up, aching from my fall, and glanced around before mounting. Dusk was setting and we looked for a place to camp. At the first clearing, Masheka dismounted. He kept his arrow fitted to his bow as I gathered wood and lit a fire. We ate some dried meat and berries, then I lay down to try and sleep. Wind Chaser was curled up beside me, and Masheka was keeping guard, but I couldn't sleep. The mountain lion was out there waiting. It cried out like a woman screaming, sending shivers down my spine. I sat up and looked around uneasily. "I will keep guard while you sleep." I put another log on the fire.

"I don't plan to sleep tonight. I have seen a mountain lion kill a deer."

We heard the snarling growl of the mountain lion close by and Wind Chaser was instantly on his feet. The horses whinnied and pulled against their ropes. Masheka raised his bow and arrow but the mountain lion did not appear.

I waited in tense silence, listening to all the night

sounds, my eyes straining for any sign of the mountain lion. Finally, I became too tired to stay awake and I lay back down. I dreamed I was standing at the edge of a stream. An early morning mist was rising up off the water. Oapiche walked into view and beside him was a large, white mountain lion. The lion looked at me with its glowing greenish-gold eyes.

Masheka awoke me when the sun had risen enough to see by. He showed me large lion prints near our camp. He kept his bow and arrow ready as we followed the prints into the woods. Deep in the woods, we saw blood on the ground near deer tracks and some tufts of deerhide. The carcass had been dragged off.

"The mountain lion has killed a deer," said Masheka. "He will be full now and shouldn't give us any more trouble."

"Then we should stay here a few hours so you can sleep."

"No, I don't want to sleep until we are a long distance from here. Though mountain lions normally only kill to eat, I do not trust this one."

"Last night I dreamed of my Spirit Guide. He came to me with a white mountain lion. I don't know why the mountain lion came to me yesterday, but I know it was not a bad thing."

Masheka frowned. "You have powerful dreams and animal guides. Perhaps some day you will be a shaman."

"Can women be shamans in your tribe?"

"Yes, both men and women can be shamans. Shamans are leaders among my people. They help make major decisions for the tribe and lead ceremonies. They also help those who go on Vision Quests to understand their visions and dreams. They get their power from the spirits and can foretell the future and cure illness."

"Women can be leaders in your tribe?"

"I have just said they could be."

"Even young women!"

"Yes."

"Women are not leaders in my band. They are not allowed in councils nor are they allowed to participate in many religious ceremonies. They are not allowed to look at or touch the men's sacred objects or use the sacred sweat lodges. When a young warrior returns from a Vision Quest, he shares his vision with the elder and shaman. His father may help him prepare ahead of time but never his mother. I have heard of a woman becoming a chief in some tribes but only after she is so old that she can no longer bear papooses."

"If women in your tribe can't become shamans, then the people in your tribe must think your ways are strange."

"A woman can become a medicine woman." I lowered my eyes, remembering times when other women of the tribe had come to father and grandfather telling them I should not be allowed to go off on so many quests. "Some say I have forgotten a woman's place."

Masheka laughed. "From your expression I'd say you were given quite a hard time. A man would have to be strong to have you as his squaw."

I glanced up at him. He was a strong enough man to have a woman who walked with visions. He seemed to read my thoughts and smiled at me warmly.

We headed off again, riding through the foothills of the Wind River mountain range. In the afternoon, we stopped so Masheka could sleep. We had not seen any sign of the mountain lion. It was warm, but Masheka insisted on building a large fire. He stacked firewood next to it and told me not to go hunting for more while he slept. I took out my bow and several arrows.

Satisfied that I was prepared, he went to sleep. Even though we had not seen any sign that the mountain lion was following us. I decided to check further. I stared into the fire, watching the red and golden flames leap and curl. I stared and stared until I felt a tingling on the top of my head, then

120

movement as I soared up and out of my body. From my new vantage point I looked down at my body and the campfire below. Masheka was asleep on the ground and the two horses were staked near the fire. Wind Chaser was curled up beside my body below. I flew higher, seeing as a hawk does in flight. There was no sign of the mountain lion anywhere near our camp. I began to search for Spirit Cave, studying the terrain from above.

I reached a place where the land was familiar to me. I knew it in the way I knew the country my people lived in. I moved toward the ground and was soon standing on a rocky ledge looking down the side of a mountain. The cave was not far from this place.

Masheka's deep, angry voice brought me swiftly back into my body. "Is this how you keep guard?" he demanded.

I opened my eyes and looked at him bewildered.

"The mountain lion could have killed us!"

"He is not near here. I traveled out of my body and searched for him."

He stared at me. "I do not know what you mean."

"Surely you've heard of spirit flights where a person slides out of their body and sees the world from above."

"Dreams and visions will not keep us alive against real dangers."

"This wasn't a dream!" I changed the subject. "Masheka, I was taught that the more obstacles a person encounters the closer they are to the truth. The bear, the buffalo, and the mountain lion have tested our courage and determination. They are strong medicine and such strong medicine would only be sent if this quest was one of great importance. We must be quite close to the cave. In this cave lies powerful medicine."

"Do you know how to get there?"

I rose. "No. I would have found it if you hadn't called me back from the spirit world."

"Then go back into the spirit world and find it."

"Do you think visions come merely by asking for them?" I demanded in frustration. "They are gifts from Apo and if a person has even one in a lifetime they are blessed. Don't ever again disturb me when I am having a vision!"

"Your tongue is sharp. Do you forget that you are a squaw and not to question a brave?"

I gathered my bundles. "I didn't ask you to accompany me on this quest."

"I seem to remember that you did. You didn't want me to return home with Pocatello and my brother."

"I liked your company then."

"And you don't now!"

I tried to stay angry but a smile slowly crept over my face. My feelings had grown stronger for him with each day we'd been together. "I like your company well enough."

We started off traveling toward the land I had seen in my vision. What had taken moments when free of my body proved to be slow travel over rugged land. We had difficulty finding a route across the rocky terrain that the horses could negotiate. We traveled for many Suns and Sleeps without any sign of the land I had seen in my inner vision

One evening I sat by the fire tired, hungry, and discouraged. I was beginning to wonder if I would ever find the cave in this vast region. What if we had come all this way and didn't find it? What if it lay only in the world of visions? I stopped the panicked wanderings of my mind and climbed up the side of the mountain to pray. I sat down overlooking the mountainous land and sang a love song to Apo.

I stayed awake all night singing and praying, hoping for a sign, but none came. In the predawn I greeted the morning with my pipe ritual. Afterwards I played my flute; its sweet notes strengthened me.

I went back down the mountain to the meadow valley where Masheka had remained with the horses and Wind

Chaser.

Masheka rose as I walked toward him. He searched my face hopefully, but upon reading my expression, he sighed and packed up our supplies.

We traveled slowly that morning. I studied every shadow on the face of the mountain that might hide a cave. In the afternoon, we left our horses and climbed up a steep, rocky slope in search of the cave. "What if I'm not worthy of finding it?" I asked Masheka.

"Then you'll have to become worthy if you really want to become a medicine woman."

"How do I become worthy?"

"Listen to your guardian animal spirits. They'll teach you and give you power."

"Perhaps a maiden shouldn't have power."

"A maiden can have power and become a shaman. You're obviously guided for a special reason. I think that you're trying too hard. You've gone many days without much sleep and little food."

"I don't want to stop to rest, and eating will only weaken my inner connection with my Spirit Guide. We're not far, yet we are not any closer than when I first learned of the cave. I still don't know where it lies hidden."

I felt exhausted and my steps were labored. The sky was darkening as thunderclouds rolled over. We started back to the horses. The rain caught us before we reached them and soon we were soaked.

"I'll be glad when I return to my people and can take a rest from traveling," said Masheka.

When we finally reached the horses, Masheka wanted to build a shelter and stay there until the rain passed, but I wanted to go on.

"I'll go ahead alone and you can follow later," I said, going over to Good Thunder.

"No, we'll both stay here and get warm. You're making

yourself sick."

"I am not. Masheka, I can feel the cave's presence. It calls out to me. If I ignore its sound it may not call again."

"She's a stubborn squaw, Wind Chaser." Masheka said, looking at our four-legged traveling companion. Wind Chaser wagged his tail. Masheka turned to me. "Let's waste no more time arguing then." He mounted and we started off. The rocky mountain trails were hazardous in the rain. The rain grew harder and the wind picked up. I didn't know which way to go and kept stopping and looking around.

"We are traveling in circles!" Masheka finally said, with an impatient edge to his voice. "Admit it, you don't have any idea which way to go!"

"I'll know when I am close to it."

"You've said we were close to it for days! Continue on your own if you will. I'm going to set up camp and dry out." I watched him dismount, then looked down at Wind Chaser. He looked as miserable as I felt. Good Thunder hung his head in fatigue. I slipped off his back.

"All right I admit it. I don't know where it is," I said. Lightning lit up the sky and thunder cracked as I spoke.

"What!" shouted Masheka. He was leading Straight Arrow into a forest of huge pine trees to get some shelter from the driving rain.

"I don't know where it is!" I shouted.

He stared at me a moment, then nodded. "I know." He went into the pine forest and removed Straight Arrows' packs.

By my feet Wind Chaser was whimpering pitifully. He went a short distance toward Masheka, turned back to me and barked, wagging his tail hopefully. When I didn't move he came back over to my side, only to start off again. I stood there despairing of ever being able to find the cave.

"Are you coming?" Masheka shouted.

"I may never be able to find it!" I yelled back.

He left the relative shelter of the trees and came back

over to me. "We'll search again tomorrow."

"I don't know where to look anymore. I don't know which direction to go. The land is so vast and rugged. Maybe we'll never find it." I was close to tears.

"We'll find it."

"I am a stubborn squaw—a stubborn, foolish squaw to have come here. The cave will never reveal itself to me. I'm not a strong medicine man."

"You're not a foolish squaw. You're a person dedicated to your spiritual training."

"Masheka, you aren't listening? I have no idea how to find the cave."

He put his arm around me and led me to where he'd left Straight Arrow. Good Thunder and Wind Chaser followed. "You're just tired and discouraged." He built a fire under the bough of a large pine tree and I warmed myself beside it.

"Do you want to turn back?" I asked.

He studied me for a long time before replying. "Obstacles shouldn't make one discouraged but more determined. You told me obstacles show a person they are close to the truth. Go to sleep, Vision Woman. When you have rested your clarity of purpose will return."

## 8

## Visions

*Wind River Range*

I awakened early to the sound of gently falling rain. Masheka didn't stir as I crawled out of our furs. He was exhausted from our dawn to dusk search for the cave. Wind Chaser rose to his feet and followed me out of the small lean-to Masheka and I had built the evening before to keep us dry. When I left the shelter of the forest, the gentle rain touched my face and hands. I felt refreshed and renewed from my night's sleep.

We had camped beside a tall, rocky mountain wall. I looked up, thinking that from the top I might get a good view of the surrounding area. I began to climb up the almost vertical wall, finding hand and toe holds as I went. Wind Chaser ran back and forth below me, barking in frustration at not being able to follow. The climb was difficult, but when I reached the top I was able to see a great distance. There were alpine valleys, forests, and snow-topped mountains surrounding me. I turned all four directions in hopes that I'd be given some sign of which way to go.

The Spirits remained silent, so I began to pray. Inwardly I heard the beating of drums and chanting in an ancient language I didn't know. I opened my eyes and rose, facing the direction the sound was coming from. I stretched out my arms and began to sing along with the chanters while doing a slow swaying dance.

I felt the power of the ancients pouring through me. High above me I heard a hawk cry. I looked up to see a red-tailed hawk, circling overhead close to grandfather sun. It flew off to the west. I followed him, walking in the opposite direction from where I had come. I was forced to stop when I came to the edge of the mountain. I could still see the hawk, gliding on the air currents. I peered down the rocky slope. It was a long way down, more than the distance across the Sogwobipa River at its widest point. But it did not look too difficult to climb. I lowered myself over the side and, clinging to the rocky face, started down. I grabbed onto shrubs and roots to keep from falling.

I was part way down when I heard Masheka calling for me. I yelled back up to him and he came over to the edge of the mountain and looked down.

"What are you doing?" he yelled.

"Following the hawk."

He started down after me. When I reached the bottom, I continued forward with my heart hammering in my chest. I'd been to this place in my visions and knew how to get to the cave from here.

Masheka dropped onto the ground and came over to me. "Wind Chaser's barking awakened me. You shouldn't have wandered off alone."

"I know where we are. Around the bend," I said, pointing to where I meant, "is a woods with a small creek rushing through it. The creek is clear and when you look down you see colored polished rocks. On the side of the creek is a boulder that has ancient drawings on it. Beyond that is the Spirit

128

Cave in the side of a rocky wall. Come on!"

Wind Chaser ran through the large pine trees and joined us. Excitement filled me as I hurried forward. I rounded the bend and the babbling brook was there just as I had described it. I stepped into its cold, clear water and carefully waded across. The boulder was there and I ran my hand over the pictures and looked up at Masheka in wonder.

"What do the drawings mean?" he asked.

"The people who made these pictures are the ones I hear chanting and playing their drums. This rock was a place of power. They'd travel here from great distances and leave offerings. The drawings show they were great hunters. See the pictures of a brave shooting the kotea and deer. It also tells of their journey here from the cold north. At the bottom, it tells of Spirit Cave and of visions that can be seen there." I paused, not knowing how I knew these things but sure that I spoke the truth.

I turned in the direction of the cave; my heart beating as rapidly as a deer's when wolves surround it. What would I learn in the cave about my people and myself?

I started forward. The rocky surface of the mountain made the cave hard to see. It lay hidden in the shadows of a ledge overhang. I shivered thinking of how I had instinctively been studying every overhang we had passed since entering the Wind River Mountain Range.

I walked forward to the cave and paused by its entrance. I could hear the drums and chanting again. I stood listening, rooted to the spot. "Do you hear them?" I asked.

"Hear who?"

"The ancient people. They're playing their drums and chanting."

He shook his head, looking uneasy. "I don't hear anything."

"I must bathe and say prayers before I enter. Only a person who is pure and willing to see the truth can go inside." I looked at him. "You have come all this way with me. In my dreams last night, we were in the cave together. Will you go into the cave to seek a vision?"

Masheka backed away from the entrance of the cave. "There's big medicine in the cave."

"I knew you could feel it."

"This must be one of the crossing places between this world and the world of spirit. I was taught that energy forces come together in a few places to make crossing over easier. I'm not going in for I'm not studying to be a holy man. I don't hear the drums and chanting nor did I see a vision of the white mountain lion. My Spirit Guide said to guide and protect you. He didn't say I was to follow in your path. I must seek my own way.

"I'll follow Wind Chaser back to get the horses and lead them here. Then Wind Chaser and I will guard you. Come, Wind Chaser, show me how you got here." He turned to go and I put my hand on his arm.

"Thank you for encouraging me last night and for accompanying me here."

"I've learned a lot about courage and dedication from you. You've taught me to see squaws differently." He turned and left, calling Wind Chaser to him.

As I bathed in the cold stream water, I could still hear the drums and chanting. Once I was clean, I dressed in my light tan tunic and sat near the cave, facing its entrance. I began to chant along with the ancient people. The air around me began to change, until everything was vibrating. I sang Hu-nai-yiee and inwardly heard the sound of the wind. I was filled with love for all life and for Apo. I went into a trance-like state and all physical reality faded away.

Oapiche appeared at the mouth of the cave with a light shimmering around him. His face was filled with compassion and his eyes shone with wisdom. He wore a white leather shirt and leggings and carried a sacred staff. Next to him was a magnificent white mountain lion who watched me with intelligent greenish-yellow eyes. His sleek muscular body was full of power. I felt a deep sense of peace and harmony.

"Come, Red Willow, the ancients call to you."

I rose, tingling with anticipation and a little afraid, then followed them into the cave, stooping to go through the entrance. They led me down a narrow tunnel into the depths. The interior was cool and dark with the only light source being what was radiating off Oapiche and the mountain lion.

As they led me to a small side passageway, the drums and chanting grew louder. We stepped through an opening and stood in a mountain meadow. It was night and I could now see the ancient people chanting and dancing around a huge fire to the beat of the drums. I became one of the male warriors dancing and singing to the Great Spirit. I wore a wolf head on top of my head. The fur of its body and its tail hung down my shoulders and back. On my feet were bone anklets that shook as I moved, and in my hands were tortoise shell rattles.

The dance was to give thanks for my people's safe journey from the land of ice and snow, with its many moons of cold, to this new land rich in game, with moons of warmth for balance. My people were strong and brave.

I became one with the sound of the drum as I danced around the center fire. The fire was the heart of the sacred nation.

Above me were thousands of sparkling stars. I stared at them as I danced and suddenly I shot up into the stars like an arrow. In the star-filled sky I soared among the wispy clouds. I had a wonderful feeling of freedom at being able to fly like an eagle. I was an unlimited being of light and so much more than my physical body.

Oapiche's voice called me and I found myself back in my own body standing next to him. The mountain lion started walking forward, and I followed him from the cavern of ancient dancers into the next cavern. In this opening I saw the Nimi. Our peaceful village was set up along the Salmon River at our summer camp. My aunt was beside our family tepee, cooking over the fire. Near her Antelope was weaving a reed basket. Naked young children were playing in the warm sunlight while their mothers gossiped nearby.

I flew away from there and soon found my brother standing alone in the mountains, his arms raised in prayer.

"Gray Eagle seeks truth in inner silence as do you," said Oapiche. In the next moment my brother left his body and stood beside me in front of Oapiche and the mountain lion. He warmly greeted Oapiche then smiled at me. "I have missed you, little sister. The tepee is quiet in your absence." My brother embraced me.

"It is good to see you." Tears came to my eyes. My brother was the only one left of my family; we had always been close. So many times we had sat and listened to Grandfather's stories or explored the secrets of nature together.

"This love you have for each other is strong and good," said Oapiche. "Because of it you have been able to meet. Through love for family we learn to love the Great Spirit who created this world. In love lies the answer to the truth you seek."

The vision of my brother faded. I felt a sudden sadness and was lonely for him and my people.

I followed Oapiche and the white mountain lion into a third cavern. The cavern walls dissolved and I flew up into the sky with my traveling companions. We traveled over the rugged mountains and across the flat plains toward the rising sun. We stopped at the edge of the land where it met the Eastern Great Lake. Water spread out further than I could see even from my aerial viewpoint. We landed on the clouds and looked down. I saw many people with pale skin dressed in strange clothing walking between large, unusual-looking lodges. They were many more than the kotea in a large herd.

"For many generations there have been only the descendants of the ancient people on this land," said Oapiche. "They have lived simply and understood the sacredness of all life, and seen the connection between the spirit world and the physical world. They recognized the importance of the wisdom of the elders and guardian spirits. They understand many things, but the people have become set in their ways and their consciousness grows rigid. They fight amongst each other instead of living peacefully in this vast, abundant land. They will not be able to withstand the Wasichus.

"The Wasichus look at life differently. They build strong lodges to keep out the cold, sun, and rain and they do not live with the animals and nature. There are good men and women among the Wasichus as there are among your people.

"Ever since the Wasichus reached this land, they have been in conflict with many of our nations. It is always the case, for customs, beliefs, and traditions vary from one group of people to another and so they clash when they come together. The stronger of the two races becomes dominant, but both groups of people grow and change and reach new understandings. This process expands the group consciousness of a people.

"The Wasichus are moving west and will invade your land. At first they will come to trade and then their holy men will come to teach you about their god. You will find many of the things they have to trade are of value and there are also some truths in their spiritual beliefs. The Wasichus will keep coming; some will come here seeking a new life and land while others will come in search of the yellow metal they use to trade with.

"As the Wasichus begin to come in greater numbers they will clash with your people and the other nations. They are a powerful race and there will be great suffering among your people. The different nations will begin to band together to try and keep their land, but the Wasichus are too strong and the old way of life will gradually give way to a new way.

"The pain that both your people and the Wasichus will have to go through is necessary because through these experiences Soul becomes purified and learns the divine laws.

"I'm showing you a glimpse of what is to come so you can understand the changes from a higher viewpoint. I want you to know why these changes are happening so you can give your people strength and courage."

"Can't this future be prevented? The Shoshoni and Comanche nations are large and strong."

Oapiche shook his head sadly. "The Wasichus are too powerful. Your people must change to survive; there's no other way. Many of your people will die but after visiting the spirit world they'll return and see things through the eyes of the Wasichus and reach a greater understanding."

"Will this happen to all the nations?"

"Ai, but the heart of the people cannot be completely extinguished. Their spirit is too strong and proud. This world is only a testing ground—a place of learning. The spirit world is the real world, and the coming of the Wasichus to your land does not touch it. This world is only a shadow of the spirit world. The spirit of the ancient people will live on. You will feel the spirits of those who have gone before and loved this land in the trees, in the wind, and on the mountains.

I found myself back in the cave with the mountain lion and Oapiche. We walked to another opening in which there were many ancient, sacred objects. I saw ancient pipes, rattles, shields, medicine bags, bear claw necklaces, and objects of power. "Pick a talisman to take back to the world with you. Something that will remind you of what you have learned in Spirit Cave and what your destiny is."

I walked slowly forward, feeling the power of the ancient objects on the ground before me. The cavern was filled with light, though I couldn't see its source. Inwardly there was a hum in my ears. I knelt down, torn between curiosity and a reluctance to even look at the objects. They were sacred objects that had been carried by shamans and healers. I was a squaw and hardly worthy of picking one.

I built up my courage and with a trembling hand touched a pipe. It was a pipe that had been used by the elders of an ancient tribe in ceremony. I could feel the energy of those men about it. I moved my hand to a crow feather. It would be good for keeping away bad spirits. I picked up a small eagle-bone-whistle used for the sun dance by the Nimi. I set it down and reverently touched a shield. It was full of power. It would be good protection. It was painted red and on it were eagle claws and owl feathers, and an ermine pelt. I touched a small bird sculpture made of stone. All these things had power but none seemed to be right for me.

I reached out for a small round stone and as I did so the humming in my ears grew louder. I rolled it softly around in the palm of my hand. It was pleasing to look at with colorful lines going through it. Yet it seemed so small and unimportant that I started to put it back. I immediately felt a deep sense of loss. The feeling was so strong that I closed my hand around the stone and it spoke to me, telling me it would give me visions. I knew then that it was my talisman and that it was as sacred as anything else in the cave. Stones hold past memories and are as old as Mother Earth. I stood up and looked at Oapiche. "This is what I choose."

"You have chosen well. The stone will give you visions as well as protection. Put it away and keep it safe."

I untied my medicine bag and put the stone inside.

"Come, I will take you part way back." I followed him and the white mountain lion through a labyrinth of passageways. He finally stopped and turned to me. His eyes were deep and full of wisdom as he reached out and touched the center of my forehead. I felt like he had opened a passageway into the world of spirit that I could go through whenever I needed to. I felt his great love for my people and me. A great sorrow came over me that he was leaving, sending me back to the world.

"I'm only a squaw. How can I give my people the courage they need?"

"Your people have brave warriors and elders with great wisdom. You'll help by keeping that courage and wisdom alive; you'll help them through the difficult times that are ahead."

"Please don't go."

"I'm always with you. Just look inwardly when you need me." He and the mountain lion began to walk away from me. The only light in the cave had been the light radiating out from them. As their forms slowly faded so did the light.

The darkness was absolute in their absence, and there was a complete void of sound. The inner humming was also gone. While with Oapiche, my body was not solid but was composed of vibrating light, now I was solid and felt trapped within in this dense, confining form.

Intense fear came over me. I didn't know if I'd ever be able to find my way out of the cave. My heart was heavy as I thought of the future of my people. I took a few deep breaths to calm myself and put my attention on Oapiche. He was still there, guiding me, only I had to listen to him inwardly. I was ashamed of my fear. I had been given a great vision, yet as soon as it left me I was as frightened as a child seeing a kotea charging toward him.

I was weak, as if I had been sick, and I was hungry for I had not eaten in many Suns and Sleeps. I felt cold for it was cool in the cave so far away from the warmth of the sun. I wondered how long I had been in the cave. Feeling light-headed, I sat down on the hard rock cave floor. The urge to sleep was overpowering; I lay down and rested.

I was shivering with cold when I awoke. I don't know how long I had slept. There was no way to tell in the darkness of the cave, and no way to gauge the passing of Suns and Sleeps without the position of the sun or stars in father sky.

I didn't know how to find my way out of the cave and wondered if my vision stone could help me. I felt for my medicine bag and found my stone inside. The stone felt warm and good in my hand. Inwardly I heard the sound of wind and the distant rumble of thunder. Then a vision came to me. I saw Grandfather as a young man. He walked right by me and into a cavern seeking visions.

Next a woman who was a healer came to me. She looked youthful but her eyes held the wisdom of an elder. "There are many plants provided for us by the Great Spirit to help us stay strong and get well when we are sick," she said. "You can learn to listen to the plants and they will tell you of their healing properties. Remember this when you go back to your people. You can help them even when it seems like an impossible task and they turn away from you." She showed me various plants and told me of their properties.

When she left a shaman came. Strength radiated from him such as I'd felt in Grandfather. He shared mystical chants that held power and were to be used for healing.

The shaman left and I was alone. The vision stone was still in my hand and its power seemed to be gone as if it had told its story. I was exhausted and weak. I had no idea of how long I had been gone from my body. I knew I had to find a way out of the cave soon or my strength would give out.

I surrendered to the guidance of Oapiche and started forward, holding out my hands in front of me. I hit my head against the ceiling. It hurt, and putting my hand to it I felt warm, sticky blood. Panic rose in me and I fought it back.

"This is a test," I said out loud, comforted by the sound of my voice in this place void of sound. I put a hand up and felt the rocky cave wall overhead. I moved slowly forward again on a path leading downward. I needed to go up to get to the entrance. Feeling around, I found a tunnel leading upward. I began to crawl. The fear came back. I felt closed in as the tunnel became narrower. I scraped my back on it and bumped my elbow. It became so narrow that I had to wiggle through the passageway using my arms to pull myself through.

The tunnel opened into a wider area on another level. I stood up and walked forward, glad to be out of the narrow tunnel. I was not careful enough and in the next instant I fell over the edge of a ledge and was tumbling through the air.

I landed on the hard stone ground below. Everything hurt and when I tried to move there was a throbbing pain in my ankle. Feeling my leg, I found that I had torn the skin all down the side of it. Unable to rise, I crawled around, trying to find a way out of the pit I had fallen into. I discovered I was in a small chamber with the only way out being the way I had come in.

As I lay there, I wondered why Oapiche had not led me from the cave. How was I to help my people trapped here beneath the earth? I wondered how long Masheka would wait for me before he began to worry. How long had I been here? Would Masheka have the courage to come in after me? I remembered the look on his face as he had backed away from the cave saying, "There is big medicine in the cave." He had looked unnerved by the spirits and unknown mysteries it contained. Had Oapiche left me here to force Masheka to enter the cave?

I closed my eyes and focused inwardly, then called out to Masheka. It took me a long time to still my inner thoughts and to remove my attention from the cold, fear, and pain. Finally an image of Masheka appeared surrounded by a radiant blue light. "Come find me," I whispered. I felt his energy and knew that I had made contact with him.

I felt like I was in a void without beginning or end. I became frightened again of dying in the cave, my life force growing gradually weaker. My mind and spirit wandered.

Something drew my awareness back into the cave. Feeling Masheka's presence somewhere nearby, I called out to him, hoping he could hear me. There was no response. I called again and again until I was hoarse but there was no answer.

I waited, wondering if I had only imaged Masheka's presence. Finally, I heard a voice. I could not tell its source. The sound echoed off the wall and seemed to bounce around. I yelled his name back in answer.

I heard Wind Chaser barking and then he started to howl.

I howled back to him. The sound was eerie in the cave. His answering howls grew fainter and I panicked, yelling, "No, no, come this way."

We yelled and howled back and forth for a long time. At last when Masheka shouted my name it sounded just above me.

"Masheka, I am down here." I called back.

"Can you see the light?"

"No."

I waited, holding my breath and keenly tuned into every sound around me. There was a faint scraping noise then I saw a dull light above. "I see it. I see it!" I exclaimed.

A moment later I heard barking above me, then the light grew stronger and I saw Wind Chaser's two gleaming eyes overhead. Masheka came into view a moment later. The sight of them brought me a wonderful sense of joy and relief. Masheka was holding a rolled up piece of lighted birch bark near the opening I had fallen through. He was far above me. He knelt and peered down at me. "Are you all right?"

"My ankle is injured."

"We will get you out of there." Wind Chaser ran around the opening above me, barking wildly.

"We need a rope," Masheka said after looking over the situation. "I will get one and be back."

"No! Do not leave me alone in the dark!" I was horrified at the thought of his leaving. I was sure he would never find me again.

"Here are some food and water." He tossed me a leather water pouch. It fell on the ground and spilled out some of its precious contents. I eagerly swallowed down a few mouthfuls as a food pouch landed on the ground next to me. "I will be back shortly."

"Stay here longer please!"

"I can't, I'm running out of birch bark. We will both be trapped here if I don't go immediately. Have courage, Red Willow. Come, Wind Chaser."

"Please leave him here to keep me company."

"I need his keen sense of smell to find my way." He grabbed Wind Chaser by the scruff of his neck and dragged him away from the opening of the hole. Wind Chaser growled.

"Go with Masheka, Wind Chaser!" I commanded.

The light disappeared, and I began to shake in fear. I clenched my sacred stone, controlling my fear with effort. I ate the pemmican I found in the food pouch. I was starving and it only awakened my appetite and made me hungrier. My ankle was throbbing. When I felt it I found that it was swollen.

I grew frightened when Masheka did not return. I worried that he had not been able to find his way back. I drank the rest of my water, then lay down and thought about how Masheka would soon hold me in his arms, and give me his strength until my troubled spirit was strong again. He would listen with a grave, thoughtful expression as I shared with him what I had seen in my visions. He would hunt for me. protect me, and lead me safely back to my people. Before the Season of Falling Leaves I'd see my brother and the others of my band again.

But once I reached home, Masheka would leave me, tak-

# WHAT MUST I DO TO BE SAVED?

1. **I MUST BELIEVE THAT I AM A SINNER.** **"For all have sinned, and come short of the glory of God"** (Rom. 3:23). **"The wages of sin is death"** (Romans 6:23).

2. **"BELIEVE ON THE LORD JESUS CHRIST, AND THOU SHALT BE SAVED"** (Acts 16:31). That is, I must believe that Jesus died, was buried, and rose again to save sinners like me. He bore **"our sins in his own body on the tree"** (I Peter 2:24). **I must trust Jesus.**

3. **I MUST CONFESS MY SINS AND ASK TO BE CLEANSED OF ALL SIN.** **"If we confess our sins, he is faithful and just to forgive us our sins, and to cleanse us from all unrighteousness"** (I John 1:9).

4. **I MUST BELIEVE HE HAS DONE IT.** I Must take God at His Word and confess Him before men. **"If thou shalt confess with thy mouth the Lord Jesus, and shalt believe in thine heart that God hath raised him from the dead, thou shalt be saved. For with the heart man believeth unto righteousness, and with the mouth confession is made unto salvation"** (Romans 10:9, 10).

5. **I MUST FORSAKE MY SINS.** To repent means to forsake or turn away from. He will give us power to do this. **"But as many as received him, to them gave he power to become the sons of God"** (John 1:12). **"For godly sorrow worketh repentance to salvation"** (2 Cor 7:10). **"Repent ye therefore, and be converted, that your sins may be blotted out"** (Acts 3:19).

—Cyrus Osterhus

Osterhus Pub. House, 4500 W. Broadway Minneapolis, MN 55422
Toll Free: 1-877-643-4229  This tract costs $2.50 for 100; $6.50 for 500; $10 for 1000
Postage: Add 30 percent (not only 30¢)  www.osterhuspub.com

ing my heart with him when he left, for somewhere during this long journey to the cave my heart had become his. I had grown to enjoy the sound of his voice, his presence, his quiet strength, and the feel of his body near mine when we slept beside one another.

At last I heard Wind Chaser barking above me and a moment later the light appeared; with it I could see Wind Chaser and Masheka again. Masheka secured the rope and dropped it down to me. The rope was made from tying the horses's reins and bridles together.

"Can you climb up?" he asked.

"I am not sure." I crawled to the end of the rope, dragging my injured leg. Then I grabbed onto the rope and tried to pull myself up. I found I had no strength. "I can't."

"Just hold on then and I'll pull you up."

I wrapped the rope around my right wrist and held on. He pulled me up until he could reach me, then he grabbed my arm and dragged me over the edge onto the ledge next to him. He drew me close and I wrapped my arms around him. His arms had never felt stronger and more welcome.

"The fire is almost out." He held a new piece of birch bark to the one burning out and it burst into flame. "Let me see your ankle."

Masheka handed me the birch bark torch, then examined my injured leg and ankle with a worried frown. "It's badly swollen. He lifted me into his arms and rose. Wind Chaser led the way back through the cave, his nose close to the ground. He lost the scent once and whined pitifully, then made circles until he picked it up again. We went through many twists and turns in a maze of paths, always moving upwards. Limestone formations like icicles hung down from the ceiling and rose up from the floor. In places the passageways were narrow and at other times we were in wide caverns.

At last we reached the entrance and, when we stepped

out, the bright sunlight fell on us. Its warmth felt wonderful on my skin but after the darkness of the cave I was almost blinded by its light.

Masheka carried me to the stream and bathed my leg. It was scraped and bruised and my ankle was twisted and swollen. The cold water felt good on my ankle but made me shake. I was still badly chilled from being in the cave.

"It's a bad scrape," said Masheka.

"I couldn't see, and I fell down the hole."

"How did you get so far into the cave without a light?"

"Oapiche led me." Wind Chaser pushed his head against my chest and I scratched him behind the ear.

"What visions did you have in the cave?"

My hand stilled on Wind Chaser's head and I looked at Masheka. His brown eyes held warmth and a touch of awe as if he had seen or sensed something of power. "I saw some good and some bad things. I'll tell you about it after I have rested. What did you see while you were in the cave?"

"I didn't go into the cave for visions," Masheka said with gruffness to his voice.

"I know, but you must have felt something while in the cave."

"I felt the spirits of holy men who have come to the cave for visions, and I felt the power of the cave and its pull into the other worlds. You don't look well."

"How long was I in there?"

"The sun has risen three times since you went in."

I felt dizzy and exhausted. Masheka carried me back over to where he had set up camp and placed me on furs under a small shelter. I fell asleep almost immediately.

When I awakened, I was lying under a lean-to and the cave was nowhere to be seen. I sat up and the movement caused my head to ache. Masheka was immediately beside me. "It's good to see you open your eyes at last. You have slept for a long time."

142

"Where are we?"

"One Sun's journey from the cave. Its presence was disturbing. You kept tossing and turning in your sleep and crying out. I felt it best to take you away from there."

"I must return to my people now."

He nodded, looking sad. "We will stay here until you have recovered fully and your ankle is better. Then we'll go to the trading post before starting back. I have hunted while you slept and I have more furs to trade with."

"No!" I felt a chill go up my spin. "I don't want to go to the trading post!"

He looked surprised at my outburst. "You don't have to. We can camp nearby, then I'll go there alone."

"You shouldn't go there either. It's too dangerous."

"There's no danger. The Wasichus set up a trading post, called the Kootenai House, in our territory. We have not had trouble with them. The Wasichus come to trade and I want a flintlock for hunting and to defend my people from the Blackfeet. It's not far from here. You can't deny me the trip when I have come so far for you."

"I'm not trying to be difficult, I just don't want to go. I saw in my vision that the Wasichus will bring great trouble to our people. They'll take our hunting grounds."

"We're strong warriors. They can't take our tribal land."

"There are a great many of them. If we kill them more will come."

"If they're so powerful an enemy, we need to know how to fight them. To kill a grizzly bear you must first understand him and learn to think like him. As a boy I was taught to face my fears not run away and hide. We'll stay here while you heal and I'll hunt game so we have furs to trade with."

I lowered my head, accepting his decision though I was uneasy about going to the trading post.

*9*

# Trading Post

*Fort Raymond on the mouth of the Big Horn River in what is presently Montana*

I apprehensively followed Masheka into the trading post with Wind Chaser at my heels. I limped slightly, for my ankle was still not fully healed. The log trading post consisted of two rooms and made me feel closed-in. Inside were many rows of furs hanging from the ceiling, beads of all sizes and colors, seashells, pans, fishhooks, tobacco, knives, hatchets, and many other things I had never seen before. Masheka had hunted for twelve suns before we had set out for the post. Hunting had been good and he had shot several antelope and deer. I had prepared the hides so we would have furs to trade with. Trading was a common practice among the tribes, but never within an enclosed log structure such as this.

Five Crow warriors were in the trading post; I was afraid there would be trouble. I froze but Masheka glanced at me. "There's no fighting between tribes allowed at trading posts," he said.

He placed his buckskin and antelope hides on the

counter. Two Wasichus, such as I had seen in my dream, were behind it. Their pale faces were covered with bushy hair and the hair on their heads was short. Their skin was much lighter than ours, and their eyes were the color of a blue jay. One man's hair was brown and the other man's hair was red. I stared at them in wonderment, knowing that none of my people would believe me if I were to tell them that there were people who looked so different from us.

Their clothing was also different. They wore what I came to learn later were pants and shirts made of fabric, and hats made of leather. It was a lot to take in all at once. I wanted to leave this place with its unfamiliar log walls and strange-looking men where Crow warriors also came to trade.

One of the Wasichus looked at me with interest as I studied them. The owner of the trading post pointed to himself and said, "Manuel Lisa." He pointed to the other man and said, "John Colter." In sign language he asked what Masheka wanted.

Masheka asked to trade for a flintlock and gun power. Manuel shook his head and said he had no muskets to trade but he would sell musket balls and powder. Masheka scowled and insisted that we needed flintlocks to defend our tribes against the Blackfeet who already had them. We were upset to have come so far and not be able to get the main thing we came for. Manuel was firm in refusing to trade for the flintlocks. Masheka was forced to trade for other things. He lay down his furs and traded for an unfamiliar shiny object.

He held it up and told me to look in it. I jumped back surprised to see my own face. The Wasichus laughed at me and Masheka smiled and said, "This is a mirror. You can see what you look like whenever you want to." I looked in it again. It was the first time I had seen a reflection of myself other than in a lake. A comely face greeted me with bright, alert brown eyes like a doe has. My features were finer and my skin was lighter than most in my tribe, and my hair was long and black. Masheka was watching me, looking immensely pleased with himself. I started to hand it back and he said it was a gift. He handed me another object that he said was an ivory comb to comb my hair with, or to wear in my hair as a decoration. Then he told me to pick out some beads. There were shiny beads made of what the Wasichus called glass. I loved the blue ones best. I picked out some, then put all of my treasures into the pack I was carrying.

Masheka traded for an iron ax and knife. I left his side to look at the fine things on the tables. I reached out and lightly touched a piece of fabric, wondering how it was made. The red material was thick and would keep a person warm in the Season of Howling Wind.7

A Crow warrior came over and touched my cheek. I whipped out a knife and he backed away. The redheaded man yelled something in a strange sounding language. He gestured in sign language that knives were not allowed in the trading post and for me to put mine away. Masheka turned and told me to come back over to him.

The Crow brave asked Masheka in sign language what he would sell me for. Masheka's expression darkened and he told him I was not for sale. I wanted to leave this place even more now. It would be a terrible fate to become a slave to a Crow warrior.

Masheka took a long time working out a trade with the Wasichus. He traded for flint, fishing hooks, and a fine bridle. While he was trading, two more Wasichus walked into the trading post. They carried flintlocks and many furs. They had bushy faces and looked as if they had not bathed in a long time.

Masheka finished his trading and nodded to me. I started to follow when one of the Wasichus who had just arrived suggested playing the hand game. Masheka hesitated as all the other men, including the Crow braves, sat down at a square piece of wood with four legs. The white men invited

Masheka to play and finally he sat down. The men who had just entered the trading post said in sign language that they were fur trappers.

The men began to put trinkets in the middle of the table to gamble with. Soon there was a pile of knives, beads, coral, and tobacco.

The hand game was a guessing game where a small stone was hidden under one of several baskets. The Wasichu whose hair was red like the color of fire was the first to try and guess which basket the stone was under. He intently watched as the baskets were mixed around, then took a guess. The other man turned over the basket showing there was nothing underneath. The redheaded man laughed, and then it was the next person's turn to guess. The game was one that I had played many times at home with other squaws to help develop my inner vision. We rarely gambled with any-thing of great value. Thinking the game was harmless, I began to look at all the unusual things in the room.

A young squaw walked into the room from the other room in the trading post. I couldn't tell what tribe she was from, for she wore clothing of the Wasichus. She was coarse in her manners and was carrying a container and some cups on a tray. She set them down on the table and used hand signs to tell the braves that she had firewater. I had never heard of firewater, but the Crow braves apparently had for they looked quite pleased.

I wondered if she was one of the Wasichus's squaws. When she started talking to them in their own language, I knew she must have been with them for a long time.

One of the Crow braves smiled and gestured that he wanted some firewater. She poured him a cup and he gave her some beads in exchange. She then offered Masheka some and when he accepted she poured him a cup. After giving her some beads, Masheka took a drink of the firewater. He began to choke and cough, turning red as tears came to his eyes.

The Wasichus and Crow braves thought it was funny and laughed at his expense. By now they all had a cup. None of them reacted as Masheka had when they drank the firewater. I was quite puzzled by this. Masheka was as strong a warrior as any of them—why it had affected him and not them was a mystery to me.

Masheka took another sip. He didn't choke on it this time and seemed to be getting used to it. I was frightened by this firewater and thought it must be very bad medicine. The game they were playing continued and when it was Masheka's turn he lost. He didn't seem to care, but rather he seemed to be enjoying the game and the firewater too much. The game grew louder and louder, and all the men were continuing to drink this firewater. The Wasichus won many of the games and did not seem as strongly affected by the firewater.

The game made me nervous. Something was wrong. The game and drinking were not done in fun but rather for a darker purpose. I saw that Masheka and the Crow braves had lost many of their newly acquired supplies to the Wasichus traders. Masheka and the Crow braves were growing angry. I wanted to leave while we still had some supplies, but it was not my place to say anything to Masheka. I was frightened of these strange Wasichus and of the Crow Braves.

Masheka laid his knife on the table and I cringed, afraid that if he lost the round there would be trouble. This reckless gambling was out of character for him. His knife had sacred feathers on the handle and a sharp stone blade. He never went anywhere without it hanging at his side. I doubted he would give it up if he were not successful in guessing which basket the stone was hidden under. I began to wonder if an evil spirit possessed Masheka. All the men were acting without the reserve that should have been between men who were strangers and even enemies such as the Crows were.

One of the pale-faced men began mixing up the baskets. It soon became impossible to tell where the stone was.

Masheka pointed to one of the baskets. The man smiled slyly and turned over the basket, showing that there was nothing underneath. He reached for the pile and Masheka grabbed the knife from the pile. Using sign language, he said that the Wasichus had cheated. "The stone was there but you have removed it!"

"No I didn't!" the trapper signed.

"Yes, you did. I saw you take it!" signed Masheka. The Crow braves were angry and started reaching for the things that they had lost. The trapper who had first suggested the game pulled out a flintlock. Manuel said in sign language that there was no cheating and told the Crow braves to get out of the trading post. "We don't want drunken Indians in here!" The Crows had no flintlocks and there was little they could do but leave.

Masheka and I were now alone with the Wasichus and I feared that Masheka would not leave peacefully, since he thought the men had cheated him. He held the knife in a threatening manner. "Give me back my things. You have cheated me!" Masheka said with his hands.

The trapper aimed his flintlock directly at Masheka. "We'll give you a chance to win back your knife." He looked at me with lust in his eyes. "The woman is all you have left of value to trade with. If you guess right you can take her and your knife and leave here in peace. If you lose, she goes to the winner."

Masheka attacked him, knocking the flintlock from his hands and holding a knife to his throat. The redheaded man grabbed Masheka's arm, spun him around, and slugged him in the jaw. Masheka fell back against the counter.

Wind Chaser leaped off the floor and went flying through the air. His powerful, muscular body crashed into the redheaded man. He fell over on to his back, fighting to keep Wind Chaser from tearing out his throat.

"No, Wind Chaser! No!" I screamed. I grabbed Wind

150

Chaser and pulled him off the man. He continued to growl as the man regained his feet. I was afraid the trappers would shoot Wind Chaser. The one Masheka had attacked had his flintlock again aimed at Masheka and the other one had also pulled out his.

"We will gamble for the squaw," said one of the trappers. "Sit!"

Masheka looked like he wanted to kill the trapper as he replied, "The woman is not mine to gamble with."

"She came with you. We'll gamble for her. I need a woman to keep me warm at night and cook my meals."

I let go of Wind Chaser and faced Manuel. "I'm the sister of the head chief of a Shoshoni tribe," I gestured with my hands. "We are part of a powerful nation consisting of thousands of people. Let me return to my people so I can tell them of your trading post. They're great hunters and will bring you many furs. Our people have need of the supplies you have for trade."

The tension was terrible in the room as we all waited for his reply. Against their flintlocks Masheka and I were powerless. I was afraid Masheka would attack the trapper again. His anger was so strong I could feel its energy. I was equally afraid of not being able to contain Wind Chaser, who was growling fiercely. The man, Wind Chaser had previously attacked, looked nervous, despite having a flintlock aimed at the wolf-dog.

"You may go," said Manuel in sign language, "but the Indian must leave all his things including his knife. He lost them in a fair game."

"The game was not fair," said Masheka. "I won't leave it. You have cheated me and tried to steal Red Willow."

I slid my pack off my back and pulled out my tomahawk. "Take this instead. It will bring you many knives if you trade it."

The redheaded man looked at the knife tightly gripped

in Masheka's hand. Masheka's eyes were cold and dangerous. Wind Chaser's hair was standing up on his back as he continued to growl.

"It's a fair trade," said Manuel. Masheka started for the door and I moved to follow him.

One of the trappers blocked my way and said with his hands. "Stay with me and you can have anything you want in the trading post." He was a big man, much taller than the braves in my tribe. He smelled of sweat and dirt. His teeth were yellow and crooked and packed with food. His eyes were narrow and the hair growing out of his face hid so much of it I had trouble seeing his character in it.

I gestured back, "I go with Masheka."

"A pretty squaw like you shouldn't be made to live the life of a savage. White men do not force their women to work hard like your braves do." He grabbed my wrist. I was so frightened that I trembled like a leaf in a storm.

Masheka jumped him and the two men fell heavily to the floor wrestling. Two of the men pulled Masheka off him and the third tried to restrain the trapper.

Manuel said something to him in his own language. I do not know what he said but from the sound of his voice and from his manner I could tell that he was extremely angry. His voice carried authority. Together the redheaded man and the trapper threw Masheka out the door and all four men turned to me. My knees felt like they had turned to water.

At that moment, Good Thunder gave out an ear-piecing scream. The Wasichus ran out the door and I grabbed my pack and followed them out just in time to see the Crow braves riding off with Straight Arrow and Good Thunder. Masheka made hand signs to Manuel to lend him a horse to go after them. Manuel shook his head. "Indians are thieves. All of you steal horses. You would steal mine now that yours is gone."

One of the trappers said, "I'll give you a fine horse for

the squaw."

Masheka gave him a piercing, angry look and said with his hands. "No, she is worth more than all your horses. Come, Red Willow. We'll leave here." He walked away from the Wasichus and I followed, keeping several paces behind to show him respect. It was dusk and I was anxious to be away from this place. Wind Chaser kept close to me; the Wasichus made no attempt to stop us.

We walked along the edge of the Big Horn River in the direction the Crow warriors had gone. The sun was setting and it was rapidly growing dark. I was terribly distraught over losing Good Thunder. The love I had for my father's warhorse ran deep and I wanted to sit down and weep or take my anger out on Masheka.

Without horses we would have great difficulty getting back to our people. Masheka and I had been gone much of the Season of Ripe Berries. We'd probably have to find a place to camp, then hunt to get furs to use in trade for horses. It might take a long time, and we could easily end up staying here during the Season of Howling Wind.

The loss of our supplies was also a problem; we had little left to survive with. Fortunately my medicine bag, and all of the things most precious to me, were in my pack.

Masheka was silent as we walked and I didn't know what he was thinking. I hoped that the evil spirits had left him and stayed at the trading post. He finally stopped at a clearing in the woods. "We'll camp here. You shouldn't walk any further on that ankle."

"What are we going to do without horses?" I asked.

"I'll steal ours back."

"How will you do that? The Crows will be many miles from here by now."

"When Hard-to-Hit told me of the trading post, he also warned me that the Crows have a village nearby. It is only one sun's journey from here. I will travel there in the morning and steal our horses back."

"They'll kill you if you try. We have lost everything except my pack."

"Including your tomahawk. Why did you give it to them?"

"To save our lives. They had flintlocks. I knew that you wouldn't leave there without your knife and you had gambled away everything else of value."

"They cheated. The Wasichus cheat my people whenever they can."

"They didn't cheat. The fire water made you reckless."

"The trappers hid the stone."

"It doesn't matter now. Either way our horses and supplies are gone. I wish that we had never gone there. How will we reach own people without Good Thunder and Straight Arrow?"

Masheka drew me against him. "I told you I would steal them back."

I wrapped my arms around him, seeking his comfort; the Wasichus and Crow braves had badly frightened me. Masheka ran his hand intimately down my back to my waist. The feelings between us were powerful. He tilted my face up so he could look at me in the moonlight. I felt his desire for me and an answering warm tingling sensation ran through my entire body.

"You are so beautiful that every man who sees you wants you, but you have no desire to be any man's squaw." He slid his hand onto my breast. "Tonight I will make you my woman." His breath smelled like firewater and I shuddered remembering the evil spirit that had made him act crazy in the trading post.

"No!" I pushed his hand away.

"Why do you protest?" he asked, backing me up against a large birch tree. I could feel the heat of his aroused body through my buckskin dress. "You want me."

154

"Not when you are possessed by an evil spirit!" I tried to twist away from him, and Wind Chaser began to growl.

"I'm not possessed." Masheka replied, his voice low and dangerous.

"Yes, you are!" I gave him a forceful shove and he staggered backwards, tripping over a log. I ran into the woods; terrified of the evil spirit that had taken over Masheka's body. Wind Chaser ran along at my side, but I didn't hear Masheka coming after me. I couldn't go far in the dark, dense woods, and soon I was forced to stop. I crawled into some bushes to hide from Masheka. Wind Chaser hunched down and crawled in after me. He lay down next to me and I curled up with my arm around him. I pressed my face against his thick fur and began to cry, overwhelmed by our fate. Wind Chaser began to howl. "Hush, Wind Chaser; Masheka will find us," I said. He quieted and I listened intently to see if I could hear anything. The wood was still; all I could hear was the beating of my own heart. It was chilly and I wrapped the shirt I was making for Masheka around me. I lay awake worrying about Masheka and our horses until I finally fell into an exhausted sleep.

In the morning, I was awakened by the sound of Masheka's voice calling for me. I didn't answer or leave the shelter of the bushes, still afraid of him.

I heard the sound of his footsteps drawing closer and closer. I realized he was following the trail I had so carelessly left the night before in my panicked flight from him. He stopped near the bushes I lay cowering in and looked around.

All at once, I felt his hand on my arm and he roughly pulled me to my feet and out of the bushes. "What are you doing here?" His face was contorted with anger.

"Hiding."

"From what?"

"From you."

"From me! Why would you hide from me?"

"Because you are possessed by an evil spirit."

Masheka grabbed my other arm so that I was more firmly in his grasp, and he gave me a hard shake. "I'm not possessed! Stop acting crazy. I feel like wild stallions are bucking around in my head and do not need any more trouble from you."

I wasn't convinced that he was back to normal. He was far removed from the quiet, protective man I had come to depend on. "You're hurting me," I whimpered.

He immediately released his rough hold and folded me into his arms. "Don't be frightened," he said in a voice that was calm and reassuring. "I'm not possessed. When you ran off last night I thought you would not go far, but when I called to you this morning and you didn't answer, I feared you were stolen or injured."

I pushed him away, flaring up with anger. "The only danger I was in last night was from you!"

"I would never hurt you."

"You tried to force me to be your woman! You have no honor. I refuse to travel with you any longer."

"No honor!" His anger matched mine. "I have shown you great patience. I should have taken you the first time we shared a sleeping robe. By now you would be carrying my papoose, and we would be safely at my village. You have no choice but to keep traveling with me. You would not survive two Suns alone in the mountains now that you no longer have a horse."

"I still have Wind Chaser to protect me. You did not manage to get him stolen though you almost caused him to get killed!"

"So now it is my fault that Good Thunder was stolen!"

"It certainly is! I never wanted to go to the trading post. I warned you that it was dangerous."

He looked away and the silence hung between us. He

156

had control of his emotions when he looked back and his voice was soft. "I thought it would be good to have a flintlock since they are more powerful than bows and arrows. I also went there so I could give you something better than what Hard-to-Hit had given you."

My anger fled at his words. "Masheka, he only gave me a few trinkets. You have saved my people from the Blackfeet and defended me from many dangers. I am sorry I ever accepted the beads if it made you feel you had not given me enough."

"Am I forgiven?"

"Only if you promise to never drink fire water again."

He grinned and the tension dissolved; his smile always won my heart. "I promise." He drew me against him again. "I was afraid I would not be able to get you out of that trading post. I wanted to kill that fur trapper for the way he looked at you. I have no desire to drink firewater again; the promise is easily given. It makes a man weak and foolish."

He released me and said, "Let's start for the Crow village."

## 10

## Horse Raid

We reached the Crow village in the early evening and hid in the bulrushes at the edge of the Bighorn River. The village was across the river from us and we knew scouts would be out; our position was at best precarious. The Crows are a much smaller nation than the Shoshonis, but this particular tribe looked to be quite strong. I soaked my swollen ankle in the water as we looked for the horses. We spotted Straight Arrow, grazing in the corral with the other hoses, but Good Thunder was not there.

In the distance, a group of people were gathered and their laughter caught my attention. The crowd parted slightly as a brave walked through it, and at that moment I saw they were gathered around Good Thunder. One warrior held Good Thunder's bridle while another jumped on his back. Good Thunder went crazy, bucking wildly and sending the brave flying. The man tried again and was thrown even further.

"Good Thunder doesn't let just anyone ride him," I whispered to Masheka.

"I can see that."

I strained for a better look. Wind Chaser crawled on his belly alongside me with his ears bent down. Good Thunder's sides were heaving and he was covered with sweat. No one was eager to try and ride him again, but finally an especially daring warrior stepped forward. I couldn't understand their language but I could see that there was betting going on. As the brave came toward Good Thunder, he reared up on his back legs. He came crashing back down almost on top of the Crow brave. The brave grabbed his mane and leaped onto his back. Good Thunder reared, but this warrior was a great horseman and clung to his back. Good Thunder started running. He leaped over a fallen tree and raced off.

"They'll ruin him if they're not careful," I said angrily.

"He's a strong horse," Masheka replied.

After awhile the brave returned with Good Thunder who was much subdued. The brave sprung off Good Thunder and began to walk him, leading him by his bridle. Masheka tapped my arm. "Come on, it is not safe here. We will return after it is dark."

We carefully made our way a safe distance from camp. I took meat jerky out of my pack and handed some to Masheka. Afterwards I examined my moccasins which had holes worn through the bottom. We needed to hunt game for food, new moccasins, and sleeping robes.

"After we get our horses back, I'll go hunting," said Masheka. He often knew what I was thinking before I said anything.

"This is the last of our food."

"If we still had fish hooks from the trading post, I could catch us some fish. We'd better try to get some sleep. We have a long night ahead of us."

I lay in the tall grass beside Masheka, thinking about the horse raid we would be making on the Crow camp. I had been on horse raids before but only on horseback and with many warriors. I had only stolen horses from corrals, which

160

were usually at the edge of a camp. I had never ridden into camp with the warriors and tried to steal the more valuable horses. That was considered too dangerous for a squaw.

"Are you asleep?" I asked.

"No, I've been thinking that it would be best for you to wait here while I go into camp to steal our horses back."

"Good Thunder would set up a commotion that would arouse the whole camp if you tried to steal him. He is so spooked that he will not behave for anyone but me."

"I could steal you a different horse. Good Thunder is too wild for you to manage, and it is too dangerous for you to try and steal him back."

"When we make our escape from the Crow camp I will be glad to have Good Thunder under me, for he is the fastest horse I've ever ridden and he has great endurance."

"Our squaws never go on horse raids."

"Nor do they use weapons. Our ways are different; you should be getting used to that by now."

"Perhaps it is good that I'm not taking you to live with my people. They wouldn't understand your ways."

"Your mother is Shoshoni."

"My mother's nature is much different from yours. She's never accompanied our braves on a horse raid. It doesn't make sense for her to want to. A horse raid tests a man's courage. A maiden does not need her courage tested. Moreover, many warriors go on horse raids to acquire enough horses so they can get a squaw."

I was reminded of the horses that Masheka had given my brother for me. "It's exciting to go on horse raids. Men get to do all the exciting things in your tribe."

Masheka put his arm around me and drew me close. "I love your spirit, Vision Woman, but I don't want you to accompany me into the Crow's camp. You could be killed or taken as a slave."

"I don't see such a dark future. During the Season of

161

Howling Wind I will be with my people. I have seen this in a vision."

"In the cave?"

"No, since then when I have looked at my vision stone." I opened my medicine bag and took out the stone. "Feel its power." I set it in his hand.

"It's strong medicine. You have changed since being in the cave."

"So have you," I replied. "In the cave, a medicine woman told me about the healing properties of many plants. It was too much for me to remember, but now when we are walking through the forests I recognize many of the plants and I know what they can be used for. I have been collecting many of them to bring to my people."

"So your vision to be a medicine woman who would serve your people was a true one. I was hoping the cave would guide you in a different direction."

"So did I." I lay with my head on his shoulder, lightly running my hand up his muscular arm and across his chest. I admired the physical strength in his well-toned body and wondered if he still wanted me.

"Did you kill the bear these teeth came from?" I asked, examining the large, curved teeth on his bear-tooth necklace.

"Yes, he was a large grizzly. It took several arrows to kill him, leaving holes in the fine hide that had to be sewn up."

"Only important braves of high rank can wear bear necklaces in our tribe."

"It's that way in our tribe as well."

"And eagle feathers are considered powerful medicine. Your shield had many on it. Are you considered a great warrior in your camp?"

"A great warrior does not lose his horse to a Crow."

"If you are unable to steal Straight Arrow back you won't be able to return to your people."

"I'll capture and break in a wild horse if I have to."

"Then that is what I will do as well."

He laughed a deep laugh that vibrated in his chest under my head. "So Shoshoni maidens capture and break wild horses. It has been interesting traveling with you."

"We haven't parted yet."

"No, not yet."

"How did Straight Arrow get his name?"

"He and I have a weakness for racing. When he runs he is as fast as an arrow that is shot straight and true."

"When we get our horses back, we will race and see which horse is faster."

"We may have a chance for that race before the night is over. Go to sleep or you'll be too tired to steal back Good Thunder." I closed my eyes and found it easy to slip out of my body. I found myself riding Good Thunder through the clouds.

I awoke when Masheka gently set me from him. A quarter moon was out.

"I was hoping you wouldn't awaken," said Masheka.

"Would you have left me here if I hadn't?"

"I would have returned for you with our horses."

I sat up. "Not with Good Thunder." I gave Masheka some water from my water pouch then drank some myself. We went down to the river and waded in. The water was cold and dark. Wind Chaser jumped into the water after us. We began to swim across, and the current took us almost even with the Crow camp. When we reached the opposite shore Wind Chaser shook his fur, spraying me with water.

"Stay here," Masheka gestured in sign language, "while I scout out their camp." He disappeared near the village and I hid in some bushes.

He reappeared a short time later. "There's only one guard; I'll take care of him. Once you see that it is clear, you go after Good Thunder and ride silently out of camp. Good Thunder is staked by a tepee over there." He pointed to the tepee. "We'll meet here and swim back across the river together. If there is trouble, ride out of here without waiting for me. You can make it back to your people alone. You're a strong woman."

He left my side and headed toward the guard. His moccasin-covered feet made no sound. I saw his knife in the moonlight. He snuck up on the Crow guard and a moment later the guard fell to the ground. I ran into the camp with Wind Chaser at my heels and reached Good Thunder without incident. I began to unfasten the rope that tied him to the stake. My heart pounded in my ears and I listened to every noise, afraid of being discovered.

Good Thunder was nervous and I stroked his mane and tried to calm him. He nickered and I froze, afraid he had been heard. I could hear someone moving about in the tepee. I drew out my knife and slashed the rope that tied Good Thunder. A dark Crow warrior stepped through the buckskin flap as I started to mount. Wind Chaser leaped at him and the warrior cried out as he was knocked back against the tepee. Wind Chaser sunk his teeth into the man's throat and ripped it open. I mounted Good Thunder as another warrior stepped out of the tepee. I urged Good Thunder into a gallop as I glanced back to be sure Wind Chaser was coming.

I rode to where Masheka was waiting with Straight Arrow and two other fine-looking Crow horses. I rode past him yelling, "Let's get out of here!" In back of us were several loud war cries that sent a shiver up my spine.

I heard Masheka racing after us as Good Thunder plunged into the river and started swimming across. Straight Arrow and Wind Chaser splashed into the water moments after me. Good Thunder swam through the deep water with no difficulty and soon we were back on dry land. I glanced over my shoulder and saw many Crow braves on horseback also swimming across the river.

Good Thunder started galloping again and I crouched

down low and twisted my hands in his mane. Behind us I could hear the Crow warriors had also reached dry land. An arrow struck my pack and another grazed the side of my head. Masheka rode close beside me and Wind Chaser ran alongside us.

Good Thunder's mane whipped back into my face. His strong body moved steadily under me, not showing any sign of tiring even though we had covered a great distance. Tree limbs tried to snatch me off his back and scratched my arms and legs. We jumped across a small creek, then began climbing a steep embankment. I glanced back and saw that there were still many Crow warriors chasing us.

At the top of the embankment, we found ourselves on a narrow trail, probably made by mountain goats. Masheka took the lead and we rode along the edge of the hill, then followed a gully down the other side.

Masheka and I started across a large open meadow. The Crow warriors following us had not yet left the woods and were beginning to fall behind. Masheka drew one of the Crow horses alongside his horse and leaped from Straight Arrow onto the other horse.

My stomach tightened as I drew the other Crow horse alongside me and prepared to jump.

"No!" Masheka violently motioned for me not to try it.

Good Thunder raced along beside Masheka's new horse, showing no sign of fatigue. We quickly outdistanced the Crows now that Masheka had a fresh horse and theirs were beginning to tire. I spared a look for Wind Chaser afraid he might not be able to keep up and found him nipping at one of Masheka's spare horses as it started to falter. The raid had frightened me but it was evident Masheka had enjoyed it. He probably felt it had restored his honor after losing our supplies in the trading post.

We rode hard the rest of the night and were still riding as the sun began to show its face. On top of another rocky slope we paused briefly to look for the Crow warriors. They were far below us. We raced on until we reached the Flow-to-Mud. There we stopped to water and rest the horses. I moved onto one of the other horses and we swam across the river, then followed its course. Good Thunder was on a rope behind the horse I was riding and tried to bite the other horse. I hit his nose with the end of the rope and he became more obedient. He didn't like being led.

We rode all day, only stopping for short intervals to rest the horses. We had seen no sign of the Crow warriors, but knew that meant little. They wouldn't give up so easily. When evening put a blanket across the sky, we slowed to a comfortable walking pace. I was tired and hungry. We were still riding along the Flow-to-Mud River.

At dawn Masheka decided it was safe for us to stop. We found a sheltered area with grass for the horses. My body was so stiff I could barely get off my horse. Masheka laughed at me. "You will never be a Kootenai warrior."

"I don't want to be a Kootenai warrior." My poor legs were unsteady and I sank down onto the ground.

Masheka came over to me and squatted down beside me. "Are your legs sore?"

"They ache."

"If you are admitting they hurt then they must be real bad." He pushed up my dress before I could stop him and examined my legs. They were red and in places the skin had been rubbed away. "We need some bear grease to rub on them," he said as he stood up. "We can't rest here for long. We need to get far away from the Crow warriors so I can hunt."

"Do you think we've lost them?"

"Temporarily, but we're not out of danger."

Masheka brought me the water bag and I drank. We made a pinebough sleeping couch and I lay down. Masheka covered me with leaves as it was cold in the mountains at dawn. Masheka kept guard, although I knew he had gone without sleep longer than I had. He woke me when the sun was high in the sky and said we had to travel. I tried to rise and found that I could not; my legs were without strength. "I've never ridden so hard before," I said apologetically.

"Take off the shirt." I was wearing the shirt I'd made for him and I slipped it off and handed it to him. He took it from me and laid it on Good Thunder's back. "This should help protect your legs." Masheka lifted me onto my horse and we started off again.

We rode until evening, and then he lifted me down and told me to keep guard for Crows while he went hunting. I called Wind Chaser to me and petted him. "Are you getting tired too, my friend?" I lifted up his paws and examined them to be sure they were not injured from our many suns and sleeps of hard traveling. His paws were in far better shape than my legs. I was so tired I couldn't stay awake and I fell asleep, leaning against Wind Chaser.

A deep voice cut through my dreams and I awoke suddenly. "Do you sleep when you're suppose to be keeping guard?"

I slumped over onto the ground. "Let the Crows take me captive if they have so much endurance that they have kept up to us." I started drifting back to sleep, despite the fact Masheka was in the middle of scolding me. He lifted me up and placed me on Straight Arrow, then mounted behind me. I snuggled against him and drifted off again.

I awakened when Masheka lifted me off Straight Arrow. It was dawn and I realized we'd ridden all night. Masheka carried me to the edge of the Sogwobjoa River. Kneeling down I drank from my hands while the horses waded in. I shivered with cold as I watched the sunrise, lighting up the clouds in pink and purple hues.

Masheka drew me against him and I was glad of his warmth. "I know it's been a difficult ride," he said, "but the

167

further we go the less likely they are to continue to follow." He rubbed my back and switched to his own language as he continued to comfort me. I wondered if he realized he was no longer speaking Shoshoni. His words were softly spoken and warm. I put my arms around him; aware of how much bigger and stronger he was than me.

I kept guard so Masheka could finally sleep. I started to nod off when Wind Chaser growled. Scanning the woods, I couldn't see anything moving amongst the trees. Frightened I grasped Masheka's arm. "Masheka, wake up."

A Crow chief in full war bonnet came running out of the dense woods toward us, brandishing a tomahawk. Wind Chaser sprang at him. The Crow chief knocked him aside with his shield as Masheka leaped up with his knife drawn. Another warrior appeared, swinging his war club, as he charged at me. I rolled out of the way as the war club came down, striking the ground right where I had just been. He swung again and Wind Chaser attacked him, sinking his teeth into the arm.

Masheka and the Crow chief were slowly circling one another. The Crow chief lunged and Masheka side stepped the tomahawk and struck back with his knife.

The other crow warrior struck his war club against Wind Chaser's shoulder. Wind Chaser yelped and fell to the ground.

"No!" I yelled, attacking the warrior with my knife. He jerked back from the blade and violently knocked me to the ground. I lay there stunned as he raised his war cub about to deliver the deathblow. I threw dirt in his face, screaming to Masheka who was still fighting the Crow chief.

Masheka drove his knife into the chief's heart, and then he gave out a spine-tingling war cry as he leaped through the air toward the Crow warrior. Masheka's body crashed into the other man and they both fell heavily onto the ground. The war club fell from the Crow warrior's hand and he closed his hands around Masheka's neck.

I scrambled to my feet, grabbed the war club, and swung it. The stone head of the club hit the warrior's skull with a sickening thud, and he collapsed on the ground.

Masheka sprung to his feet before I could ask if he was hurt. "Stay here and hide while I see if there are others," he said. He disappeared into the woods, leaving me alone and afraid. The horror of the warrior's violent death swept over me. I felt sick and my body broke into a sweat. I knelt and threw up on the ground.

The wind blew through the trees and the leaves rustled on the ground. I looked around nervously, expecting another Crow warrior to appear as I moved over to where Wind Chaser lay. He raised his head and licked my hand. I checked him over and found that his shoulder was bloody from where he had been hit. I got my water pouch and cleansed his wound, then washed my mouth out.

Shortly Masheka reappeared leading two Crow horses. "They were alone," he said. He tied the new horses to the two we already had and took two furs and pemmican from their supplies.

"Do you think any more will come after us?"

"No, most likely the rest went back. We are a long way from their village. It is hardly worth tracking us this far for so few horses." He picked up the war club and tomahawk and fastened them to one of the horses.

"You killed a guard and Wind Chaser killed one of their warriors when we took back our horses. This is not too far to come in revenge."

Masheka crouched beside me and placed a fur over my shoulders and gave me a piece of pemmican. He had put the other fur over his own shoulders. "Can you keep going?"

"Yes, but Wind Chaser was hit with the war club. I won't leave him even if you beat me."

"I would never beat you and I don't want to leave him either." He examined Wind Chaser's shoulder and affectionately scratched him behind the ear. "We're indebted to you again, my friend." He put his arm around me. "You look shaken."

"The sound of his skull spitting open was terrible. I shall never forget it if I live to see a hundred winters. Perhaps Kootenai ways are best, and squaws should not use weapons."

"I was just thinking the opposite. You saved my life. Killing is never easy. A warrior goes into battle prepared to die but fighting to live."

"I want to help people, not be a warrior."

"A warrior also helps his people."

"I know and there is great honor in being a warrior. I do not want to stay here any longer; there has been too much violence." Masheka helped me onto Good Thunder, then placed Wind Chaser in front of me. He mounted Straight Arrow and we rode away from that place of death. We had reached the north edge of the Absaroka Mountains. This land was Shoshoni land; if we ran into any of our bands, we would be safe. We soon left the Flow-to-Mud and rode west.

Late in the afternoon we stopped at a stream so Masheka could sleep. I went over to the two new Crow horses and looked to see what the warriors were carrying in the way of food and supplies. They were traveling light and had little more than some pemmican, sleeping robes, a bow and quiver of arrows, a spear, and water pouches. I ate some of the pemmican, for I was starving, and put the quiver of arrows on my back. I intended to be able to defend all of us if we were attacked again.

Light raindrops splashed on my face and I began to make a shelter out of pine boughs under a large tree. The rain started coming down heavier, waking Masheka. He helped me finish the shelter. Wind Chaser limped over and crawled in with us. I checked his shoulder and saw that it had stopped bleeding. Masheka brushed Wind Chaser's fur with a pinecone. I could see that he and Wind Chaser had developed a deep bond. Masheka went back to sleep while I continued to keep guard.

Masheka awoke in the early evening and ate some of the pemmican. The rain showed no sign of letting up but we were tired of being cramped beneath the shelter, so we went and sat by the stream. Several deer came up to the water a short distance from us and started to drink. Masheka took the bow from me and pulled an arrow from the quiver on my back. He slowly rose so as to not frighten the deer and let the arrow fly. A large buck went down while the other deer ran off. Masheka slit open the buck's throat to insure it a quick death. Still kneeling beside the animal, Masheka thanked the deer for giving its life so we could survive.

"The spirits have sent the deer to us," said Masheka. "When I shot him, his spirit flew from his body. I, too, left my body and flew out with him. I felt a joy and freedom I have never known before, as if we were celebrating his journeying into the spirit world. I'm grateful that he was willing to give up his life to feed and clothe us."

I looked at Masheka, awed by this unique man and his experience. "Death is a gateway to new life."

We skinned the deer and cut up the meat. As we worked, Masheka said, "The days are growing shorter and it is becoming colder. I will have to leave you soon if I am to reach my people before the ground is blanketed with snow."

My knife became still in my hand and I stared at him. It had seemed so far off that we would part, but now our journey together was almost over. My chest constricted and I felt like I needed air.

Masheka cut me off a piece of the deer liver and I ate a bite, then threw the rest to Wind Chaser. I had lost my appetite after Masheka's words though I was hungry.

When we had finished butchering the deer, we washed the blood off in the river. I gathered wood for the fire, and started it with my firestones, thankful that I had my pack of supplies with me when the Crows had stolen Good Thunder. We cooked some of the meat over the fire and ate it. The remainder of the meat we wrapped up in the hide and hung in a tree so the bears would not get it.

We decided to stay at this place for a few Suns and sleeps to give Wind Chaser and us a chance to rest. In the morning Masheka went off to scout the area, and I began tanning the hide. I rough-tanned it; merely scraping, cleaning, and stretching it because we did not want to stay in this place too long. I intended to use the leather to make moccasins for Masheka and I. They wouldn't be as soft as a properly tanned hide and wouldn't last as long, but they'd be serviceable.

I was heavy hearted as I worked, knowing I'd soon be separated from Masheka. Even the thought of being with my people again did not lighten my spirits.

## 11

# The Parting

We traveled west for many suns following narrow animal trails through the Shining Mountains. The trees were a canopy of golden-red colors. The air was starting to grow cool, especially at night. One day as I rode along a twisted mountain trail with horse flies buzzing around my head, I saw that Masheka had stopped. I rode up to him and discovered that there was a huge bull kotea in the trail, blocking our way—the biggest bull I had ever seen.

Masheka held a spear ready, "Stay back," he said softly. The kotea bellowed, then lowered his horns and charged. The ground shook beneath his feet. Masheka rode forward to meet him. When the bull had nearly reached them, Straight Arrow swerved so he was alongside the kotea and Masheka drove the spear into the bull's heart.

The kotea swung his head, trying to gore Straight Arrow's side. The horse moved swiftly away and the bull turned around and came after him. Weak from the loss of blood, the kotea finally fell to the ground with a reverberating thud. Masheka leaped off Straight Arrow and approached the animal slowly. The kotea attempted to rise then fell back dead.

I started trembling as I watched Masheka say a prayer of gratitude and put grass in the kotea's mouth. Our men usually hunted the kotea in large groups. One rider would attack the animal and cut the hamstrings, then another would kill it when it was down. I had never seen a single warrior kill one.

My heart pounded as I dismounted and came over to Masheka. I stared at the large, powerfully built animal. "He might have killed you." My voice was unsteady, revealing my distress.

"Instead he gave his life for us. It's good; I'll feel better knowing you have plenty of food and a kotea hide to keep you warm on your journey home." He grinned. "My part is done. You'd better get to work. It'll take you awhile to cut up and dry all this meat and to prepare the hide."

My eyes widened; the kotea was enormous. Cutting it up was squaws' work, but not one woman alone. I knelt down by the backside of the kotea and ran my hand over the thick, brown fur. It would make a warm robe to both wear and to sleep on. I could still feel the heat of his body and was sad that such a fine creature had to die. With my knife I cut into the hide at the back of the bull's neck then sliced it all the way to the tail. Warm blood poured onto the ground beside me. Masheka stripped to his breechcloth and squatted down on the other side, ripping the belly from the tail to the head.

"Would you do a squaw's work?" I asked.

"We would have to camp on the edge of a mountain tonight if I didn't." He cut off the horns. "The horns are powerful medicine. We have much to be grateful for."

"Why did you put grass in his mouth?"

"For his journey to the spirit worlds. We will leave the head. He was a noble being."

Together we took off the top half of the hide and cut all the meat from the bones. Masheka tied one end of our rope to the kotea's feet and the other to Straight Arrow. I guided

Straight Arrow backwards until the kotea flipped over onto its other side. We lifted the hide off that side, then cut the rest of the meat from the bone. We wrapped the meat up in hides and packed it onto the four extra horses.

Evening approached as we continued our journey. We rode until we came to a creek that ran into a mountain lake and set up camp. I sliced the meat into sections, throwing Wind Chaser a few pieces, then made a fire and put some meat on sticks to roast over the flames. Masheka made a drying rack for the rest of the meat.

My arms grew tired from cutting up the meat, so I went down to the lake and waded in. The water was warm and shallow but as I walked further out it became cold. I leaned over and washed the kotea blood from my arms and dress. Masheka stripped and dove into the deep water. He resurfaced a moment later and let out a war cry.

He swam toward me and stood up. "That feels good. Try it."

"The water is freezing."

"Do you expect me to travel with a filthy squaw?" He lunged at me and grabbed me before I could escape to the safety of the shore. I fought him as he lifted me into his arms and carried me out farther. Wind Chaser swam into the water after us.

I screamed as Masheka threw me into the water and I sank into its freezing depths. The cold water shocked my body. I came up sputtering and mad. I swam toward shore and stood up when I could touch the bottom. Masheka stood in water up to his thighs laughing. I threw myself against him, trying to knock him down. He almost lost his footing on the slippery rocks, then he tried to catch my hands as I continued to shove against him. He was laughing so hard he could hardly defend himself.

His laughter infuriated me. I knocked one of his legs out from under him and he finally went down, taking me with him. I went under the cold water again. Masheka rose and lifted me up with him, carrying me to shore. He good-naturedly dumped me on the ground.

"You're going to make some poor brave a disrespectful squaw."

"I'm all wet and have nothing to change into!" Wind Chaser chose this moment to get out of the water and shake himself all over me.

"Then take your leather dress off." I stared at him as he crouched down in front of me. The inviting light in his eyes set my heart to racing. "Or should I do it for you?"

"No!" I scrambled to my feet. "I had to get wet anyway." I dragged half of the kotea hide to the water and submerged it, then cleaned off the leaves, dirt, and blood. Masheka helped me drag it back to shore for it was too heavy for me to manage on my own. We put it fur side down on a log. Using a kotea foreleg bone, I began to scrape off bits of meat, fat, and connective tissue.

Masheka threw more wood on the fire, then braided kotea hair into a rope. I worked near the fire for I was cold. After a while Masheka took over scraping the hide. When he had finished, we stretched it out on the ground and staked it. I had no energy left for the other hide. We ate the freshly cooked kotea meat along with thistle taproots, cow parsnips, and berries that I had gathered that morning.

I lay down on the coarse grass, exhausted and shivering, thinking that soon I would not have to sleep on the hard ground. The kotea hide would make a warm sleeping robe. The kotea was a great gift and we would use all of it. The sinews and tendon would be used for thread and bowstring, the gallstone would be used to make yellow paint, the tail would be used for a fly swatter, and the stomach would make a fine water container.

"Don't fall asleep in your wet tunic," said Masheka, interrupting my thoughts. "You'll take a chill."

"And whose fault would that be?"

He handed me a buckskin. "Your own."

I took off my tunic and wrapped the soft buckskin around my shoulders. After hanging my tunic to dry on some nearby tree branches, I sat next to Masheka. He put his arm around me and I leaned against him at peace. I watched the fire cracking on the logs. It had grown dark and the fire gave us warmth as well as light. It was comfortable where we sat for Masheka had spread pine boughs on the ground and put an antelope skin over it. I wished I didn't have to return to my people and could just keep traveling with Masheka forever. My heart was filled with love for Masheka and I couldn't imagine life to offer more than it did in this moment.

"It's good that we can both return to our people with meat," said Masheka.

I yawned. "Meat is always needed in the Season of Howling Wind. Tomorrow I will finish preparing it and work on tanning the hides. Thank you for helping me cut up the kotea. I couldn't have done it alone."

"Do not tell my brother. I'd never hear the end of it."

I grinned. "I won't betray your secrets."

He laughed and turned from the fire to look directly at me. "You are lovely in the firelight." He dug out my ivory comb and began to comb out my thick damp hair. Soon it was shiny and free of tangles.

"You're always so modest with me," Masheka said softly. He pushed the buckskin off my shoulders and it dropped down to my waist. I shivered as the cool night air touched my bare skin. He slowly reached out and caressed one of my breasts with a reverent expression on his handsome face. "Your skin is so smooth. I have wanted to touch you like this for a long time. Your beauty makes my heart beat like a drum." He drew my hand to his chest so I could feel it. Masheka was beautiful as well; the red and golden firelight danced on his strong, young body.

177

He drew me to him and his bare chest felt good against my breasts. "Your people are fortunate to have such a strong, courageous, medicine woman." He lay down on his sleeping couch, drawing me down beside him. One side of my body was warmed by the fire and the other by the heat of Masheka's body.

"Why is it you are not protesting?" he asked, running his hand down my back.

"You have stolen my will as well as my heart. I have no wish to deny you anything."

"Yet you refuse to share a lodge with me."

"I'm guided in a different direction."

"The horses are growing thick coats and the leaves are turning color; fall is setting in early. It will be a long, cold winter with a thick blanket of snow covering the ground. Many of your best hunters were killed and food will be scarce this winter. You were thin when we met this spring, you will fare worse this winter. Your chief brother does not need another mouth to feed— especially one who is my responsibility!"

"It is because the Nimi are so weakened that I must return to them! Our medicine man was killed in the attack. There's no one but me to tend to them when they are sick, and it is my responsibility to help them understand their visions and dreams."

"Women cannot help men understand their dreams and visions. At least not a young squaw."

"I can guide the women."

"I don't want to return to my people without you."

I put my arm around him. "I don't want to be separated from you either, but it must be this way. You're a Crazy Dog scout and a Fish Chief with responsibilities to your tribe, and I'm needed to help my people through a difficult winter."

He held me tightly, understanding the truth of my words. Survival in a band was difficult without each member sharing the burden. I could feel his inner struggle. His desire for me as his wife weighed heavily on his mind. Finally he sighed and loosened his hold, and I knew he had resigned himself to our separation.

He pressed his cheek against mine. "You smell like mountain flowers. I shall think of you whenever I smell them. In my memories you will never grow old and plump as surely the woman I take for my squaw will."

I felt my heart pierced at his words. "You're going to ask some other squaw to share your lodge when you return to your people?"

He braced himself on one elbow and looked at me. "I don't wish to live alone. There is a young squaw back at my village who likes me. I will probably take her for my wife."

I sat up and he drew me back down beside him. "Stay with me tonight. We have so little time left."

I rose, wrapping the buckskin around me. "You expect me to lay with you after talking of your plans to marry a Kootenai maiden! Go sleep with her to satisfy your lust!" I walked away from him and lay down beneath a tall pine tree. I was furious that he thought of marrying another squaw, yet my body was on fire for him and I had trouble getting to sleep. Somehow during our journey Masheka had become a part of me.

The next morning I awakened early. I was cold and had slept poorly. I dressed quickly and glanced at Masheka who was still sleeping soundly. It was unusual for him to sleep past dawn and I wondered if his sleep was troubled. I built up the fire and warmed myself beside it, then washed a rock clean and laid a strip of kotea meat on it. With another rock I began to pound it until it was soft. I put the meat back on the rack to finish drying and pounded another strip. Masheka awakened after awhile and I handed him a piece of cooked meat.

"It's good. I can see that when it suits you, you can be

as good a squaw as you are a warrior."

I glared at him and went back to pounding strips of meat. I worked all morning until my muscles burned and my arms felt like boulders. Masheka offered to help but I told him it was a squaw's work, so he made a knife and fish hooks from the kotea bone and went fishing.

I was sad and angry at the thought of Masheka taking another woman for his squaw. Needing a break, I took out Masheka's shirt and began sewing a row of red, yellow, and blue beads down one side of the front. I had done the other side already. Next to the beaded strip I had sewn tufts of kotea fur. I wondered if the Kootenai squaw could sew this well and wondered if she was prettier than I was.

Masheka approached me with several trout and set them down nearby. "As if I don't have enough work without fish to clean and dry," I snapped, shoving his shirt into a pouch so he wouldn't see it. I picked up my knife and tore into a fish as if it were a Crow brave.

"The fish has given his life so we can have enough food. Why do you treat it with such anger?"

"Is she pretty?"

"Who?" he asked, looking puzzled.

"Is she lovely, naked in the firelight?"

"What are you talking about?"

"The Kootenai squaw you plan to marry."

"Oh, Wild Plum; she will be pleasant enough to wake up next to."

"Is she young?"

"A little younger than you. She will be an obedient wife who will work hard."

"You'd be bored with an obedient wife." I stabbed my knife violently into the next fish and sliced it open. Its gills still moved even though it was dead. "I know how to do everything a squaw must do. I can put up a tepee by myself and—"

"Do you know how to build an earth lodge?"

"No, but I can weave fine baskets and sew a sturdy pair of moccasins like the ones I made you" I gestured to the moccasins he wore. "I used the hide from deer's neck for the soles because it is the thickest."

"Can you grow tobacco to smoke in the sacred pipes?"

"I could learn. I know how to gather seeds and pound them into flour to make bread out of them."

"One of the elder Shoshoni braves might be willing to take you for a second wife since you have so many skills. A young buck probably won't want a squaw who has spent the Season of Ripe Berries alone with a Kootenai brave. Being a second wife is hard. The first wife will not like you because you're pretty and she'll make you do all the work." He looked at the fish I was stabbing. "That fish won't be fit to eat. You've prepared it with anger instead of gratitude." He got up and went into the woods.

I put the fish filets on the rack to dry. The fish entrails I buried away from camp so they wouldn't attract wolves or bears. I worked on the kotea meat again, pounding out my frustrations. I saw a vision of a young, pretty squaw beside Masheka. It should have eased my guilt and made me happy to know he would not be alone when he returned to his village, but it didn't.

I began to sing prayer songs as I worked and gradually my anger left me. I apologized to the fish and kotea for my lack of gratitude.

Masheka returned with birch tree sticks and came over to sit beside me. "You have a pretty voice. I take your singing to mean your cheerful disposition has been restored and it's safe to work beside you."

"It's safe."

He began making arrows from the sticks. "Do you have any obsidian in your pack or did we lose it all when the horses were stolen?"

I took some obsidian rocks out of my pack and handed them to him. "I still have some and you're welcome to them. They're heavy to carry."

He turned a piece in his hand. "This stone will make fine arrow heads."

"Tell me about your home."

"We live in one of the most beautiful places in the Shining Mountains. The Sacred Mountains lay just to the east of where our permanent village is located, always gracing us with their peaceful presence. They're immortal and unchanging while we are but a small ripple on the water.

"Trout and huge fish, called sturgeon, live in the large lake near our village and there is a lot of game in the woods. In summer we travel to the plain to hunt the kotea."

"Do your people ever run out of food by The Season of Melting Snow?"

"No, we never go hungry." He used a piece of an antler to chip away at the obsidian, forming it into an arrowhead as he continued. "We explore the rivers to the west of us by canoes and trade with the Salish and Nez Perce who live along them. We also travel great distances to the east through Blackfeet and Lakota territory to get red stone for our sacred pipes. The Blackfeet first came to our land in my father's lifetime. We have had an ongoing fight with them since then. They are driving the tribes of my people west off the plains."

"The Blackfeet are a powerful nation. They make it difficult to hunt the kotea."

Late in the afternoon I lay down on the sleeping couch—edgy from sleeping so poorly the night before. The sun felt good on my skin and I soon fell asleep. I found myself back in my tepee at my village. The wind howled outside and shook the tepee as it tried to get in. I put another stick in the fire. Mother and Father lay on their sleeping couches. They were both feverish and breathing poorly. Their lungs were congested and their chests rattled. I squatted down next to mother and put a cold cloth on her forehead, worried and distressed that I couldn't do more to help her. She stared up at me with glazed eyes. Deep sorrow filled me as she took her last breaths and died.

Masheka shook me awake. "You were moaning in your sleep," he said gently. I reached out for him and he drew me to him. "What dream did the spirits send you?"

"I dreamed of those that can no longer be spoken of." I wrapped my arms around his neck.

"Did you dream of the man you were to share a lodge with?"

I shook my head.

"Your parents?"

I nodded and tears came to my eyes. "I know I should not speak of them, but sometimes it is hard to keep all my sadness inside. They were caught in a blizzard and were half-dead when Father carried Mother into the tepee. He had carried her for a great distance. His feet were frozen and his face and hands frostbitten. Mother was even worse. Father was recovering at first but then they both came down with fever. I watched helplessly as mother died. Father lost his will to live after that. He left us for the Land of the Shadows shortly after her. I could do nothing to help them. The Season of Howling WInd is hard on my people. Food is scarce and wood runs low. Many get sick. They need a healer...I must return to them." I looked up at him. "Do you understand why I must go back?"

"I understand why you feel you must go back to them, but I don't think you have to."

I stayed in Masheka's arms. My dream had brought back memories that were still poignant. It began to drizzle, so Masheka and I made a lean-to out of the buckskins and slept under it that night. In the morning it continued to rain softly as I lay under a skin curled up against Masheka. The short time we still had together was sacred to me. Later when the

183

sky cleared, we finally got up.

I went over to Good Thunder and stroked him behind his ears. He was feeling frisky and pulled away, prancing around. I grabbed his rope bridle and he tried to bite me, then jerked away and kicked me in the thigh. Searing pain went through me. I fell to the ground and grabbed my aching leg. "Stupid horse!"

"Is your leg broken?" Masheka squatted down beside me.

"No, he would never kick me that hard. I think he just likes to remind me that he is not a tame beast of labor." Good Thunder came over and pushed his head against my back, trying to make up. I grabbed his bridle and pulled myself to my feet. My leg was throbbing and I knew a bruise would form.

"You should have a gentle, little filly that will not give you so much trouble."

I glared at him. "Good Thunder is the fastest horse there is. Why would I want some gentle filly?"

"Good Thunder's fast, but not as fast as Straight Arrow."

"I'll bet you he is!"

"How much are you willing to bet?"

I frowned, trying to think of something of value. "My mirror against your armband," I replied, deciding I'd like something to remember him by. Masheka always wore his armband. He took off his breastplate and necklace to sleep or swim, but the armband was always on his arm. It was a leather band finely decorated with dyed quills. Long tassels hung from it where it was tied.

"You mustn't think you have any chance of winning to make such a small bet. Make the stakes really matter. How about my bear claw necklace against your vision stone."

I gasped. "I can't gamble with that!"

"You aren't sure you'll win."

"I'm sure! But it's sacred, and besides, what would I do

184

with your necklace? A maiden can't wear or even own a necklace with such great medicine."

"All right, the mirror against the armband. I can give the mirror to Wild Plum since you are so willing to gamble it away. We will race to the tree, circle around it and race back." He pointed across the meadow to a distant tree. "The first one back to our camp wins."

"Agreed." I was angry that Masheka would give my mirror to another maiden if he won. I couldn't mount Good Thunder without a saddle with my bruised leg, so I reluctantly asked for help.

"Perhaps it would be better to race at another time."

"Now is fine!" I snapped. Masheka lifted me onto Good Thunder's back and I swung my leg over.

Masheka mounted then shouted, "Ready..., go!"

Straight Arrow took off but Good Thunder reared up and plunged down before starting off after him. Precious moments had been lost in our slow start.

Good Thunder loved to run and he sailed forward like he was the wind. I crouched down on his back, becoming a part of him. Winning the race was more than not losing my mirror and gaining Masheka's armband. Now was my chance to prove to him that I was a skilled rider and that Good Thunder was a fast horse. The wind whipped my hair back and tore at my dress. I was exhilarated. I felt as if I were soaring like a bird in flight.

Straight Arrow kept his lead on Good Thunder. I spared a look at Masheka. I loved watching him ride. He was the finest horseman I had ever seen. Straight Arrow was still ahead when we reached the tree. Good Thunder and I circled around it just moments behind and started back toward camp. Good Thunder's hoofs thundered beneath me.

"Come on, Good Thunder!" I screamed. He put on a burst of speed and caught up with Straight Arrow. They ran neck and neck.

"Go, Good Thunder, go!" The horses continued to run side by side as well matched as any two horses that had ever raced.

My desire to win the race faded as I got caught up in the pure joy of racing alongside Masheka. I felt very close to him; we were as one, enjoying the freedom racing spirited horses brought.

We had just about reached our camp when Good Thunder pulled ahead and took the lead. We thundered into camp and then raced beyond. Good Thunder didn't slow as we approached the creek and we flew over it and rode into the woods. Good Thunder finally slowed down as the brush grew thicker. I turned him around and rode back to camp.

I slid off Good Thunder's back and hugged him. Masheka watched me. "He's a fine animal. Sometime I'd like to try riding him."

"He'd probably be too hard for you to handle. Perhaps we could get you a filly."

"It looks like I'll have to find something else to give Wild Plum. The mirror obviously has no value to you since you were willing to risk it in a bet."

"I wouldn't have bet it if I wasn't so certain of winning."

"Are you forgetting that you almost didn't win? The armband is yours. You'll have to untie it. It's been on my arm a long time and the ties are tight." He turned so the arm with the band on it was facing me. I hesitated, not feeling right about taking it. "Go on, you won it. It belongs to you now." I worked at the knots. They were indeed tight. It took me a while to work them free. I pulled the armband off him and found the skin underneath much lighter than the rest of his arm. I could see now that it was quite old. I could feel its power. The quillwork was exquisite.

"Who made it?"

"My grandmother made it for my grandfather."

I looked up at him. "I can't take something of such value."

"You won it fairly."

"But I didn't know its value or I wouldn't have asked you to bet it."

He took the band from me and tied it onto my arm. It slid down my arm into my hand. "It's too big. You keep it. It isn't really the band I want; it is the man who wears it."

"Then maybe you'll come to my village someday and give me a chance to win it back." He turned away and began packing up the extra horses.

I put the armband in my leather bag that carried my flute and other things of value, then tied the bag on Good Thunder. My leg was sore and it hurt to move around.

Masheka was quiet and moody as we traveled that day. I wondered if losing the race bothered him or if there was something else. We set up camp in the late afternoon and, while we were unpacking the horses, he announced that he would start back to his people on the following morning.

I had known this was coming and that he'd delayed separating from me as long as possible. Still it shocked me to hear him say it. I felt the prickling sensations of tears starting to form. I picked up a leather pouch and went into the woods to pick berries that I'd seen as we had ridden here. I wanted to be alone so that Masheka wouldn't see me cry. When I was out of sight the tears began to roll down my cheeks. I filled the pouch with berries, then sat down and prayed to Apo to give me strength to follow my path.

My pain eased a little. I went down to the river and washed my face to hide the evidence that I'd been crying.

Returning to camp, I found Masheka wasn't there. I got out my flute and left camp again. I climbed up on a large boulder and began to play. Soon, Masheka came over to me. "Your music is like a song from the spirit worlds."

"I gathered some berries."

"I saw them."

"I needed to be alone."

He nodded and took my hand in his. We walked back to camp together. I served him the berries and dried kotea meat, then ate some myself. Neither of us ate much. We went to the river and watched the sun go down together. The trees were brilliant in their fall color. Masheka put his arm around me and I rested my head against his shoulder. The evening air was cool and we had our kotea robes wrapped around our shoulders. Several deer came down to drink at the creek. Masheka made no attempt to kill any of them as we had enough meat. We could enjoy their life and the beauty of the forest.

We returned to camp and Masheka lay down on his kotea hide. I fed a few sticks into the fire, then lay down beside him.

"Lay your sleeping robe someplace else, Vision Woman. I wish to sleep tonight and not be tormented by your nearness."

"My nearness could be a pleasure," I said in a sensual voice.

"Do you offer me tonight what you have withheld for so long?"

"You know I have wanted you for a long time and would withhold nothing."

"What I know is that you want to return to your people, though you are my woman."

"Then come with me! Among the Nimi a daughter is considered a blessing because her husband comes to live with his wife's band and not the other way around."

"I am a Kootenai warrior. I don't want to live as a Shoshoni, hiding in the Season of Howling Wind from my enemies without enough food to keep my squaw and papooses fed. We'd arrive at your people's camp without a tepee, supplies, or clothing. Your people had most of their tepees and supplies destroyed; they wouldn't welcome us."

"They'd welcome us because you saved our band and

because they need a medicine woman. Gray Eagle and I have a tepee and supplies and you can hunt for food."

"Your tepee is crowded with your aunt and uncle and others living there."

"We can make our own tepee after the kotea hunt this fall."

"It takes many kotea to make a tepee and many moons of work to prepare the hides. Moreover, I am responsible to my people. I am a Fish Chief studying to be a Band Chief. I have my own visions to follow."

"What are your visions?"

"They're not to be spoken of except to a shaman or the elders."

I didn't ask further questions though it made me curious. I had not thought of Masheka having a vision, though I knew Apo guided him, and that he had to have powerful medicine to enter the cave searching for me.

Masheka spoke again. "I felt a closeness to you the first time I saw you in the Sacred Mountains. I often go there to get direction and visions. Targhee usually comes with me so we can protect each other. On the day I left with the Crazy Dog scouts for the Sacred Mountains, I had risen early in the morning and prayed to the Master Spirit for guidance and protection. A Spirit Guide came to me and told me I must go into the mountain alone because there was someone there who needed protection. I have felt this guardian's presence ever since. My vision led me to expect to find a brave in the mountains and I was surprised to find a maiden. When I stepped out of the woods and first saw you, there was golden light surrounding you. I slipped away quietly so as to not disturb your vision."

I was amazed by his words. I wondered if Oapiche was his guardian. There was a deeper connection between Masheka and I than I had realized. I wanted to know him as a man even if I could not marry him. "Let's not talk about visions and responsibility. Tonight, I want to be yours." I ran my hand down his muscular chest to his taut stomach, taking pleasure in the feel of him. "I will always be yours in my heart."

He roughly flipped me onto my back and lay over me. "Your vision is clouded! If we share the sleeping couch tonight, you could leave tomorrow carrying my papoose. A squaw with child needs a brave to hunt for her and to protect her from enemy tribes. I will not take the chance of getting you with child."

"Only two nights ago you would have taken the chance."

"I was the one with clouded vision on that night. You were so lovely naked in the firelight that I didn't think of responsibility."

"Perhaps neither of us has clouded vision. Perhaps we are meant to have this time together before we part. I'm not like your Kootenai squaws; I don't need your protection. I know how to use weapons and how to hunt for food. Besides my brother will protect and shelter me."

"Your brother has the whole tribe to be concerned about. If they're attacked, he will lead the defense and when he hunts he will be obligated to give much of the meat to the many squaws who were left widows by the Blackfeet."

"I can hunt with a bow and arrow, set snares, and fish. I won't go hungry, and the Blackfeet do not attack in the Season of Howling Wind. It is only in the Season of Melting Snow when our men are weak from hunger and we come out of hiding to hunt the kotea, that we are in danger of attack."

"But the Season of Melting Snow is when you would be large of belly and awkward with my papoose if we mated. If that does not deter you, think of the disgrace you bring upon Gray Eagle who is the tribal chief. He needs the respect of his people to lead them. If you come back with child they will say he cannot even control his sister, let alone a war party."

Tears came to my eyes. "I wouldn't be disgraced. The tribe considers us married."

"It is no better, a tribe does not welcome back a squaw, carrying a papoose, when she has deliberately left her brave, placing a burden on her tribe to provide for her."

I moistened my lips, feeling the weight of his strong, male body on mine. My desire for him seemed more important than any rational reason for not mating with him. "But I want you." My voice came out a breathless whisper.

"Want?" He thrust his leg between mine. "You want me for the night and tomorrow you want to leave me for your people. If want were the only issue then I would have mated with you the first time we lay together for I have wanted you since then." He rose and stalked off, moments later there was a splash as he dove into the cold river.

I rolled over on my fur and started to cry. His rejection hurt, but I knew he did it because he cared about me. I fell asleep to the sound of the wind blowing through the trees. In the middle of the night, I half awakened as Masheka lay down next to me and drew me against him. I sleepily rolled over and put my arm around him before drifting off again.

In the morning I awoke just before dawn to Wind Chaser's howling. I got out of my sleeping couch and took out my peace pipe. Masheka also rose, and he followed me as I walked to the river. I held out my pipe to Mother Earth and Father Sky and to the four different directions, ending facing the east as the sun rose. Inwardly there was a soft humming sound in my ear. I gave prayers for our safe journey.

Masheka and I walked back to camp. I ate and drank a little as I watched Masheka pack his horses. He seemed anxious to be off, whereas I wanted to delay the moment of parting as long as possible.

I had a kotea robe over my shoulders but the day was warming so I rolled it up and tied it to Good Thunder.

Masheka turned to me after he'd finished taking down our camp. "You take the Crow horses to help replace the ones you gave my brother for me," I said, my heart heavy.

"I'll leave a horse for you to carry some of the kotea meat to your tribe."

"I've much to thank you for."

He nodded and knelt down, calling to Wind Chaser. When Wind Chaser came over, Masheka affectionately scratched him behind the ears. "Watch out for Vision Woman," he said. He looked at me. "You'll be all right. Your tribe is not far from here."

"They'll be getting ready to leave for the winter camp."

"Where will they go?"

"We'll probably head south and camp near other tribes on the Piupa River."

"Come here," Masheka said softly. I went to him and he held me tightly against him. "Every time I hear a wolf howl I'll think of you, Vision Woman. And every night when I sleep under the stars I'll remember lying beside you and hearing you call them by name. When I climb the sacred mountains I will feel your presence at my side and when summer comes and warms the lands again I will remember swimming in the river with you and racing our horses. We are parting, but forever you will walk in my soul."

"As you walk in mine." I slipped away from him and went to my pack and pulled out the shirt I had made for him. "I've finally finished your shirt."

His eyes lit up. "It's beautiful." He pulled off his old shirt and slipped the new one on over his head. The fringe hung down around the top of his thighs. The sleeves reached to his wrists and it fit him across the chest comfortably. He admired the pattern of the beads running down the front of the shirt.

"I have something for you as well." He brought over a finely made rope bridle he had made from the kotea hair. He slipped off Good Thunder's worn one and put it on. "Good

192

Thunder is as fine a horse as I have ever seen. You handle him well. You have changed my thinking about squaws for your heart is brave. I will share what I have learned with my tribe and if I have daughters, I will teach them differently.

"Go to your people, Vision Woman. You'll be a blessing to them." He mounted up and rode off without looking back.

Wind Chaser started after him, and then came back to me when he saw that I was not going along. I mounted up and started off in the other direction. Wind Chaser followed me a short way then started after Masheka again. Confused, he finally sat down and began to howl.

"Come, Wind Chaser," I called. He got up and trotted toward me. I urged Good Thunder into a gallop and rode away from our camp.

## 12

# Winter Among the Shoshoni

*On the Snake River in Idaho*

I found my people's encampment one evening soon after Masheka and I separated. When I entered my brother's tepee the familiar aroma of drying herbs and smoke greeted me. Gray Eagle, Antelope, Talking Goose and White Bull were sitting around the fire. Antelope ran to me and we hugged one another joyously. Gray Eagle also rose and came over to me. He embraced me and tears came to my eyes so great was my happiness at being with my family again.

"Why are you here?" Gray Eagle asked with concern.

"I was guided to come here to serve the Nimi."

"Where's Masheka?" asked Talking Goose, embracing me.

"We traveled together to Spirit Cave, then he returned to his people." I joined my family by the fire and Wind Chaser lay down beside me. I learned that Antelope and my brother had married and they shared the tepee with White Bull and Talking Goose since my aunt and uncle's tepee had been destroyed. I told them much of my journey, including the visit to the trading post. "The trading post is run by the Wasichus," I said. "They have skin that is very pale—almost the color of this dress."

"You speak with forked tongue. All men have skin like ours!" said White Bull.

"I tell the truth; their skin is pale and they have hair on their faces. And their hair is many different colors. I saw one who had hair the color of fire and eyes that are the color of the sky on a sunny day."

White Bull frowned. "I think you make up stories to impress us."

"It's from the Wasichus that the Blackfeet get their flint-locks. They have many useful things to trade furs for. Look at this." I took out my looking glass and handed it to him.

He looked into it and jerked back when he saw his own image. "What is this?"

"A looking glass so you can see yourself when you put on war paint." I handed him my ivory-carved comb. "This is to brush your hair with. They also have knives made of some-thing much harder than stone or bones." I gave some colored and silver beads to Talking Goose and Antelope.

"We will have to go there to trade," said Gray Eagle, examining the looking glass.

"No, they'd give you fire water which makes a brave crazy when he drinks it."

"It is not for squaws to decide," said White Bull. He looked annoyed that I, a young squaw, knew about things he had never heard of.

"What are your plans now?" Gray Eagle asked.

"To be a medicine woman for our people."

"You belong with Masheka," said Talking Goose. "It's the way of the Nimi for a woman to stay with her husband."

"He is not my husband."

"Gray Eagle gave you to him in exchange for nine ponies," said White Bull. "You dishonor our lodge by returning here."

"My place is with our people! We have no other healer."

"You should force her to return to Masheka." Talking Goose said to Gray Eagle. "You're too lenient with her. A squaw has no need to go on so many Vision Quests."

"It is too late in the season for her to travel to Masheka's people."

"Then find her a brave among our people. She's old to still be living in her brother's lodge."

"Enough, Talking Goose," said White Bull. "Our chief does not need a woman's advice on how to handle his sister."

On the next afternoon I heard a scratch at the tepee flap. I pulled it back and Sweet Clover entered, carrying Little Cloud. "It is so good to see you," said Sweet Clover, giving me a hug. "I'm so glad you came back to the people."

"I missed you all so much." I released her and lifted Little Cloud from her arms. "He's gotten so big and strong."

Sweet Clover beamed. "He'll be a great warrior like his father, Chased-by-Bear." I smiled, wondering what it would be like to hold Masheka's papoose in my arms. I set Little Cloud down. He ran over to Talking Goose on his short, chubby legs and sat on her lap. Talking Goose made a fuss over him and gave him a licorice root to chew on.

"I see you are going to have another papoose," I said, for she was large with child.

She beamed happily. "It will be born in the Season of the Howling Wind."

"I'm happy for you."

"You must be there when my papoose is being born. I had a difficult time with Little Cloud. I'm frightened."

"Don't worry. I'll be there."

"Let's go outside and take a walk." We left Little Cloud with my aunt and went outside. "I thought I should warn you that Talking Goose was making trouble for you this morning. She came to our tepee and gossiped with Yellow Flower and Sharp Nose," said Sweet Clover. "She said you brought things that are Bad Medicine from the Trading Posts, made up stories about men with pale-skin, and dishonor our people by leaving your husband and returning here. She said you're wild because Gray Eagle does not make you obey him. The women are jealous of you, and Talking Goose makes it worse."

"Do you believe the things she says about me?"

"No, I know that you are guided by the spirits and do what you think is right. But you must be careful. Yellow Flower is full of malice. She has been bitter ever since Chased-by-Bear married me. She turns her hatred from me to you because Chased-by-Bear speaks of you with admiration. He says you are a great medicine woman and have visions. He would like to take you for a wife."

"Does this upset you, too?"

She grinned. "No, better she directs her anger toward you. I would welcome you as a sister to my lodge. But why is it that you are not with Masheka?"

"I'd like to be with him, but I knew the Nimi needed a medicine woman. I wanted him to come live with our band, but he is a proud Kootenai Fish Chief. He did not want to become one of our people."

"It's usually the squaw who must bend. My mother says a squaw must be like the barren winter trees that bend when the winter wind howls. If you're covered with leaves like the summer trees, when the wind blows you'll loose many branches or maybe even be uprooted."

"I'd have bent like the trees in winter if I had only myself to think of, but I've been guided to help our tribe. I can't think of what I want, yet I can't help thinking of Masheka. He walks in my soul."

"The Season of Howling Wind will be hard for you without him, but perhaps by spring you will look favorably on another brave"

"It'll take more than one Season of Howling Wind to

forget him."

I spent the evening alone in the tepee. I took out Masheka's armband and reverently studied the pattern on it as I thought of him. I missed him terribly and started to cry as the thought came to me that I would never see him again. I didn't feel like I belonged with my people anymore. I wondered why I had been guided to return to them when they did not seem to want me.

Gray Eagle came into the tepee, hesitating by the flap when he saw that I was alone. He started to leave when he realized I was crying. "Why do you weep?"

"I miss Masheka."

Gray Eagle came over and put his arm around me. "The way of a medicine woman is not easy. There are many tests along the way."

"Why am I asked to give up what I love most?" I pressed my head against his chest.

"We were taught as children that it is more important to serve the greater good of the tribe then to serve our self."

Talking Goose came into the tepee. "What goes on here! Get away from her, Gray Eagle. She's your sister."

He moved away, looking stricken like a child caught doing mischief. "We do no harm. She is upset and I am comforting her."

Talking Goose looked sharply at me. "Why does she cry?"

"She misses Masheka."

"She should have stayed with her husband. You two cannot be alone together! If you come in and see she is alone you must wait outside or ask her to leave. You should not talk directly to each other either. You know these are the ways of our people. You are the chief and must support the custom and not break the rules."

"I do support our customs. I also know that it is not for a squaw to tell a chief what to do." He walked out of the tepee, looking quite perturbed.

Soon after I arrived, we headed west for our winter camp. The women broke down the camp and made pony drags by tying lodge poles behind the horses. Our supplies were tied on and the small children rode on top. Even Wind Chaser had a small drag to pull. My band had joined the Agaiduka band for the summer camp but now we broke up into a smaller band for the winter so there would be less competition for game.

On our journey we ran into a lone kotea bull and three of our best hunters set after it. They killed it and the women cut up the meat. The koteas were leaving for warmer grounds and I knew we wouldn't see any again until Season of Melting Snow.

We were a much smaller tribe after the battle with the Blackfeet. We numbered about sixty warriors and one hundred and eighty women and children. We had less than thirty-five tepees.

We traveled south along the Salmon River until it ran into the Sawtooth Mountains, and then we followed the Big Woods River as it curved south. This was the land of my people. We passed other bands as we journeyed. Finally, we reached the sheltered campsite on the Piupa Rivers where we had camped other Seasons of Howling Wind.

Antelope, Talking Goose, and I set up a large tepee. It consisted of elk skins that shed the rain and snow. When we traveled we had only put up half of it, but now that we had reached our new camp we put it all up. Inside we put up a painted dew cloth to give us extra protection from the cold and to add beauty to our tepee. The inner wall could also be adjusted for more ventilation. Last we tied our baskets, weapons, cooking supplies, herbs, and clothing to the lodge poles to keep the tepee orderly.

A blizzard came bringing cold weather and deep snow that covered the ground in a white blanket. Food became scarce for the men could not go out hunting. Gray Eagle gave away all the meat he had hunted and dried during the Season of Ripe Berries so the widows and their children would not starve. I kept Good Thunder close to the tepee and chopped willow bark off trees for him to eat. As soon as the snow stopped, my brother and White Bull went hunting. After they had been gone two suns, Antelope and I became worried for it was bitter cold.

I put on a kotea robe and heavy mittens and went to the river with Wind Chaser to fish. Wind Chaser ran off and I tried to spear one. The fish did not show themselves though I told them of our need for food. I felt cold and numb as I crouched there. The wind was strong, stinging my cheeks and whipping under the bottom of my robe. When Wind Chaser reappeared, the sun was high in the sky. I was eager to return to the warmth of the tepee.

As I walked back, I saw that there was a commotion in the middle of camp. Gray Eagle and White Bull had returned to camp with a Bannock warrior who was slumped over his horse. The man tumbled off his horse and I ran over to him. I thought the man must be wounded but when I reached him I saw that there were blisters covering his face. Many of the women and children gathered around including Sweet Clover and Little Cloud.

Sweet Clover squatted beside me. "He is so young," she said. "You must try and save him." White Bull and Gray Eagle carried the unconscious man to our tepee and laid him on a sleeping couch. I did what I could for the brave, tending him throughout the night and praying to Apo to guide me, but the brave grew worse and died in the early dawn. I went and got his things, some we would bury with him and others we would give to those in camp that needed them the most. I was surprised to see among his things, a red blanket, an iron knife, fishhooks, and colored glass beads. I knew he had been to the trading post. White Bull and Gray Eagle carried the Bannock warrior outside and buried him in a crevice with his weapons.

I felt sad that I had not been able to help him but there were other things to think about. There was always work to do: hides to tan, clothes to sew, food to prepare, and animals to tend to. Antelope was already with child and she worked hard but tired easily, leaving much of the drudgery to me. Antelope's mother came to see us often. She was making her future grandchild a small turtle-shaped pouch to put the umbilical cord in. She had already made a cradleboard to carry the papoose in. I gave her some glass beads I'd gotten at the trading post. She worked day after day sewing glass beads, stone beads, porcupine quills, and bones into an intricate pattern so the pouch and cradleboard would have protective power.

Antelope, Talking Goose, and I worked on tanning kotea hides to make Talking Goose and White Bull a tepee. It was peaceful in the warm tepee with the snow falling outside. I was looking forward to the birth of Antelope's new papoose. It would come at the beginning of the Season of Melting Snow.

Half a moon after the Bannock warrior had ridden into camp my brother and White Bull came down with a fever. The fever was mild and I was not too worried. But later, they broke out in blisters on their faces and torsos.

My bleeding started and I was forced to go to the women's lodge, which was located outside the village. It tore my heart to have to leave for I wanted to nurse my brother and White Bull. After traveling with Masheka I knew my bleeding would not hurt White Bull and Gray Eagle, but to ignore this custom would damage my brother's position in the tribe.

That evening Sweet Clover came to the women's lodge. "My papoose wants to be born." She sat down on a sleeping couch, looking tired and worried. I went over to her and put my hand on her forehead and found that she was hot. That night as her contractions grew stronger, she developed blisters on her face and torso. One of the elder women, Black Crow Feather, came to help me with the birth. Crow feathers were believed to bring protection and were often placed in cradleboards. Since Black Crow Feather had delivered so many papooses safely into the world, she had earned the name.

Her calmness eased my nerves at being there for my first birth. Sweet Clover's mother, Mountain Lamb, also came to help at the birth of her grandchild. We told stories as the long hours went by. The birth was a difficult one because Sweet Clover was so sick. At dawn I supported Sweet Clover as she squatted down and Black Crow Feather helped the child into the world. Her face darkened with distress when she saw the infant. "The papoose is not well. The evil spirits have cursed it like its mother and our chief. Tend to it while I deliver the after birth." She directed Mountain Lamb to go and tell Chased-by-Bear that he had a daughter and to wash his genitals, as was the custom, while I washed the baby. Mountain Lamb left the tepee, wailing loudly for her granddaughter.

Sweet Clover also began to weep and Black Crow Feather handed me the papoose. The infant was a perfectly formed little girl but covered with sores. Some were on her arms and legs as well as on her torso. My heart was heavy as I washed, greased, and powdered the tiny papoose. Once this was completed, I wrapped her in a soft skin packed on the bottom with dry moss. I handed the child to Sweet Clover who held the papoose to her breast so it could nurse, then looked up at me. "Do you think she will live?"

"It is hard to know. This sickness is different from any I have seen before."

"Pray to Apo for her."

"I will do everything I can to help you both."

"I will name her Rising Fawn, because she reminds me

of a little spotted fawn I once came across. The fawn was curled up, hiding in the forest plants, waiting for its mother."

Chased-by-Bear came swiftly to the women's lodge with his mother-in-law still wailing in back of him. "How sick are my wife and daughter?" he asked when I opened the flap.

"They have the same illness that my brother and White Bull have."

He blanched. I could see how much he wanted to see his wife and child but it was forbidden until a full cycle of the moon had passed. After that she could live in his tepee but not share a sleeping couch for a year, so she would have plenty of milk for her new papoose and not have another growing in her belly.

"You have a beautiful daughter," I said, wishing there was more I could say to comfort him.

"A daughter is good. When she marries her husband will live with our band and accompany me when hunting and on the warpath. Tell Sweet Clover my heart is on the ground; I will not be happy again until she and the child are well."

I sang prayers beside Sweet Clover and Rising Fawn. The baby was feverish and I bathed it with cool water and put bear grease on its sores. There was a scratching on the tepee flap before the sun was high in the sky. Chaser-by-Bear was standing there with Little Cloud in his arms. "Save my son," he said. He brought the child into the tepee and laid him on a sleeping couch. Little Cloud was covered with blisters, as were his mother and new baby sister.

"I will do what I can to help him."

"They say you have brought this bad medicine to our tribe. When I was a boy, we had a powerful medicine man whom someone cheated. He retaliated by cursing a stone and hiding it in that man's tepee. The man had bad luck hunting and fishing after that. He couldn't shoot straight when he saw a deer and fish would not come to his hook. The tribe says you are a powerful medicine woman and bring bad medicine to our tribe."

"You have known me since I was a papoose. I don't bring bad medicine. I want to help our people not bring bad fortune."

"I know, that's why I brought my son to you." He crouched down by his sleeping wife, gazing at her with his heart open for all to see. He left the tepee right as Jogwotee, the head of the elders, arrived to examine the newest member of the tribe. Black Crow Feather wrapped the infant in a fur and carried her outside to him.

Sweet Clover opened her eyes. "Where does Black Crow Feathers go with my baby?"

"She's showing Rising Fawn to the head of the elders," I replied. I couldn't join the men because of my bleeding. Jogwotee examined the child, his expression grave. He was wise and had been a close friend of Grandfather. I had great respect for him, but I was afraid of what he would decide.

"This papoose is covered with sores!"

"She is cursed by the evil spirits," said Black Crow Feather.

Jogwotee looked at Chased-by-Bear with kindness in his eyes. "The child must be put out to die."

"No, it is not a curse but merely an illness!" I cried out. "She deserves a chance!" I came out of the lodge. "Please, let me try and save her."

"Go back into the tepee before you cause Chased-by-Bear and I to die. She cannot be saved." He turned and walked away, carrying the child.

Chased-by-Bear's pain-filled eyes met mine. "Do not let him kill your child!" I pleaded.

"Whether the infant is cursed or merely ill it cannot be allowed to live for it will weaken the whole tribe." Grief stricken, he followed Jogwotee.

"We must try and stop him!" I said to Black Crow Feather.

"Rising Fawn is cursed. You are the cause of this bad medicine that has come to our tribe. Your uncle and our tribal chief will die because they let you break so many of the ancient tribal customs. Our customs have kept our people strong as long as the oldest of our tribe can remember."

"It is not a curse but a disease and I did not bring the illness, the Bannock warrior did. Please save Little Fawn."

"There is nothing I can do to save her."

I stood there with my stomach twisted in knots, wondering what to do. Gray Eagle was sick and couldn't help me fight the elders. If I tried to fight the elders alone I could be banished from the tribe, and then I would not be able to help the others who were sick. I heard Sweet Clover and her mother in the tepee weeping. Greatly distressed, I went to them. I comforted Sweet Clover, then did what I could for Little Cloud.

The disease was not something I knew how to cure. I knew I needed powerful help. I sat on a fur and took out my vision stone. Then I began to pray to Oapiche, asking him how to cure those who had become sick. My consciousness moved back to Spirit Cave. I was there inwardly with the healer who told me how to listen to the plants speak so they would tell me of their powers. The shaman joined us as we talked. He gave me some mystical chants to sing to drive away the blister sickness.

When I came back from my vision, I sent Black Crow Feather for some of the dried roots I had hanging in my tepee. Once she brought them to me, I listened inwardly to the roots, asking each one if it would help cure the blister illness. Snakeweed and Alkanet vibrated with positive energy when I held them. I cut the knurled black root of the snakeweed into little pieces, and then I pounded it into a power that was reddish in color. I made a strong tea from the root. The tea had an astringent taste but I made Little Cloud and Sweet Clover drink it every few hours because snakeweed is known to have properties that expel venom from a person's body. I also gave them some broth made from venison and garlic to give them strength. Little Cloud kept scratching his blisters until they bled, so I had to bind his hands. I put some of the tea in a leather pouch and told Sweet Clover's mother to give it to Gray Eagle and White Bull. Then I drank some.

After I had done what I could to help them, I chanted the songs I'd learned from the shaman. I felt the power of the words as I sang, giving strength to Little Cloud and Sweet Clover and driving away the evil spirits. For two days I stayed beside them, doing all I could to help them. My connection was strong with the spirit world during this time. That evening it was a full moon and Jogwotee held a Naroyo dance ceremony to drive away the evil spirits.

The next morning Yellow Flower came to the tepee, her face was distorted from weeping, and I was afraid more in Chased-by-Bear's family were ill. "Please, Red Willow. Talk to Chased-by-Bear. He has not returned to the tepee since his papoose was put out to die. He sits by her grave mound and neither eats nor sleeps. He has cut off his fine, long hair and prays and sings. He does not talk to me when I go to him. It's like he has gone to the Land of Shadows with the child. My two little girls' stomachs growl, for our food is gone. Please help us!"

"I'll go at once. Where is he?"

She led me through the woods to a rocky place at the base of the mountains, then left us. Chased-by-Bear was sitting on the ground next to a crevice where the dead baby had been placed. He had a kotea robe over his shoulders and there was snow on it over an inch high. I sat down beside him and, holding my vision stone in my hand, began to sing Hu-nai-yiee. The song had no power of its own but when sung with love; it provided strong medicine. I sang until I felt an inner connection to Chased-by-Bear, then sat listening to the inward sound of the wind.

I shivered with cold as I sat on the ground, but I rose above the discomfort of my body. After a long silence, I felt a change in Chased-by-Bear and knew it was time to speak. "Sweet Clover and Little Cloud are getting better. I think they will live."

He turned and looked at me. "It's an illness then and not bad medicine."

I nodded. "Chased-by-Bear, I do not mean to be disrespectful of your mourning but I came here because I think it would be good for Sweet Clover and Little Cloud to see you. Moreover, Yellow Flower asked me to tell you that she and your little daughters have no food."

The far away look in his eyes disappeared as my words registered. "I kept slipping further into the Land of Shadows until I heard you singing and drawing me back." He sighed deeply. I felt his inner pain. "When Jogwotee placed the infant on the ground, she began to cry, so he pinched her nose and held her mouth shut until she became silent. I felt her spirit rise up and I wanted to follow it. I understand why the infants that are weak or sick have to die, but it does not make it any easier." He did not say anything further. I sat quietly beside him, feeling his pain. A strong bond formed between us as we sat there sharing the sorrow of his tiny daughter's death.

He finally rose. "I will go see Sweet Clover and Little Cloud, then go fishing so my family can eat." We returned to the women's lodge together and comforted his wife and son.

That night Antelope came to the women's lodge in great distress. "White Bull's name can no longer be spoken. Talking Goose grieves for him; she cut off her little finger at the joint, as our ancestors did, and she acts as one deranged. She tears at her clothes and hair and rocks back and forth. Gray Eagle is very ill and I fear he will not live through the night. He asks for you. How many more days do you think it will be before you can leave here?"

I pulled my fur robe over my shoulders. "I will leave now."

"But you are still bleeding," said Black Crow Feather. "You cannot go."

"I will not stay here while my brother dies." I left the tepee and Antelope followed.

"You must not go to him," said Antelope. "You will cause him to bleed to death through the nose."

"That is only a superstition." I hurried toward the village.

She grabbed my arm, forcing me to stop. "What if the elders are right and you kill him?"

"I traveled with Masheka when I had my bleeding, for there was no laying-in-lodge to go to, and Masheka did not die." I wrenched my arm from hers and started walking.

"But you could be banished from the band for breaking custom. You'd disgrace Gray Eagle as well. The council will reprimand him and the people will pick a new chief."

"It is night; no one will see me go to him."

"Black Crow Feather knows."

"It is more important that Gray Eagle lives than that he remains chief." We had reached his tepee.

"Please I beg you, do not go in. Perhaps tomorrow your bleeding will be over."

"You said you feared Gray Eagle would not live through the night. I won't wait."

"If he dies the people will blame you. You could be put to death. He is our chief and you go against the wisdom of the elders. You're breaking an old custom. They only need an excuse like this to take action against you. There have been many complaints brought before the elders and Gray Eagle about you. Gray Eagle is naturally upset because he loves you. The people are afraid. They want someone to blame for their suffering, for the attack by the Blackfeet, and for the cold winter and bad medicine that mysteriously causes blisters. You have frightened them with your stories of pale-faced men, and your looking glass that reflects our faces like a pond. They say the mirror steals a person's soul. Some even say it stole your soul. Black Crow Feather says you brought the bad medicine that kills our people."

I stood there, trembling and afraid. I wanted to go back to the women's lodge, then I thought of my brother and knew with an inner certainty that I could help him as I had Sweet Clover and Little Cloud. My fears evaporated like the mist in the morning sun. The love I held for my brother made me strong. My band needed Gray Eagle's wisdom and leadership. If it cost me my life to try and save him, I was willing to make that sacrifice. I held Antelope by her shoulders and looked her directly in the eyes. "Dear one, listen with your heart not your fears. I might be able to save Gray Eagle. It is not good to go against the customs of the Nimi, but I will not follow them if it means letting my brother die."

I pulled back the flap and bent down, stepping into the tepee. Talking Goose was sitting by Gray Eagle's pine-bough sleeping couch rocking back and forth and crying. My heart froze, thinking my brother must be dead. I flew across the tepee to him. His sleeping couch was in the honored position directly across from the door.

His face was gray and sunken with blisters on it. He did not move at all. I held a feather over his nose, to see if he still breathed, and it moved slightly. "He yet lives." I untied an alkanet root that was hanging on the tepee wall and handed it to Antelope. "Boil some water and make a strong tea using this root." Antelope put pine pitch on the fire to make it hotter. The flames leaped up heating the pouch that hung above it. I pulled the kotea robe off my brother and cooled him by wiping off his body with cool water. I was horrified to see how thin he had gotten. I realized he had been giving most of the meat he'd gotten when hunting to the widows whose husbands had died in the battle with the Blackfeet. A chief

WINTER AMONG THE SHOSHONI

holds himself responsible for the men that fight under his leadership.

He muttered my name and I clasped his hand. "I am right here. Everything is all right. Rest, my brother, and get strong again. He opened his eyes and looked at me with a slight smile playing on his lips then he drifted off again.

"Antelope, go to Chased-by-Bear. Ask him to give us some fish if he was able to catch any today. If he does not have any then go to Sharp Nose's tepee and see if they have any meat or fish. Gray Eagle needs nourishment if he is to live."

Antelope returned swiftly with a rabbit from Chased-by-Bear. We made a soup of it and fed it to my brother. I told Antelope to eat some as well then told her to rest, for I was worried about her and the child she carried. I ate and drank what was left. For I knew I had to stay strong to help the others.

I held my vision stone and chanted beside my brother all night. By morning Gray Eagle was doing better. I fed him again and gave him more tea, then went to the women's lodge to check on Little Cloud and Antelope. They were also stronger.

I was sad that my uncle had died but grateful that the others had lived through the night and that no one else was sick. I spent the day between the two tepees, one in the center of camp and one outside camp. I sat beside Gray Eagle through the second night, I was weary and bone-tired, but afraid his spirit would leave his body and not come back if I fell asleep.

Before the sun had risen in the sky, one of the tribal women came to our lodge and said her daughter was sick. I went to her tepee and saw her daughter had the fever as did her other children. I was tending to them when another squaw arrived and asked me to come quickly to see her husband who had broken out with blisters. I gave the mother snakeweed to make tea for her children then went to see the sick brave. I soon found that many in the band were sick and I tended to as many as I could for the rest of the day and all during the night. On the next day, even more were sick and I heard that an old woman had died in the night.

I went to the women's lodge to check on Little Cloud and Antelope. They were much better and I sent for Chased-. by-Bear to take them back to their own tepee. There were four lying-in-lodges. I went in each one doing what I could to help the sick women who were in them.

Panic began to overwhelm me. I went outside and sat on a kotea robe, then began to contemplate on this deadly disease that was spreading through our camp. Holding my vision stone, I stilled my mind and opened myself to spirit. Into my mind came an image of the Bannock warrior falling from his horse. In the cave, Oapiche had said many would die of the pale-faced diseases. Perhaps the Bannock warrior had been to the trading post and gotten the disease then brought it to my people. I saw Sweet Clover and Little Cloud standing close to him, and Gray Eagle and White Bull carrying him into the tepee. Those four had been the first to get the disease. I had taken them about half a moon after they were exposed to the blister sickness to get ill. During that time they had visited with many in the village, spreading the blister sickness to more people even before they knew they had it.

While in deep contemplation about this, Raven, a young girl of not more than twelve or thirteen summers, came walking to a lying-in-lodge. She looked proud to be coming here; it was probably her first time. As she reached one of the tepee flaps and started to open, it a terrible feeling swept over me. I jumped up. "No! Do not go in!"

She looked at me and smiled. "I am a woman now. Mother told me I must stay here until my bleeding stops."

"There are sick women in all of the women's lodges. If

you go in, you will be exposed as well and get the blister sickness."

Her smiled disappeared and she looked frightened. "What should I do?"

"Stay at home with your family."

"I cannot. Mother said I must come here."

"I'll go to your tepee with you and explain why you cannot go to the women's lodge." We went to her tepee. Both of her parents were there as well as her two sisters, and her grandmother.

"Raven cannot go to any of the women's lodges because there are sick women in all of the tepees. Your daughter would be exposed to the sickness," I said.

"You go there and you have not gotten sick," said her father, War-i-gika.

"I am a medicine woman. I have to go there, but your daughter should not. If there was an extra tepee we could set up a lying-in-lodge for well women, but we have a shortage of tepees"

"The elders will be angry with me if I disobey this custom," replied War-i-gika.

"The elders are very wise but sometimes there are things more important than custom. If you send your daughter to the women's lodge, when she comes back she will carry the disease to all your family before she even shows any sign of being sick."

"The elders say it is not a disease but bad medicine. The same bad medicine came to Jogwotee's band when he was a young boy. It killed almost all of his tribe and that is why he came to live with our band." He looked at his daughter. "Go to the women's lodge."

I looked at the girl's mother. "Do not let him send your daughter there."

The woman did not say anything. She pulled a kotea robe over her head and began to wail. Her two sons had been killed in the Blackfeet raid on our camp and she did not want to lose another child. Grandmother joined her in her wailing.

"Enough!" yelled War-i-gika. "Raven, go to your mother." The girl ran to her mother who put the kotea robe over Raven's head as if to hide her from War-i-gika's sight. "I am tired of living in a lodge of women. I will go live with my brother until Raven can be around men. Raven, you must stay in the tepee at all time. I do not want you to run into any of the braves and get blamed if he comes down with the blister sickness." I left the tepee, feeling relieved. Stopping the spread of the sickness was as important as helping the ones already sick.

Over the next few Suns, more and more of my people became ill. The blister illness was spreading like fire through the forest. I was greatly distressed. I went from tepee to tepee trying to help the sick and wishing I could do more to save my people. I had run out of snakeweed and alkanet and switched to tormentil to expel the poison in the sick people's bodies.

One afternoon I left the tepee, with Wind Chaser at my heels, to give Good Thunder some dried grass to eat. I always kept him near the tepee, but he was not there. A feeling of horror came over me. I wondered if he had died while I tended to the sick and been eaten by my starving people.

Terrified, I ran down to the corral. When I got there, I saw Chased-by-Bear feeding Good Thunder some cotton-wood bark. The horse had a thick kotea robe over his back and was standing among a group of horses to stay warm. Chased-by-Bear looked up and smiled when he saw me, but his smile left when he saw that I was upset. "I'm sorry. I should have told you I had brought Good Thunder to the corral so I could care for him along with my horses. I also brought Gray Eagle's war-horse and have been feeding the stallion and the other horses in your brother's herd. I thought they would be safe here, for no enemy would be out in this weather stealing horses."

I wrapped my arms around Good Thunder's neck, kissing and stroking him. "I am sorry for forgetting you, my sweet baby." Good Thunder nuzzled my hand to see if I had a treat for him. I gave him the grass I had brought.

I turned to Chased-by-Bear. "How can I thank you?" Tears filled my eyes.

"Why do you cry?"

"I thought he might have died."

"He is fine. He is a strong horse."

"And I cry because I am only a young squaw, and yet somehow I must help my people. My Spirit Guide, Oapiche, knew this illness was coming and that is why he trained me as a medicine woman and sent me back to the Nimi. Our people don't trust me because I went against custom, but Gray Eagle would have died if I had not." I babbled unable to stop crying once my dammed up emotions erupted.

Chased-by-Bear drew me into his arms. "It is too great a burden for you to endure alone."

"I am afraid of not being able to cure those who are sick."

"You were able to save Antelope and Little Cloud. You may not be able to save everyone, it is up to Apo who lives and dies, but you should feel proud for you are a great medicine woman. You saved my life as well, for I would have crossed over to the Land of Shadows if you had not searched for me there and brought me back with your song. If I had died my family might have starved, so we are all indebted to you."

"I am sorry for crying."

"You do not have to be strong all the time. You have worked so hard to help the sick that you have not taken care of yourself. You have a lot of responsibility weighing on you."

I clung to him, gathering strength from him. Gradually the sharp edge of my distress left me and my tears dried up.

215

Shoshoni people do not show their emotions except with family or when in mourning, but Chased-by-Bear and I had a bond between us. I was glad for his comfort. I had felt alone as it had been so long since a man had held me.

# 13

## Smallpox

*On the Snake River*

Exhausted, I went back to the tepee and I lay down on my sleeping couch. The world was spinning around and it was difficult to rest, but once I had fallen to sleep I slept like one who is dead. I had gone too long without sleep.

Angry voices aroused me. Dizzy and confused, I raised my head, trying to comprehend the source of the trouble.

Antelope looked out the flap opening. Her pale face had a worried expression on it."

I sat up. "What is it?"

"They are demanding that you come out."

"Who is?"

"Jogwotee and the tribal council. They blame you for the bad medicine that has made so many of our people break out in blisters."

I rose and put my kotea robe over my shoulders.

"Do not go out there!" exclaimed Antelope. "They will do something terrible to you."

"No, they won't." I went out and looked around at all

the angry, fearful faces. Scared, I began to sing Hu-nai-yiee inwardly.

Jogwotee came forward. "The council has decided that the bad medicine has come to our people because you have broken tribal customs. You also tell lies and make up stories about pale-faced men. For breaking the harmony of the circle of the Nimi, you are to be banished from our tribe. You must leave at once."

My stomach twisted; it was a death sentence. The wind was howling furiously around me, blowing snow in my face and trying to rip my kotea robe off my body. A person could not survive cast out in the Season of Howling Wind.

"I broke tribal custom because my brother is sick and needed a healer. I told the truth about the pale-faced men. When Masheka was here he told you his people had traded with them."

Talking Goose came over holding my looking glass. "You steal our people's souls with this."

"No, it's only a looking glass. It is like a clear lake that lets a person see their reflection."

"Our chief is dying because of you," said Sharp Nose.

"No, he grows stronger."

"You bring a curse to our people that killed White Bull!" said Talking Goose, shaking with emotion.

"I did not bring the blister sickness. The Bannock warrior brought it."

"You bring great shame to the Nimi by breaking so many customs," said Jogwotee. "You go on quests, you fight like a man, and you do not stay in the women's lodge. Furthermore, you bring shame on our tribe by leaving Masheka after your brother gave you to him. Masheka saved our tribe from being destroyed by the Piegan and deserved to be honored. Apo is angered by your actions and punishes the whole band. We will appease him by forcing you to leave us."

"I left Masheka only because my Spirit Guide said you

needed a medicine woman."

"You must go. I turn deaf ears to your pleas. You speak with a forked tongue," said Jogwotee.

"Our people are dying. I need to stay to help them. Please listen."

"We do not listen to a squaw. You cannot bring council to the men of the tribe."

"Let me stay a few more days until my brother is strong again."

"No, your relationship with your brother is unnatural. You broke custom by being alone with him, talking directly to him, and giving him advice." He grabbed my arm and pulled me away from the tepee. "Go! Get away from our band!" He pulled out a knife. "I will kill you if you try to poison us any further with your words"

Growling at Jogwotee, Wind Chaser crouched, ready to spring. "Quiet, Wind Chaser!" I ordered. I looked around at the unfriendly faces surrounding me. I saw so much hatred and fear that I knew nothing I said would change how they viewed me.

Chased-by-Bear came running over and pushed his way through the people gathered. "This isn't right. Red Willow is helping our people. She has saved Sweet Clover and Little Cloud's lives."

"You do not see things with clear vision. You are seduced by her beauty and look at her with lust though you have two wives," said Jogwotee.

"I would be proud to have Red Willow as my third wife. She is a strong woman with courage who has powerful visions. There is nothing wrong with this."

"Our decision is made. Interfere with it and you will be banished as well."

"Give her a chance to gather her supplies and let her take Good Thunder so she can make it to another band."

"She may not go in the lodge but Antelope can bring out

some supplies." Antelope went into the tepee. I looked at Chased-by-Bear, who was deeply troubled, and thanked him with my eyes.

Chief Gray Eagle stepped out of the tepee instead of Antelope. He had a kotea robe around him and stood tall. There was a powerful presence about him. He did not say anything but looked silently over his people, his fierce gaze going from one person to another. The weaker ones lowered their heads or backed away. Even the strong ones could not meet the intensity of his gaze. Finally he spoke, looking directly at Jogwotee. "What are your charges against my sister?"

The man seemed to shrink and look suddenly old and weak. "Red Willow has broken custom by leaving the women's lodge and going to yours."

"She came back from her quest as a medicine woman. She is no longer Red Willow, she is now Vision Woman. A medicine woman can tend to the sick at any time, both men and women. A medicine woman can attend council, give advice to chiefs, and even become a chief. A medicine woman goes on Vision Quests and acts in ways that are different from other squaws because the Great Spirit leads them. This is truth. I have spoken."

"She can't be a medicine woman because she is too young and can still have papooses."

"My mugua was floating in and out of the Land of Shadows. Vision Woman came to me there and brought me back. Our people are special, and Apo sent us Vision Woman so we would not all die when the blister sickness came. Apo knew that the Blackfeet weakened us from the attack. He led Vision Woman to Spirit Cave and trained her so we could live. Apo, the sun..." he paused for effect, gathering power around him, "has given us Vision Woman as a gift. He will be extremely angry if you throw away his gift!"

There was muttering among the people gathered. "He is

right; she is a gift."

"Look at how strong our chief is," said another.

"He came back from the Land of Shadows."

"See how powerful her medicine is."

"You are very wise," Chief Gray Eagle said to Jogwotee. "You and the other elders have helped me understand my visions for many years. What do you say now?"

The elder's honor was restored and he squared his shoulders and tried to look as one with great wisdom. "You speak the truth. I had not realized she was now a medicine woman. There has never before been a medicine woman who is so young. Apo has blessed us."

There was agreement among the people. Chief Gray Eagle motioned to me and I followed him into the tepee. Once inside, I saw that his strength had just been an act of forced bravery. Ashen-faced, he could hardly stand. I went to help him, but he waved me away and walked unsupported to his sleeping couch. He lay down and I went over to him, crouching beside him. "Thank you," I said softly.

He smiled and took my hand. "Thank you for saving my life."

Antelope came over. He drew her down beside him. "I thought you were going to die," she cried. "I thought you would never see our child. If you had, I would have asked to be killed so I could go with you to the Land of the Shadows."

Being known as a medicine woman gave me new stature in the tribe. My advice was now listened to. I ordered a small sweat lodge to be set up for Gray Eagle and some of the other warriors with the blister sickness. Once the sweat lodge was ready, Gray Eagle went in and sweated out the last of the poisons in his body. When he returned to the tepee, we poured water over him to wash away the sweat. It was too cold in the river for a sick man to jump in to cool off as was usually done.

The next day the tribal council held a meeting in Gray

Eagle and Antelope's tepee. They allowed me to join the council meeting as a medicine woman. The council decided that since the illness spread from one person to another that we would separate the well people from the sick. The people who had never been sick and those who were recovered would set up a camp further down the river, and the sick would stay here. Only the tepees where no one had the blister sickness would be taken to the new camp, in case objects as well as people might spread the disease. The healthy braves would hunt and fish, leaving food for the sick at the riverbank. They would take all the horses and be responsible for their care. Black Crow Feather, Jogwotee, Gray Eagle, and I were all going to stay with the sick to feed and care for them.

Chief Gray Eagle stood before the people and told them what decisions had been made at council. The people saw wisdom in his words. They broke camp in an orderly fashion. By the time the sun was straight overhead the pony drags were loaded up. The healthy people departed from camp amongst many tears, leaving behind about a quarter of the camp.

I worked for many Suns and Sleeps tending to the sick, barely taking time to sleep or eat. Too many were ill for me to care for them all, and we divided them up between my brother, Black Crow Feather, and Jogwotee. Despite our best efforts many died. We didn't have the time or energy to tend to the bodies, so we designated some of the tepees for the dead. It was a time of great suffering and sorrow.

One sun I walked to the river on a trail that had been made in the deep snow by the many people going for water. While filling my water sack, a feeling of danger came over me, like a shadow moving across my soul. I scanned the woods wondering if an enemy was near, ready to attack my weakened people. I called several times for Wind Chaser, but he did not appear. I picked up my water pouch and started back down the well-beaten trail. Snow rose to the height of my shoulders on either side of the path. I rounded a bend and found Talking Goose, crouched down with a knife in her hand. Her eyes were that of a crazy person. Her clothes were tattered and her whole appearance was wild looking; ice and snow clung to her hair and to the bottom of her tunic and sleeves. "You must die. You bring bad medicine and are killing all our people."

"No, I didn't bring the bad medicine."

"They have all gone to the Land of the Shadows. All are gone, all are gone." She leapt out at me. I fell backwards into the snow bank with her on top. She had the unnatural strength of a mad person. She tried to stab me, but I grabbed her wrist and stayed her hand. She forced my hand back until the blade was against my throat. A trickle of blood ran down my neck.

"No, most of the tribe lives!" I pleaded.

I grabbed a fist full of snow and rubbed it in her face. The shock of the cold snow caused her to loosen her hold. I thrust her off me and regained by feet. She also rose. She stood on the narrow beaten path between me and the village, blocking my way.

My aunt was a short woman, thickly built and solid. I had a more delicate frame and was greatly weakened from having had little food and rest for so long. Talking Goose swiped her knife at me and I jumped back. "You killed White Bull!" she screamed.

"No! He died of the blister sickness. It's a new and strange illness not caused by bad medicine. White Bull loved you. He wouldn't want to you to suffer so. Put down the knife, Talking Goose, and let us go back to the tepee. You need food and warmth. Gray Eagle and I will take care of you."

"Gray Eagle is dead. All are dead."

"No, he is alive and well." Tears came to my eyes as I

opened my heart to this woman and served as a channel for Apo to work through to touch her. I no longer saw the hatred in her but saw a woman who loved her husband. A woman full of sorrow who had borne five children, three of which had died as papooses and two as adults. She needed love so much.

She started to cry in gasps. She lowered the knife as she knelt down on the snow-covered trail. Wind Chaser came bounding down the trail and flying past me. He stopped in front of Talking Goose and licked her face. She hugged him, crying louder. I took the knife from her and slid it in my belt, then squatted down and put my arms around her and Wind Chaser.

Gradually, her weeping quieted and I helped her up. All her strength had left with her anger. I picked up my water bag and we returned to camp. It was growing dark, a fiery sunset cast reddish hues over the snow. In our tepee I gave her some stew, which hung over the fire in a kotea belly pouch. Since Gray Eagle had not returned from tending to the sick in other tepees, I took time to eat. Talking Goose no longer looked so wild. She merely looked like a grief-stricken woman who hurt so much she had been broken by her pain. After she had eaten, I helped her undress and lay down on a sleeping couch. "I do not want to sleep alone. White Bull always slept with me."

I turned to Wind Chaser. "Sleep with Talking Goose." I patted the sleeping robe, and he crawled onto it, pushing his snout against her face. She rubbed him behind the ears, then dozed off.

I checked on the other sick people in the tepee. I was of heavy heart that so many had died despite my valiant efforts to save them. The illness had killed almost all the elders and many of the adults who had gotten it. The children did better and I was able to save many of them.

I was too tired to keep going. There were no empty

sleeping couches so I slept next to Talking Goose with Wind Chaser warming my feet. I awoke in the morning to find the tepee warm. Talking Goose had built up the fire and was cooking fish. She fed all the people in the tepee, and then straightened the tepee. Over the next few days she accompanied me to each tepee and worked alongside me, helping the sick. I began to call her Silent Woman. She was a different person; one who quietly did what needed to be done without worrying about what others would think.

The winter was the worst that any of the elders could remember. It grew quite cold and stayed cold for a long time. The men found it difficult to go out hunting in such freezing weather. Game was scarce. My people lived on fish, and at times there was not even enough of that to eat. The winter was hard on the four-legged creatures, too. Many deer, elk, and antelope died because the snow was so deep.

At first, some people from the main camp got the blister sickness and come to our camp. Eventually, no more came. All the sick were recovered enough by the Season of Melting Snow to make the short journey to the new camp. Wearing snowshoes, we walked there leaving behind our dead in the tepees. We also left all our supplies for fear of bringing the sickness with us. I took with me only the clothes I wore and my medicine bag with Masheka's armband in it. I left behind the looking glass and others things of the pale-faces. I was sad to leave behind the looking glass Masheka had given me, yet part of me was glad to leave behind anything that had to do with the Wasichus who had brought us the blister sickness.

Before entering the new camp, we went into pine-bough lean-tos that had been set up with new clothes in them for us to wear. Sweet Clover took me to a lean-to separate from the others. She had a fire going under a kotea paunch full of boiling water. Sweet Clover gave me a white tunic that had strong medicine symbols sewn on it with bone beads and porcupine quills. I was deeply touched that my people had honored me with such a finely made dress. There was also a new pair of leggings and moccasins. Sweet Clover helped me bath and wash my hair. Then I washed my everyday tunic, my medicine bag, and vision stone.

At the new camp, I was greeted with great joy. A celebration was held in my honor. We feasted on fish and venison and stories were told in the ceremonial tepee. Chased-by-Bear told tales of our creator the Wolf. He also told about the coyote that was Wolf brother and a trickster. Many of the stories of Coyote's deeds were not of good deeds. I loved hearing the stories although I did not believe they were all true.

Little Cloud sat in my lap enraptured as his father told the stories by acting them out. Chased-by-Bear crouched down low and used his hands for horns, pretending to be a kotea. I smiled remembering when I was Little Cloud's age. I used to love to hear Grandfather tell stories about the coyote in the Season of Howling Wind when we had time to spare. The stories always taught something about how to live. Coyote had once killed wolf, but because they were brothers and he loved wolf he brought him back to life. The story was to show the strong love that there must be between brothers.

"Tell us how you got your name," said one of Chased-by-Bear's daughters.

"When I was young, not much bigger than you," said Chased-by-Bear, "I decided that I would walk up to a bear and swat him to prove I was brave. I set out into the woods all alone and searched for many days until finally I found a bear. It was a huge, mean grizzly bear. I was more than a little scared, but I crept up behind him while he was eating berries and swatted him on the rear. He swung around and rose on his back legs, roaring. I tore off with him right behind me. I escaped by jumping over a cliff into a river.

"When I got back to camp no one believed my tale, so I took them back to the place where the grizzly had chased me. His huge footprints were all around the top of the cliff. And that is how I got my name."

Gray Eagle told a story of his bravery when the Blackfeet attacked. As he talked, I felt Chased-by-Bear's eyes upon me. He was a full-blooded Shoshoni with dark skin, a stocky build, and prominent features. He had a look of pride and self-confidence. All the men of the tribe respected him, and the women liked to share tales of his hunting skills and acts of courage. He was a good man and my heart warmed to him. I tenderly kissed his son, Little Cloud. I had been teaching him and the other children about the customs of our people.

Chased-by-Bear rose when my brother finished speaking. "It is time to light the ceremonial fire." We all went outside, dressed in our best clothing. Though there was still some snow on the ground, it was not cold. The fire was lit and drumming began. The men danced shuffling steps around the fire. The women and children formed another larger circle and danced around the men going the opposite way. The warriors always entered the dance first just as men must always go first in life in case there is danger. The drumbeats quickened accompanied by singing. The dancers began to whirl around, keeping rhythm with their stomping feet.

I became caught up in the sound of the drums as I danced and sang around the fire. Chased-by-Bear came over and danced nearby me. When I stepped back from the fire to rest, he came to my side. "My feelings for you have grown during the Season of Howling Wind," he said. My chest tightened; I was afraid of what he was about to say. He smiled as he continued, "I would like you to be my wife. I know that you are a medicine woman; I would not interfere with your path. I would make you a good husband for I have a fine herd of horses and am the best hunter in camp. You'd have your own tepee and I would provide well for you. If you're willing to be my wife, I'll speak to your brother."

"You honor me. Your squaws and papooses never go hungry and your horses are the finest, but I don't want to have to share my husband with other squaws."

"There is too much work for one squaw. You are young and have been given a lot of freedom. You don't know how much drudgery it is for one squaw to keep a tepee. Besides many braves were killed in the fight with the Blackfeet and each brave must provide for more than one woman."

"You know that I have great regard for you. There is no one in camp I would rather marry, but I do not think I am meant to share your lodge." I slipped away from him back into the circle of dancers.

At the height of the ceremony, Jogwotee presented me with an ancient rattle that Grandfather had used to call the spirits when he was healing someone. Then the council officially renamed me, Vision Woman. As I held the rattle I felt its power and mystery. It carried the knowledge of many ages. Sensing Grandfather's presence beside me, I accepted the responsibility of a full-fledged medicine woman. Our band was small but the love that I felt among its members that night was very strong. The adversity we had all been through had strengthened us.

Antelope had been living in Chased-by-Bear's tepee while we had two camps. Now we were invited to live there as well. His tepee was crowded with his two wives and three children and the four of us. When the grass grew again we would make a temporary grass hut to live in until we had enough skins to make a tepee.

Black Crow Feather and I delivered Antelope's baby a short time later. The papoose was a boy and the whole village brought Gray Eagle gifts since he was the head chief. Gray Eagle gave away all he had in honor of his new son. Antelope stayed in the women's lodge for the required duration of the moon. The day she came home was joyous for both her and my brother. They had barely been able to endure their separation.

One evening my brother returned from hunting, carrying two rabbits. After giving the rabbits to me, he sat down beside Antelope and lifted the child from her lap. I began to skin the rabbits and cut up the meat.

Antelope started laughing when Gray Eagle teasingly told her he'd caught one of the little people and sent it down a hole in order to catch the rabbits. The elfin NunumBi were known for shooting arrows of misfortune, and were usually avoided. I glanced over at them. Gray Eagle was looking at her with such an open look of love that I felt a great emptiness in my own life. It suddenly became unbearable to be in the tepee. I grabbed my fur robe and went outside. Wind Chaser followed me out, and I scratched him behind the ears. The sharp wind stung my face. It felt good after the warmth of the tepee. It was silent and peaceful outside. The snow fell lightly and covered the trees with icy crystals.

I took a long walk and returned to the tepee feeling more at peace with myself. That night I had a powerful dream of unusual clarity. In my dream, Gray Eagle and I were in the spirit worlds. Oapiche and the white wolf came to us. Oapiche carried a feathered staff and he handed it to Gray Eagle. My brother held it close to his chest. Oapiche handed me the ancient rattle saying, "It is time for you to leave." An image of the Sacred Mountains appeared, and I heard Masheka's voice say, "I am waiting for you." I woke up so excited about the dream that, even though it was only early dawn, I awakened Gray Eagle and asked him if we could talk.

We walked down to the river. I looked out at the swiftly flowing water. "I had a dream last night that was powerful medicine. The dream showed me that I'm to go to Masheka. My Spirit Guide, Oapiche, sent me to our people to help them during the time of the blister sickness. Now that they are strong again, my place is no longer here."

"I was wrong for reproaching you for leaving Masheka.

Our tribe needs a medicine woman. We need you to heal the sick and to give people aid in understanding of their dreams and visions. We need you because you can speak to the plants and find out their healing properties."

"There is more to my dream—it's about you. Do you want to hear it?"

He nodded, looking at me with perceptive eyes that held wisdom and power so much greater than his years.

"Oapiche handed you a feathered staff. You drew it to your heart to show that you accepted the path of a shaman."

He nodded gravely. "I've been getting inner guidance to join up with the Wolf band this summer so I can study under their Buhagant who is a great medicine man."

"Then you should do so. My dream was not a dream at all but as real as you and I standing here talking."

"I wish you didn't have to leave the people. I value your council and friendship; you are my closest kin."

"We have a link even when we are apart. I saw you in the spirit worlds while I was in the Spirit Cave."

"I must journey to the Spirit Cave someday."

"You will be led if you are meant to go."

"Grandfather still comes and talks to me in my dreams and visions."

"He is with us both," I replied. "He has taught us since we were small. It's now time for each of us to take the next step."

We walked back to Chase-by-Bear's lodge and I started packing supplies. My people had given me gifts for curing their loved ones of the blister sickness, so I had all I needed for my journey. Anything I did not need, I put in a pile for Gray Eagle to keep or give away.

"Where are you going?" Antelope asked.

"To Masheka."

"Masheka! But you left him, why would you now go to him?"

SMALLPOX

"He walks in my soul and now that our people no longer need me I am free to go to him."

"His village is a great distance to travel this time of year."

"I'll be careful."

"You should wait until the chance of winter storms is over. The Season of Melting Snow has just come. Your journey will be treacherous through the Shining Mountains."

"Leave her be, Antelope," said Gray Eagle. "She is inwardly guided."

There was not much food so I took only a little; I could hunt along the way. I hugged Antelope, then Gray Eagle held me close and tears came to my eyes. I found it hard to leave them, not knowing when I would see them again.

I said goodbye to Silent Woman whose eyes were sad. "You have grown to look and act so much like your mother," she said. She often spoke of the departed even though it was forbidden. "I love you as I loved her. I wish you didn't have to go."

I went outside and loaded my things on Good Thunder. Sweet Clover and her boy came to me and I explained to Little Cloud that I was going on a long journey. I embraced Sweet Clover as Chased-by-Bear came over to us.

"If things don't work out and you return, Vision Woman," he said, "there is a place for you in my lodge." He drew me close.

"Thank you for believing in me when no one else did and for sharing your food when there was so little."

"I am the one indebted to you. You saved Sweet Clover and Little Cloud's lives and brought me back from the Land of Shadows."

I mounted Good Thunder and looked around. All the people of my village had gathered to see me off, even Yellow Flower who watched me leave with tears in her eyes. I rode off with Wind Chaser running alongside me. I turned back to my people for one last look. The great sorrow in my heart was balanced by the knowledge that I was following my vision and that each step I took away from my people brought me closer to Masheka.

## 14

## Kootenai Village

Good weather greeted the beginning of my journey. I headed north traveling toward the Sawtooth Mountains. This was Shoshoni land and I occasionally passed travelers from other bands of my people. Snow covered the ground, but it was melting and the sun was shining. I wore a kotea robe over my tunic, an otter-skin hat, rabbit fur-lined mittens, and knee high moccasins. I carried many supplies including weapons and snowshoes.

During the first few Suns of my journey, I shot a grouse and a jackrabbit. After that game became scarce. The farther north I went the colder it got. Deep snow in the mountains made travelling difficult. I left the shore of the Piupa River and headed northeast. I felt happy and excited about seeing Masheka soon.

I reached the Salmon River after many Suns and Sleeps. The river was wide and swift and there was no way to cross it except by swimming. I urged Good Thunder into the water with Wind Chaser reluctantly following. In a few steps the water reached my feet. It was freezing cold. I gasped as it soaked through my moccasins and leggings. Good Thunder was a strong swimmer, but the water was powerful and carried us downstream. He finally reached shallow water. I jumped off his back and led him to shore. There I dried him off and placed a kotea skin over his back. Shaking from the cold and badly chilled, I gathered wood, lit a fire, then stripped off my wet clothing and changed into dry ones. I made Wind Chaser run around the fire until he was dry and had warmed up.

I dug to the bottom of the snow where there was grass so Good Thunder could eat. Wind Chaser disappeared into the woods to hunt since I had nothing to give him. I melted snow and put dried roots in a bowl for my own meal since I had run out of meat a few days earlier. I built a lean-to with the open entrance facing the fire, then staked Good Thunder next to it.

When the sun disappeared from father sky, I curled up under kotea furs, trying to keep warm. During the night wolves began howling. Usually I liked the sound of howling but these wolves sounded too close. I nervously put more wood into the fire and wished Wind Chaser would return. In the firelight I saw bright eyes in a semicircle beyond the fire. Good Thunder whinnied. I heard the sound of a snarl. I knew then that a pack of wolves had surrounded us. Good Thunder reared up and pulled against his rope in an attempt to run off. Frightened, I got up and tried to reassure him. Wolves were often hungry this time of year and I feared for Good Thunder and Wind Chaser. Rarely would a wolf attack humans, but horses or dogs were often attacked and eaten.

I stayed awake all night, continuing to keep the fire blazing. Wood began to grow short and I feared that I'd run out. In the gray light of the early morning I saw that the wolves were thin and sickly-looking with poor coats. The harsh winter had taken its toll on them and they were starving.

Wind Chaser came running out of the woods and the

wolf pack ran toward him and surrounded him. I sprang to my feet and tore after them, carrying my tomahawk. They began to attack Wind Chaser. Growling, he charged his muscular body into one of the wolves and knocked it off its feet. Another leaped at him and he bit it, sending it running off. Two more attacked as I ran into the middle of the fight, swinging my tomahawk. I hit one on the head and another on its back. Snarling wolves with their sharp fangs were all around us. I feared we'd both be killed. I fought with the strength and courage that come from pure desperation, driving the wolves back.

I slammed my tomahawk into a large male that was fighting Wind Chaser. He seemed to be the leader of the pack and when he ran off, the other wolves followed. They stopped and turned to watch us from a safer distance.

I heard Good Thunder's shrill clarion call of fear and ran back to camp. Wind Chaser beat me there and leaped at one of the three wolves that had Good Thunder surrounded. The stallion trampled another beneath his hoofs. I ran into their midst yelling and brandishing my tomahawk. The wolves fled into the woods. Good Thunder stood with his large body trembling and his head held high, ready to battle the wolves again. I talked to him softly as I checked him over and he quieted. He was not injured so I turned my attention to Wind Chaser. The wolf dog had been bitten on his shoulders and back. I shook as I cleansed his wounds, greatly distressed. The bottom of my tunic was ripped and torn but I was uninjured. My thick, fur-lined leggings and moccasins had protected my legs.

Packing up my supplies, I continued northeast into the Bitterroot Mountains. I was exhausted but afraid to rest even now that it was daylight. I kept seeing glimpses of the wolves in the woods. Wind Chaser stayed close instead of running off as he usually did. One wolf tried to get close, but Wind Chaser growled ferociously and drove him off. I was afraid the wolf pack would kill him. A female kept hanging around and trying to lure Wind Chaser away. He ignored her at first, but she kept coming in closer and closer. Eventually she came right to him, keeping her head lowered and her body crouched submissively. They smelled each other, then she ran off and he ran after her. I yelled for him to come back. He paused and looked at me, obviously torn between the two of us. I called to him again and he finally ran back to me.

In the late afternoon I stopped to rest, too tired to go on. More than once I had to get up and drive the female wolf off with my tomahawk. After a few hours I continued on, cold and growing weak from lack of food and sleep.

I was in the mountains, but I could scarcely enjoy their rugged beauty, fearing what would happen when it grew dark. In the woods I gathered sticks and small branches, which I tied into bundles and put on Good Thunder's back. I wanted to be sure to have plenty to burn when nightfall came. I found a place to camp with a rocky mountain cliff on two sides. I started a fire before setting up the rest of my camp. Good Thunder was nervous and his eyes blazed. Wind Chaser began barking at the wolves, which had drawn in closer.

When the sun went down, I prayed to Apo to keep watch over us. I understood that death was part of life and felt no anger toward the wolves. They killed to eat even as I did. As the night wore on, I could barely stay awake. Toward dawn I jerked awake when Wind Chaser snarled. A pair of eyes glowed close to our fire. I threw a piece of burning wood toward them and heard a thud followed by a yelp. The wolf ran off. I began to pray. "Brother Wolf, I know that you are hungry but please go elsewhere to find your food. We are your friends in spirit."

During the next day the wolves continued to follow and torment us. The weather turned windy and cold. It started snowing in the afternoon. The snow became so heavy we were forced to stop. After covering Good Thunder with a kotea robe, I set up a lean-to. Wind Chaser and I crawled inside, and I snuggled against him under furs for warmth. The strong wind prevented making a fire. Even if I could have, the snow made it hard to find fallen branches to burn.

Worried about the wolves, I tried to keep alert, but grew tired and fell asleep, sitting up with a knife in my hand. I awoke curled up next to Wind Chaser. A thick blanket of fresh snow covered the ground. I checked Good Thunder and dug down into the snow until I found grass for him to eat, then packed up my supplies. My water pouch was frozen solid and without a fire I could not thaw it.

The bright snow hurt my eyes. We still had a long way to travel to get to the Sacred Mountains. Masheka's village was just west of them on Flathead Lake. I wondered how long it would take me to reach his village. Studying the position of the sun, I realized I'd gotten off course the day before when the sky had been overcast. After putting on my snowshoes, I led Good Thunder, for it was difficult traveling through deep snow. I was ravenously hungry and knew Wind Chaser was as well. We traveled all day, making slow progress.

In the late afternoon as we followed an animal trail through a pine forest, a moose appeared in front of us. He was a huge animal with massive, flat antlers. He charged at me and Wind Chaser sprang between us. The moose lowered his antlers and sent him flying into the snow. Wind Chaser landed on his back and flipped over, springing back to his feet. He began barking wildly, keeping the moose distracted while I led Good Thunder off the trail and into the woods. The moose plunged off the trail after me.

Good Thunder broke away from me and gave a shrill scream of challenge. The bull moose charged, his antlers lowered. Good Thunder dodged away, then savagely reared up and smashed his powerful forelegs against the brown side of the large bull. The moose swung his heavy, broad antlers into Good Thunder, slashing his side. Good Thunder attacked again, biting into the moose's neck. The moose's antler found flesh again. Mad with pain and fury, Good Thunder slammed his body against the moose with renewed fury. Wind Chaser ran around behind the moose barking and biting at his hoofs. The moose swung toward Wind Chaser and Good Thunder bit into the moose, tearing fresh. The moose freed himself and Good Thunder began circling him, avoiding the antlers.

I stood motionless, frightened by the battle. My weapons were all on Good Thunder's back and I had nothing with which to help my traveling companions. The moose warily backed away from the stallion. Between Wind Chaser harassing his every step and Good Thunder's vicious counter attack, he had enough. He turned and ran crashing into the woods.

Good Thunder hung his head, his breath coming fast—his body bleeding from his wounds. At first he wouldn't let me near him, but finally he quieted so I could examine him. He had nasty gashes across his belly and side that would leave scars but weren't life threatening. After treating the cuts with a poultice of horsetail, I continued my journey until I found a stream and a place to set up camp. At the stream's edge, I broke a hole into the ice with my tomahawk, then squatted down to fish. Using a bone fishhook and horsehair line, I caught a brown trout. The wind had died down and I was able to get a fire going to cook the fish. Wind Chaser and I shared the trout. Then I went back to where I'd seen a cottonwood tree and hacked off bark for Good Thunder. Afterwards, I set up the lean-to with its opening facing the fire.

The next day I felt much stronger but was worried about Good Thunder. His wounds were angry-looking and he walked with a limp. I checked the leg he was favoring and found the flesh torn. I wrapped it up with a piece of buckskin. Wind Chaser was nowhere to be seen and I knew he'd gone off to hunt. I peeled more bark from the cottonwood tree for Good Thunder. I stroked his fine, muscular neck as I talked softly to him, letting him eat from my hands. When he finished, I sat down to await Wind Chaser's return before setting off. My state of being was similar to that on a Vision Quest. The shortage of water, food, and sleep over so many days had made me light-headed. Pulling the small bag from around my neck, I took out the vision stone. I began to chant, "Hu-nai-yiee...hu-nai-yiee." The stone began to give off light that vibrated in my hand. I thought of Masheka and an image of his face appeared before me.

"Where is Masheka's tribe?" I asked. His face blurred. Then I saw a vision of a large, long lake surrounded by mountains. I put away the stone as Wind Chaser came bounding up to me. He dropped a hoary marmot at my feet. I hugged him with tears coming to my eyes. After skinning the marmot, I cooked it over a fire, then Wind Chaser and I happily ate it.

I set off again headed north still walking on snowshoes. Our journey through the mountains was slow. The days blended one much like the last. Game continued to be scarce and I dug under the snow in search of roots to eat. As I journeyed, the mountains came to look more and more familiar. After many Suns and Sleeps I came to the edge of a large lake, which I recognized as the lake in my vision, though it was still covered with ice. I walked out onto it and began chopping a hole with my tomahawk so Wind Chaser, Good Thunder, and I could have water to drink. The ice was so thick I couldn't break through it to the water below.

I started walking again, knowing I was close to Masheka's village, but not sure I had enough strength left to reach it.

By mid-afternoon, I felt dizzy and disoriented. Snow began falling. I became quite cold. My hands and feet were numb, my cheeks felt frozen, and ice clung to my eyelashes. I tripped and fell into the snow and was too tired to get back up. I knew I must not sleep or I would freeze to death. Wind Chaser curled up next to me, giving me some heat. I buried my face in his thick fur. The snow continued to fall, covering me with a blanket of white. I felt myself drifting off and wondered if Kicking Horse and Grandfather would be waiting for me if I crossed over to the Land of the Shadows.

I woke up when Wind Chaser began barking. Sitting up, I saw a hunting party of four Kootenai warriors coming toward us. I struggled to my feet and put my hand on Wind Chaser's back. "Quiet, these are friends." I watched them come nearer with great relief. My long journey was almost over.

They were all wearing buckskin hooded jackets. When they had reached me, I recognized Pocatello among them. I used sign language to tell him I wanted to see Masheka.

He talked to the other warriors, then signed that he would lead me there. The other warriors rode off and Pocatello gestured for me to follow him and set off into the woods. I followed slowly behind him, walking across the snow in my snowshoes. Good Thunder sank into the snow with each step. It was snowing and I was nearly frozen. I finally collapsed on the ground and couldn't force myself to rise. Pocatello noticed I was no longer following and rode back to me. He signaled I was to ride behind him. I took off my snowshoes and he reached down and helped me climb up.

We rode through the woods until at last we came to the village, which consisted of many round-shaped earth lodges spread along the shore of the lake. People in thick kotea robes and buckskin jackets were walking around between the lodges.

Pocatello rode to a lodge, then dismounted and lifted me off his horse. Scaffolds for drying meat and vegetables stood outside. The lodge itself was large and dug partway into the ground. Pocatello grasped Good Thunder's bridle and led him through the leather flap opening of the lodge. I followed with Wind Chaser at my heels. The entrance to the lodge consisted of a covered passageway that offered protection from the wind.

A barking dog greeted us at the door. Wind Chaser growled at him, his ears laid back. I quieted him with a sharp command. The lodge was dark inside after the brightness of the snow. It took my eyes a few moments to adjust. Wind Chaser shook the snow off his body. The only light in the lodge came from a large central fire pit, which was edged with stone, and from an opening in the roof directly over the fire pit. Smoke rose up and out the opening. The structure was made with a pole frame covered by cedar bark. Woven mats of hemp covered the ground.

The lodge felt invitingly warm after being outside more days than I could keep track of. People were sitting on kotea robes spread around the fire. With the warmth inside, some of the men were wearing only breechcloths. The talking and laughing I'd heard as I entered suddenly stopped. Everyone was looking at me and my two traveling companions. Masheka was among them, sitting intimately close to a young squaw. Targhee was also there, beside him was a pregnant squaw and two small boys. Across the fire were a middle-aged man and woman and a much older woman, who looked to be Masheka's parents, and grandmother.

Masheka's eyes widened with surprise when he saw me and my traveling companions. "Vision Woman!"

Pocatello said something to him in the Kootenai language. Then he took Good Thunder to the side of the lodge where there were other horses tied up, including Straight Arrow.

Masheka rose and started toward me. The young squaw also stood and put her hand on his arm. She said something in Kootenai with a worried expression on her face.

He paid no attention to her question. The significance of this woman beside him made me lose my courage. I wished I hadn't come to his village since he already had a squaw.

Masheka came over to me and put his arm around my shoulder and pressed his cheek to mine. "Ah-hie," he said, greeting me in the Shoshoni fashion. I embraced him not caring that his whole family was watching us. One of his hands slid under my robe and he held me close to him. His nearness brought the warmth and comfort I'd missed for so many moons. "Have you traveled here alone?" he asked.

I nodded. My emotions overwhelmed me.

"Is there trouble at your village that you travel so far when there is still a blanket of snow covering the ground?"

"No, no trouble." I stepped away from him. "I came because of a dream."

"You are covered with snow. Take off your winter things and come warm yourself by the fire."

I glanced at the woman I took to be Wild Plum and realized I could not bear to stay. My path was clearly not with Masheka. I had lost him by returning to my people. Tears threatened and I turned away. "I have to go. The Sacred Mountains call to me."

Masheka clasped my arm to detain me. "You just got here! You can't leave before we've even had chance to talk. You need to eat and rest before you journey further." I was shivering and he pulled off my mittens. "Your hands are like ice. You don't look well." He lifted the snow-covered robe from my shoulders and shook it before hanging it on the wall.

Masheka's mother came over to us. "No wolves in here. Send him out; he is not safe around the papooses."

"He's safe with the little ones," said Masheka. "Wind Chaser can stay." He knelt down and affectionately scratched him behind the ears. Wind Chaser pushed his nose against

Masheka's chest, his tail wagging in great excitement. I wished I were as free to show my emotions.

Masheka rose. "This is my Mother, Moon Woman. Mother, this is Vision Woman; will you prepare her something to eat? She has traveled a long way." His mother moved back to the fire. Masheka and I stared at each other as if there was no one else in the lodge. The understanding and love in his clear, dark eyes and the strength of his presence were all that I remembered. I didn't ever want to part from him and yet I knew I couldn't be happy sharing him with another squaw.

It was too much to accept all at once. I was devastated and physically exhausted. I felt weak and the room began to spin.

"Are you all right, Vision Woman?" Masheka asked, reaching out for me.

I started to fall as blackness closed over me. I was vaguely aware of being lifted and carried a short distance. I came back to consciousness to find myself on a sleeping couch inside an area enclosed by skins. The sleeping couch was raised off the ground. Under my head was a pillow made of leather skins that smelled like sweet grass.

Masheka looked down at me. "You're ill from being in the storm."

"My journey was difficult. Do you have any food to spare for Wind Chaser and Good Thunder?" I asked weakly. "I can give you something in trade."

"I already told Pocatello to feed Good Thunder, and Wind Chaser can eat when you do. How long has it been since you've eaten?"

"I no longer remember. Game was scarce and then the storm came. It was good because it drove away the wolves but Good Thunder could no longer carry me."

"Good Thunder has many wounds."

"He got in a fight with a moose."

"He is a fierce stallion." There was admiration in his

voice.

Moon Woman opened the leather flap and came over to me with a wooden bowl of stew. She gave me the bowl and tossed a few pieces of meat to Wind Chaser. I thanked her, then sat up with Masheka's help. The stew tasted delicious. Its warmth spread through my shivering body, but I couldn't eat much. Masheka tried to remove my knee-high moccasins. They were frozen on and he had to cut the ties along my calves to get them off.

Wild Plum came over and started talking in Kootenai. Masheka answered her sharply in the same language and she left us.

I set my bowl down so Wind Chaser could finish it. My hands, feet and legs hurt as they began to warm up.

"Your buckskin dress is stiff and frozen; you'll never warm up with it on." He sliced the straps at my shoulders before I could stop him.

"Will you ruin all my clothes?" I exclaimed angrily.

"If I have to. Raise your arms."

"I can undress myself." He was a strong-willed man and I was too exhausted to fight him. I did as he asked and he pulled the tunic off over my head, then wrapped a heavy kotea fur around my shoulders.

"You are all skin and bones. Are your people starving?" he asked.

"It was a terrible Season of Howling Wind. The weather became so severe that game became scarce and there was never enough to eat. But worse than that a Bannock warrior brought a strange illness that caused people to break out in blisters. Many of the people who got the blister sickness died." Tears came to my eyes and Masheka drew me against him. He was healthy and well fed. After being with all my emaciated people, I realized just how much we had suffered.

I wanted to share with Masheka all that had happened but I was too weak. He helped me lay down and I clasped

244

his hand as I drifted off.

Later, I awoke feeling somewhat restored, aware that I had slept hard. I could feel Wind Chaser curled up beside me. Great sadness filled my heart when I remembered Masheka had a squaw and I had reached him too late. I moaned and rolled over. I felt a hand on my forehead and opened my eyes to see Masheka above me.

"Are you too hot?" he asked.

"No." I reached up and pulled him down to me so I could embrace him. "I love you, Masheka." He drew me more tightly against him as he lay down, and his hand slid down my bare back to my waist. I pressed my naked body against his, feeling fire in my loins at his nearness.

"Do you come here to torment me?" he asked.

"No, I came because of my dream." I ran my fingers lightly along his cheek.

"What was your dream?"

"I dreamed I heard you say you were waiting for me, but you didn't wait. You married Wild Plum."

"She is not yet my squaw though I have asked for her. I never expected to see you again, Vision Woman. You made it clear that you didn't want me."

"I thought it clear enough I wanted you." I felt my face grow hot. "I didn't go with you last fall because my people needed a medicine woman. I followed my inner vision and I was able to help my village when the blister sickness came."

I drew away from him and sat up with the kotea robe held in front of me. "I did what I had to do and now it is too late for us to build a life together. I'll leave tomorrow for the Sacred Mountains."

Masheka also sat up. "We can still share a lodge. A man can have two squaws."

"I don't want to be a second squaw. I refuse to be ordered around by a young squaw who's not even as old as me."

He smiled. "Wild Plum would have a hard time ordering you around. But if you won't be a second squaw, you can be my first squaw. Wild Plum will accept being a second squaw, she's an obedient woman."

"I don't want to share you with Wild Plum. The lodge is not big enough for us both. It would be easier to be Chased-by-Bear's third squaw than to be your first squaw."

"Who is Chased-by-Bear?"

"He is a brave in our band who wants me to share his lodge."

"And you would be his third squaw but not my first squaw."

"I respect Chased-by-Bear, but I love you so I would not be happy sharing you."

"Do you plan to share a lodge with Chased-by-Bear?" Masheka asked, looking troubled.

"I might. I like his second wife."

"You make no sense!" he angrily exclaimed. "If you love me, another squaw in our lodge would not matter!"

I looked up at him and felt the heat rise to my face as I thought of him sharing Wild Plum's sleeping couch. I looked down, trying to cover my embarrassment.

"Why do you blush?"

I kept my face averted as I replied, "I'd want to yank out Wild Plum's hair when you shared her sleeping couch. If you only shared mine, perhaps I could bear her presence."

Masheka's anger faded. "Wild Plum wants papooses."

"As does any squaw. I will leave here tomorrow."

"You won't be fit to journey on for many suns. You were starving and sick when you reached here yesterday." He drew me against him. "Stay with me. We belong together." His eyes were filled with warmth and desire. I felt an answering fire course through my veins.

"Do you love me, Masheka?"

"Ai."

"Do you love Wild Plum?"

"Love was not a consideration when I asked for her. You are my heart and soul. I won't let you leave a second time."

"You must because it will break my spirit to share you with Wild Plum. I would have you totally or not at all."

"I am a man of honor and have given Wild Plum and her father my word. I must think on what to do." He left the small sleeping area.

Shortly, his mother entered with a bowl of food. I took it and gave some of the fish to Wind Chaser. I was ravenously hungry and began to eat. Besides the fish, there was bread, and dried berries. I was amazed that they had so much food in the spring. I ate it all and asked for more.

"You must not eat too much at once or you'll become sick," Moon Woman replied.

Wild Plum came over to me. Her pretty face was contorted with anger. "Masheka does not need a dirty, lazy Shoshoni squaw," she said with her hands. "Go back to your own people." She left before I could answer.

"Do not take her words to heart. She is angry," said Moon Woman.

"Masheka doesn't need disharmony in his lodge and I do not want to share him."

"No woman with as much fire and spirit as you would."

"I told Masheka I plan to leave here tomorrow."

"You can't leave! The tribe already considers you Masheka's wife. He has taken you into his lodge and shared his sleeping couch with you. By our customs you already belong to him."

"He put me in his sleeping couch only because I was sick."

"It's also known you traveled with him during the Season of Ripe Berries and that he gave your brother nine horses for you."

"Masheka told them about the horses!"

"No, Targhee did. Will you travel all this way to be his squaw, then leave merely because of Wild Plum?"

"Yes."

"Wild Plum will be a sister to you if she is taken as the second squaw."

"She will make my life miserable. She has a sharp tongue and quick temper." I pushed my bowl away and lay back down.

Moon Woman went over to the fire, which had a leather bag suspended over it. She dug hot rocks out of the fire and put them in the bag. "I've heated water and sent the others outside, so you can wash. Your pack is here with your clothes." She faced away from me and started working on the basket she was weaving. I went to the fire and I washed myself. It felt good to clean off and the fire was pleasantly warm. I put on the new white deerskin tunic that my people had given me. Fringe hung down from the sleeves of the arms, across the front yoke, and along the bottom edge. There were little shells hanging on the fringe.

Moon Woman emptied the water then combed out my hair. She parted it in the middle and braided it, then tied the ends with leather. Around my neck she placed a shell necklace.

"I've made this for you, my daughter. I have seen that Masheka would have a special woman at his side. A woman with courage to help our people though the years when there will be many changes brought by the Wasichus. I knew Wild Plum was not this woman. When Targhee told me about you and when Masheka did not return home for so long, I knew that you were the one. I was saddened when Masheka returned alone, but knew that you would come to him. I saw this when I looked into the wind and listened for its answers. You will not refuse to follow your path a second time."

"I can't bear to share Masheka."

She smiled affectionately. "I understand your feelings. I

248

wouldn't want to share Masheka's father with another squaw, but I would rather do that than live without him." There was much wisdom in her words and I lowered my head. I would think on what she had to say and not speak hastily.

"These are also for you, daughter of my blood." She made a weaving motion with her hand, the sign of the Shoshoni tribe. She placed a pair of finely made moccasins into my hands. They'd been decorated with porcupine quills, beads, and shells and were lined with rabbit fur. I slid them on my feet and they came up to my knees. They felt soft and warm. Tears came to my eyes and I embraced this loving Shoshoni woman.

"Come, daughter, there is food to prepare."

I went over to check on Good Thunder and, satisfied that he'd been well tended to, I went to help Moon Woman. After pounding some seeds into flour, I put them in a basket, then added water and bird eggs, and kotea fat to make flat bread. I set it out by the fire to cook, then cut elk meat into chunks and put it on sticks over the fire.

Moon Woman asked me about my people and if I knew anything about her tribe and family. I had seen them at gatherings but didn't know them well.

"I worry about my people when the Season of Howling Wind is long and cold as it was this year," she said. "Life is easier here. We have a permanent camp and game is plentiful."

Inside the lodge were large baskets hung on a pillar. On another pillar were weapons and masks used for ceremonies. The lodge was quite spacious compared to the tepee I was used to living in. Grandmother and Targhee's wife came into the lodge with her two sons.

"This is Grandmother and Red Bird Woman," said Moon Woman. Grandmother smiled at me and gestured a welcome with her hands. "And these two boys are Targhee's sons, Grasshopper and Rabbit Tail." The boys stared at me with curiosity. They were excited about something. Grandmother took the two children over to a kotea fur and began to tell them stories. Red Bird Woman squatted down to help with preparing the food. She kept looking at me and smiling.

Masheka, Targhee, and his father entered after a while and I rose to greet them. Masheka's eyes lit up when he saw me. "I'm glad to see you are up and looking so much better. Why are you so finely dressed? Is there something to celebrate?"

"Yes," said Moon Woman. "I am celebrating having a new daughter. I have waited for her all winter, knowing she would come."

"How could you have known it?" he asked, taking his eyes off me with difficulty.

"I knew. As I know many things."

"You should have told me."

"I did tell you but you did not listen."

"She is pretty enough to make other squaws jealous and she can cook well," said Targhee, grinning. "Have you tried her out on your sleeping couch to see if she is good there as well?"

My face burned and my mouth went dry.

"Quiet, Targhee, you are embarrassing her," said Moon Woman. "We have planned a celebration in the long house to welcome Vision Woman into our tribe and family. Go and change, Masheka." I looked at Masheka to see what he would do.

He smiled at me. "Will you come to the long house with me?"

My heart hammered in my chest and I felt my legs become weak. I nodded as the significance of what he asked began to sink in.

Masheka's whole family went to the long house, which was already filled with members of the tribe. Their clothing was colorfully decorated with paint, feathers, quills, and squirrel, weasel and rabbit fur. There was much smiling and talking when Masheka and I entered. Moon Woman and Red Bird Woman carried baskets of food, which they placed by the central fire where more baskets and gifts had already been placed.

Moon Woman took the kotea robe I had worn over my shoulders for warmth. I stood next to Masheka in front of his father. I looked up at Masheka and smiled in happiness. He looked handsome in the leather shirt I had made him. His father spoke in Kootenai, then said in Shoshoni so I could understand. "I have told them that you were accepted into our tribe at the morning council meeting. My family has agreed to provide for you and any future children if anything should happen to Masheka." I handed Masheka a basket of food I had prepared for him. His father told me my duties as a wife, then told Masheka of his duties as a husband. He switched again to Kootenai and spoke again, then said in Shoshoni, "I give this woman to Masheka in place of her brother." Masheka took my hand in his and lifted it up. His father placed a leather, beaded sash over our two arms.

I looked into Masheka's eyes and saw the depth of his soul. I knew for certain that sharing my life with this man was what I wanted. He was part of my spiritual journey. He'd helped me on my Vision Quest and would continue to help me.

"I welcome you into our family. May you have many Seasons of Ripe Berries together."

The people of the tribe closed in around us and gave us many presents. Feasting followed but I was not hungry, thinking of the decision I had made. I didn't know how I would adjust when Masheka took Wild Plum as his second squaw. I saw her standing off to the side. Her eyes were full of venom and I looked uneasily away. I had no wish to live with a woman so filled with malice.

We left the celebrating before anyone else and returned

251

to Masheka's lodge. It was dark and cool in the lodge with the onset of night and together we built up the dying fire.

"You are so beautiful and strong that I wanted you for my woman the first time we journeyed together," said Masheka. I looked up and gazed at him in the firelight as he continued speaking. "I despaired of us ever sharing a lodge and now here you are by my fire as my woman. I give thanks to the Master Spirit for guiding you to me and protecting you from danger." His words were spoken like a prayer.

"I was not happy without you." I touched my heart and made the sign of love then held out my hand to him.

He made the sign back to me and drew me against him. My heart sang at his touch. He unfastened the straps at my shoulders. My buckskin dress slid down and I clasped it to me.

"Not here. Someone might come in."

"Ai." Masheka lifted me into his arms and carried me to his enclosed sleeping couch. He set me on my feet on the soft kotea robe and pushed the dress off my shoulders. It slipped down to my feet. He reached out and touched my cheek and I trembled in anticipation. "You are so perfect. I found it difficult to not share pleasure with you those last days we traveled together."

"I found it difficult as well."

"Ai, that I knew and it didn't make it any easier. The time of waiting is over." He took off his bear-claw necklace and then pulled his buckskin shirt off over his head.

I watched in fascination as he continued undressing in front of me. His body was beautiful and strong. Once undressed he drew me down to the kotea sleeping robe and removed my moccasins, then we lay down. My arousal was strong at the feel of his muscular body beside mine. Joy filled me in being able to at last express my love for him physically. In fascination and delight we learned what gave each other pleasure.

252

In the sacredness of our joining I wondered if he would give me a papoose that would not go hungry and die in the Season of Howling Wind when game was scarce. I became lost in sensations and my heart soared as an eagle.

Afterwards I lay in his arms, feeling troubled. Our love-making had been powerful, bringing us to a new level of intimacy and love. I couldn't bear the thought of him sharing a sleep robe with Wild Plum. Tears sprung into my eyes. "I cannot live with Wild Plum. Part of me would die every time you were with her."

"I know."

I sat up. "You knew that I might leave and yet you gave me your seed anyway! What if I am carrying your papoose?"

He drew me back down. "I meant I know you would be unhappy if I took Wild Plum into our lodge. You aren't leaving. You're my woman."

"What will you do?"

"I'll tell Two Elk, Wild Plum's father, that I can't marry her."

"He'll be upset. So will Wild Plum. She wants you."

"It'll cause trouble in the tribe but it will pass. Two Elk has often admired Straight Arrow. I'll give the stallion as a gift. So fine a war horse will appease his anger."

"You can't give him Straight Arrow—you love the horse too much!"

"It's because of my feelings for Straight Arrow that Two Elk will understand the depth of my feelings for you. It can't be otherwise. My lodge would be crowded with any squaw but you."

"I don't want you to give away Straight Arrow, perhaps I could learn to live with Wild Plum." Tears slid down my cheeks. "It would be good to have help with the work."

"Grandmother, mother and Red Bird Woman will share in the work." He wiped the tears from my cheeks with his thumb. "Promise me you'll stay with me."

"I'll never leave you, Masheka." From one of my pouches I took out his armband. I tied it on his arm. "I wanted the armband because it was worn close to your skin and I'd never seen you without it. But what I really wanted was you. I don't need the armband now that I have you."

"What do you see in the future, Vision Woman?"

I took out the stone from my medicine bag. With the asking of the question the stone grew warm in my hand and a vision of the future opened up. I became lost in the vision. I saw a small child sitting on Masheka's lap. The glow of the fire shone on both their faces. Then I saw Masheka out riding with our young son, teaching him how to ride and hunt. I saw myself out gathering herbs to use for healing. I carried them back to the lodge and hung them up to dry like Grandfather used to do. A squaw came to the lodge seeking my help for her child who had fallen from his horse and been injured. I quickly followed her to her lodge. The vision faded and I looked at Masheka and told him what I saw.

"It is a good vision," he said, smiling.

At dawn Masheka, Wind Chaser, and I stood on the edge of a mountain and I held out my peace pipe to Father Sky, Mother Earth, and to the four directions, ending facing east as the sun rose up. I knew, as I stood there and watched the earth light up with color, that I had finally fulfilled my quest and discovered the direction of my life. I missed my people, but perhaps during the Season of Ripe Berries when all the Shoshoni bands meet, Masheka and I could journey to be with them. I smiled thinking of my coming life with Masheka.

I knew there would be hardships ahead when the Wasichus came in greater numbers, but there would be the passing of many seasons before that would happen. I would be a strong medicine woman by then and give my people courage and strength. I looked up at Masheka and my heart swelled with love. My fears about all the changes to come did not frighten me with him at my side.

As we stood there a large bald eagle flew over us. Masheka and I watched its graceful flight in awe. I thought of the time that I had seen the eagle fly overhead as I had stood beside Grandfather about to leave on my quest to the Sacred Mountains. The eagle is the power of the Great Spirit and teaches us to soar above life's challenges. This was a good sign at the start of our new life together.

# About the Author

Heidi Skarie is a passionate writer and storyteller who has taught classes and workshops on writing and spoken on radio and television. Her experiences backpacking in the Rocky Mountains, and interests in the esoteric and the freedom-loving Plains Indians led her to write *Red Willow's Quest*.

Skarie graduated with highest honors from the University of Wisconsin with a major in education and a minor in fine arts. She did graduate work at St. Thomas, Minnesota in education and studied art at the Minnetonka Art Center.

Skarie shares her home with her husband and three children in Minnetonka, Minnesota a suburb of Minneapolis. Their home is located near Lake Minnetonka, which is of special interest to her because the land surrounding the lake was sacred burial ground for the Native Americans.

Recently she finished *Dragon Ships*, a book on the Norwegian Vikings that captures the spirit and adventure of those couragous people. She is also working on completing a science fiction/fantasy series entitled *Star Rider*.

# Bibliography

Brown, Dee, *Bury My Heart at Wounded Knee*, Bantam Books, New York, 1973.

Carley, Maurine, and Virginia Cole Trenholm, *The Shoshonis, Sentinels of the Rockies*, University of Oklahoma Press, Norman Oklahoma, 1964.

Neihardt, John, *Black Elk Speaks*, University of Nebraska Press, Lincoln, 1972.

Sams, Jamie, and David Carson, *Medicine Cards*, Bear and Company, New Mexico, 1988.

Thomasma, Kenneth, *Pathki Nana, Kootenai Girl*, Grandview Publishing Co., Jackson WY, 1991.

Waldo, Anna Lee, *Sacajawea*, Avon Books, New York, 1984.

Wilson, Nicholas, and Charles Wilson, *The White Indian Boy and its Sequel The Return of the White Indian*, Fenske Printing, Inc., Rapid city, South Dakota, 1988.

*Red Willow's Quest* is available through:

Bookstores:
Local and national.

Internet:
http://www.sunshinepress.com
http://www.barnesandnoble.com
http://www.borders.com
http://www.amazon.com

SunShine Press Publications, Inc.
P. O. Box 333
Hygiene, CO 80533-0333; U.S.A.


**If you would like to contact the author:**

Heidi Skarie
3504 Larchwood Drive
Minnetonka, MN 55345; U.S.A.

Website: http://www.users.uswest.net/~jskarie
Email: heidiskarie@uswest.net